I0654509

Demons of DunDegore

Book Two: Sword of Kassandra Series

M Joseph Murphy

Demons of DunDegore

Copyright © 2014 Council of Peacocks Press
All rights reserved.
Editors: Jen Ryan
ISBN 978-1-987811-01-8

Cover art by M Joseph Murphy.
M Joseph Murphy's Official Website: mjosephmurphy.info

First electronic Edition: November 2014
First Paperback Edition: November 2014

Praise for *M Joseph Murphy*

"You dive into this world and feel for once someone has not re-told the same story with just a different colouring."

- CHRISTOPH FISCHER,
author of *The Three Nations Trilogy*.

"The Council of Peacocks has it all: epic battles, conspiracy theories, romance, and a great story line. The first page will suck you into a complex and unpredictable, page-turning plot."

- TIFFANY HUSON

"This is precisely the kind of book I enjoy reading. It hits all the buttons: Epic battles, …moments of self-discovery, …tales of heroes and villains, and of course there's loads of angst ridden teenagers with badass paranormal/psychokinesis abilities."

- TRAVIS LUEDKE,
Author of *The Nightlife Series*

Works by M Joseph Murphy

ACTIVATION SERIES
Council of Peacocks
Beyond the Black Sea
Terra Incognita (Coming 2015)

SWORD OF KASSANDRA SERIES
A Fallen Hero Rises
Demons of DunDegore
The Backward Pawn (Coming 2015)

Dedication

This book is dedicated to my father, Terry Murphy. He taught me to shoot a gun at 5, use throwing knives at 8, and how to break a man's back when I was 15. I think he wanted me to become a ninja but I became a writer instead. Close enough.

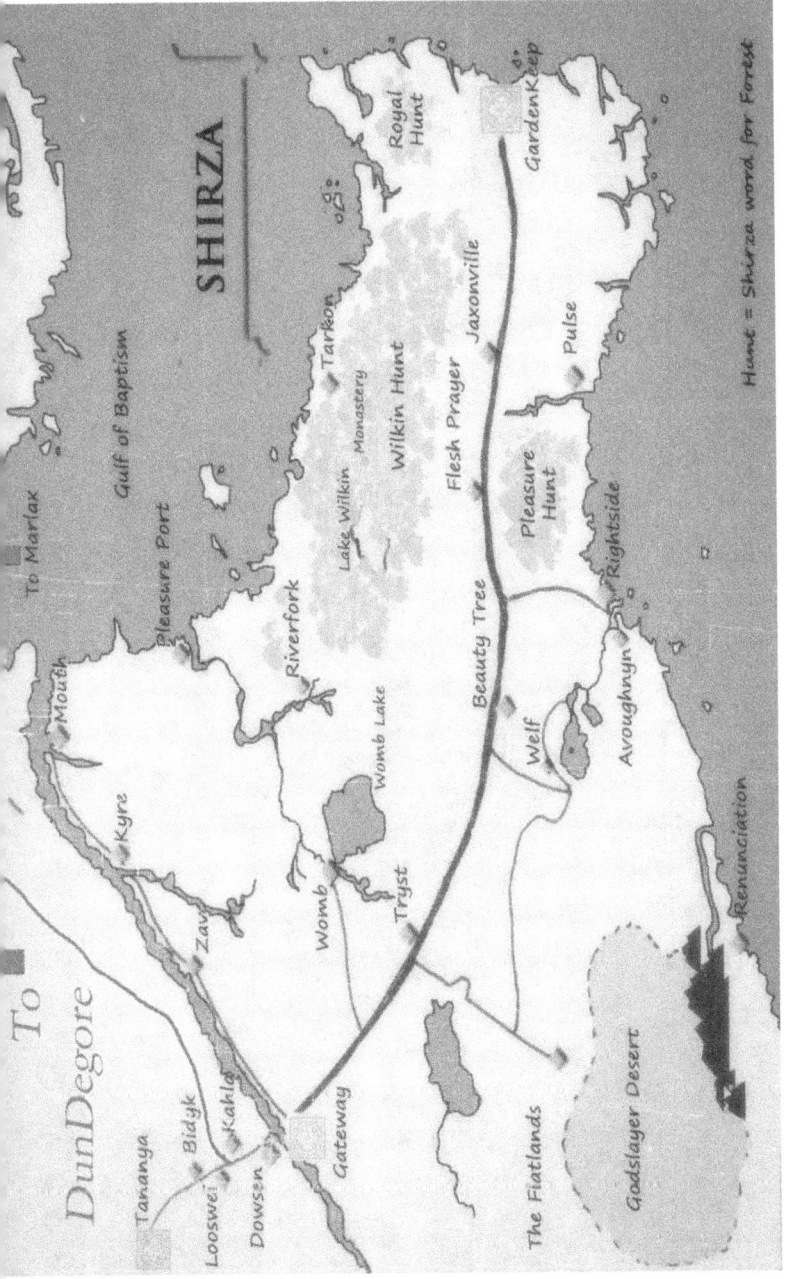

Hunt = Shirza word for Forest

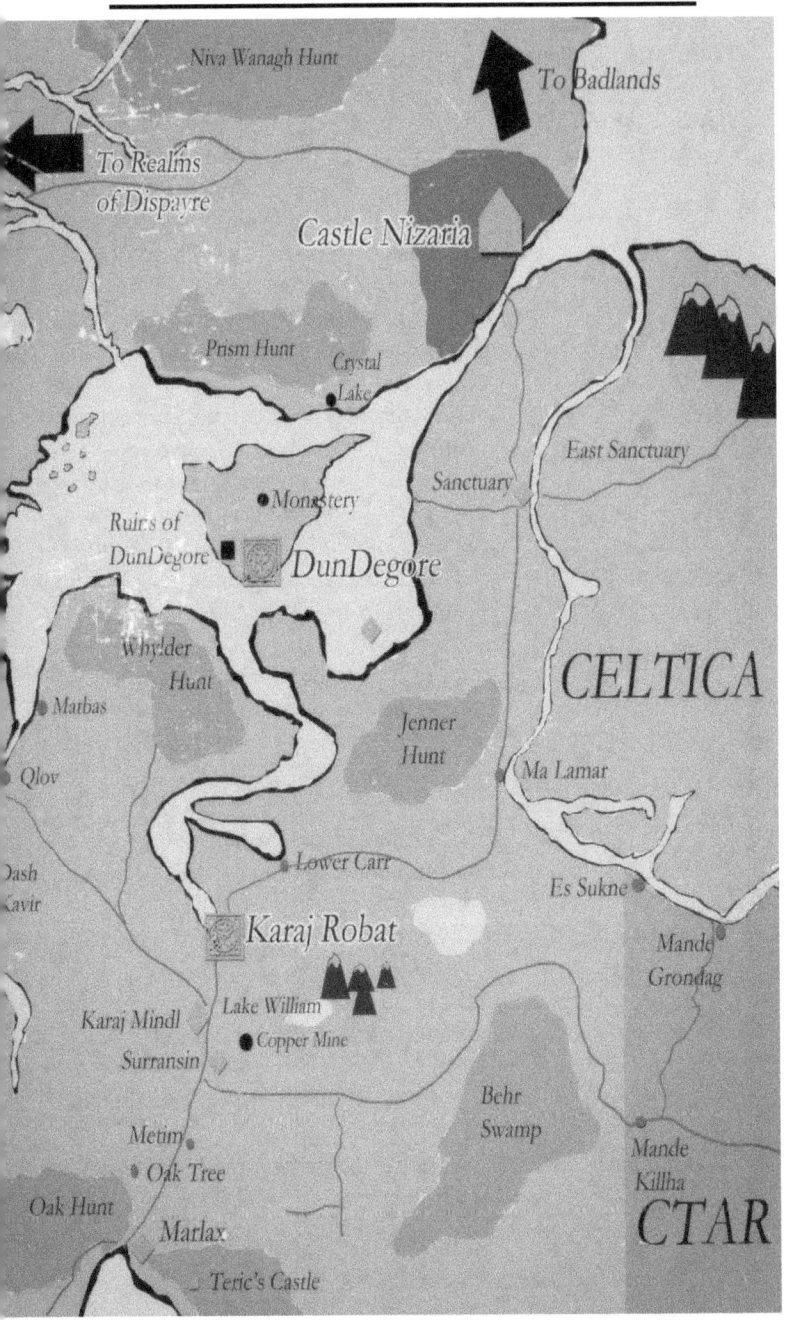

Dramatis Personae

MAIN CHARACTERS

Tadgh Dooley	Pronounced Tig (like "tiger" without the "er"). Werecat. High school student from Cleveland, Ohio. Possesses ability to make his wishes come true...at a price. With each wish, he damages the reality field. After the death of his lover, he made a deal with a demon named Bes. Age 17.
The Sage	Mysterious wise man from the city of GardenKeep. Real name unknown. Former consultant to fieldbender guild of Karaj Robat. Possesses magical abilities including elemental control over fire. Age: Unknown.
Menphis Bannmerci	Up-and-coming member of the Brotherhood of Tyche. Assigned as Tadgh's mentor. From the small town of Tarkon in the country of Shirza. Age 24.
Grandwyn Billyan	Young fod sel-onde. A child of two elmire ahk, his power is potentially dangerous. Telekinetic, energy projection, ice generation. Age 8.
Gnocko Fnesh	A frie stav from the subterranean country of Trelium, north of the Badlands. Works as hired muscled for the Sage. Age 55 (young for a frie stav).
Eiodeesh Mai'Var	Work partner to Gnocko. Trofast warrior raised by a sirian adopted father.
Tamara Billyan	Mother of Grandwyn. Instructor of Sisterhood of the Flesh in FleshPrayer. Age: 26.
Bethel Shakuul	Tamara's bodyguard. Born in Gramagh. Age 23.
Samar Fesh	Tamara's carriage driver. Former slave from Norshire. Age 18.

THE BROTHERHOOD OF TYCHE

Instructor Mal	Head of the monastery in Shirza. Leader of the Brotherhood. Age 53.
Mirelda	Head of the monastery's kitchen.

DUNDEGORE

Siron	Fieldbender. Member of the inner circle at Karaj Robat. In charge of safely securing the Sword of Kassandra.
Mikhel	Young fieldbender stationed in DunDegore. Previously sent to Karaj Robat to inform Karaj Robat about the Sword of Kassandra.
Torch Karehn	Head of the Pheonides in DunDegore. Age 52.

MINOR CHARACTERS

Barnes	Assistant to the Sage.
Shonndira Bannmerci	Cousin to Menphis (their fathers are brothers). A fod sel-onde with powers of premonition. Currently training with the nizarians to gain control of his abilities. Age 21
Pwella	Barnes' lady friend. Also works for the Sage.
Teric	Greater graunskyeg who previously kidnapped Menphis.
Bes	Demon who appears as an orange housecat with glowing green eyes. He bound the cat spirit to Tadgh
Myan	The oracle. A member of the Quadumvirate, four people who rule the realms of Dispayre in the absence of Lord Dispayre.
Andy/Echo	The love of the Sage's life. Previously believed dead. Now associated with a mysterious man who wears a sheath with no sword.

Chapter One

The day before the demons came, Grandwyn arrived in the city of DunDegore. He stood on the deck of a ship, his tiny fingers gripping the railing. No one seemed to take notice of him. Amid the wide-eyed faces of tourists coming to the holy land, he looked like an ordinary peasant boy. But he was much more than that.

A thin layer of early-morning mist blanketed the water between the boat and the approaching shoreline. Behind him, a crowd of strangers searched for signs of the legendary city. Two days ago, the ship had left the dock in Karaj Robat. After being on the water for so long, Grandwyn was eager to be back on solid ground.

Beyond the shore, thin pine trees shot up over thirty-feet tall. Grandwyn looked past the trees for his first glimpse of the ruins: enormous structures of white stone as tall as mountains. Even from here, he could tell the ruins were ancient. Large chunks had crumbled away to reveal a metallic framework underneath. According to the brochure Grandwyn held in his hands, the metal never rusted or degraded despite being thousands of years old.

A woman in a blue dress stepped out of the crowd to stand beside him. "First time on the island?"

Grandwyn nodded.

The woman glanced down at him. "Aren't you a little young to be traveling by yourself?"

"Who said I was traveling by myself?" Grandwyn crossed his arms and looked up at the woman. She looked to be the same age as his mother and was nearly as beautiful. Something in the way she looked at him made him feel uneasy. As if she wasn't truly seeing at him. "Besides, I'm not too young. I'm eight."

"Oh." The woman smiled. "That old? I stand corrected. Do you know the story behind the ruins?"

"Of course. Everyone knows the story. DunDegore was a Behersker city, one of the last to be abandoned when the ancient ones left for the stars. There are fifteen large buildings, the ones we can see from here, and a few dozen smaller ruins. No one knows exactly what they were used for. All we know is they've been there for as long as anyone can remember."

"You're very bright." The smile slid from the woman's face. Her eyes grew cold and distant.

"Did I say something wrong?" Grandwyn asked.

"No." The woman shook her head and her eyes refocused. When she spoke again, her voice was warm and comforting, almost motherly. "I just realized it's been a very long time since I've talked to a child. I had a sister once. She was about your age when she…well, the last time I saw her. We were so innocent. Everything was one great big adventure." She looked over her shoulder at a patch of shadows. "It's not too late for you, you know. You could always stay on the boat. Head back home."

Grandwyn took a step away from the woman. "Why would I want to do that? I've come all this way. It doesn't make any sense to head home now."

"No. I suppose you're right." The woman sighed and hung her head. "You and I are both on this ship until the very end. If you'll excuse me, I hear someone calling me."

The woman walked away and vanished into the crowd.

'Strange,' Grandwyn thought. 'For a moment it sounded like she knew why I was coming here. Like she was afraid for me or something. But my mother was wrong. There's nothing to fear. The fieldbenders will take me in and that will be that.'

The ship slid through the water as it followed the shore. As time passed, the sun burned off the early-morning mist and the docks came into sight. Twenty docking platforms stretched over more than a quarter mile. Crowds spilled out from dozens of large ships similar to the one Grandwyn was on. Many smaller boats were parked along the wooden piers.

Grandwyn climbed up on the railing to look past the harbor, to where the city truly began. While not the largest city he'd ever seen, DunDegore was more grandiose than his hometown of FleshPrayer. Multi-storied buildings pressed close together. People milled through the narrow streets while scores of street merchants tried to sell them souvenirs.

As the ship approached the dock, the crew grew suddenly active. Moving with practiced speed, they tied the boat off and lowered the walkway. Passengers, most of them smiling, left the ship, suitcases in hand. Grandwyn stood with the rest of the tourists at the end of the pier next to a middle-aged woman selling flowers. He looked around for the woman in the blue dress. There was no sign of her.

He disembarked from the ship and entered the city, walking past open-air restaurants and the tacky gift stores. His destination was far from the tourist part of town. Grandwyn stopped in the doorway of The Sixth Tower Inn and took a piece of paper out of his pocket, verifying he'd come to the right place.

"This is it." He refolded the piece of paper, put it back in his pocket, and stepped inside. The Inn still reeked of sweat and spilt beer from the night before. There were only two other people in the bar: an old man drinking by himself in the corner and a tall, plump southerner wearing a faded black uniform standing behind the bar.

"Boy," said the man behind the bar. "Get your butt out of here. This be no place for children."

Grandwyn took out his money purse. "Your name is Bentley, correct? I need a room, sir. My mother told me you rent them. You'll remember her, my mother. You visited her the last time you were in FleshPrayer."

The man narrowed his eyes, studying Grandwyn's face. "Aye. I see the resemblance, now that you mention it." He looked toward the front door. "Is she here, your mother?"

Grandwyn shook his head. "Not yet. She'll be here in a few days. I'm to wait for her." Approaching the bar, he reached up and placed a gold coin on the counter. Then he stepped back so he could look the man in the eyes. "This will cover us for the week, I believe."

Bentley took the piece of gold, examining it for a moment before placing it in his pocket. "Will do. But why here? This gold could buy you much better rooms in DunDegore. Especially for someone as esteemed as your mother."

"This is where I'm supposed to go. Can you show me to my room, please?"

Bentley wiped his hands with a towel and stepped away from the bar. He grabbed a key from the wall and motioned for Grandwyn to follow. They walked up two flights of steep stairs, stopping at a wooden door. Bentley opened the door and passed the key to Grandwyn.

"It's not much, but it's the best we got. No running water. Outhouse be out back. Take the stairs at the end of hall. Be careful heading down at night. It's not lit. Rarely used, actually. Most of my guests only need a bed and a closed door. They usually leave after a few minutes."

Grandwyn raised an eyebrow, confused. Bentley blushed.

"Sorry. I assumed you being from FleshPrayer and all you'd be used to that kind of talk. Forget what I said, kid. How old are you anyway?"

"Eight. Just turned."

Bentley exhaled slowly. "What are you doing traveling by yourself? It's a dangerous world out there. More so than ever if you believe the rumors."

"You don't say." Grandwyn raised a hand. It crackled with purple energy. "I can take care of myself."

Bentley took a step back. "What are you? Fieldbender?"

Grandwyn nodded and slipped out of his traveling cloak. "They don't usually take initiates as young as me, but they say I've got potential. Both my parents trained as elmire ahk."

Bentley straightened his shoulders and smoothed the folds of his uniform. "Might be best if you don't show your abilities down below. Even though there's a guild here in town, most people are scared of benders. And you being so young they might assume the worst. Think you're fod sel-onde or something. Listen, why don't I bring your meals up to you? We don't get many children at The Sixth Tower Inn. We attract a certain type of patron. I don't want them trying to take advantage of you. I wouldn't offer to do this for most guests, but your mom is something special."

"Thanks." Grandwyn nodded and waited for Bentley to leave. Then he closed the door, locking it. Looking around the room, he found a thin layer of dust covered everything, including the bedspread. "I suppose it could be worse. And it's only for a night. Tomorrow, the fieldbenders will take me in. Or they'll kill me. Either way it will be over."

Grandwyn had lied. He wasn't a fieldbender, not yet anyway. His abilities surfaced several months ago. Like fieldbenders, he could manipulate the reality field: His abilities included being able to move things with his mind, shoot beams of energy from his hands, and create ice out of thin air. At first, he practiced in secret. One day, his mother discovered him creating ice sculptures. Terrified, she made him promise to stop.

"I love you, baby," she had said as she kissed him on the forehead. "Nothing will ever change that. But if other people see what you can do, see what you are, they will want to hurt you. Kill you."

"But why? Fieldbenders can do what I do. People don't hurt them."

She shook her head and pulled her clothes tighter around her body. "But, you're not a fieldbender, Wynnie. They spend years in meditation and study, learning to do what comes to you naturally. You are fod sel-onde. You know what they do to people like you."

"I'm not!" He stomped his foot and sparks of energy formed around his eyes. "I'm not a monster. I'm just self-taught. Let me go to Karaj Robat. They have the best fieldbender guild there and…"

His mother had placed her fingers over his lips. "Absolutely not. You can never go to Karaj Robat. If the fieldbenders there learn about you, they will end you. Promise me you will never go there."

In the end, Grandwyn had promised. Which was why he was on the Isle of DunDegore instead. The local fieldbender guild was smaller but still respected. The journey here took almost two weeks. He escaped when his mother left town to attend a political conference to ensure he had a good head start. By now, she would have read his note and learned why he left. It was only a matter of time before her network of contacts tracked him to DunDegore. If he wanted a chance to plead his case to the fieldbenders, it would have to be tomorrow.

He warped the reality field in the room. In a flash, all the dust disappeared. He opened the window and leaned out. Fresh air blew his strawberry-blond hair around his face. Below, a gray-haired woman wearing a red uniform glanced up at him. Her face wrinkled with confusion. Grandwyn smiled and waved to her. She turned and walked away, but not before looking back at him over her shoulder.

***

Torch Karehn looked back over her shoulder at the young boy in the window. For a moment, she thought she'd felt the reality field being manipulated. When she saw the child, she realized she must have been mistaken. He was far too young for a fieldbender.

'Look at me,' she thought. 'Jumping at shadows. I need to control my nerves. With luck, we'll find it soon. If not, if the worst happens, my flock will need me to be strong.'

The Sword of Kassandra was missing.

Torch Karehn was head of the local Aerie, a religious center for the Church of the Pheonides. When the Sword of Kassandra appeared months ago, she volunteered to transport the weapon to safekeeping at a local monastery. Working with Sirion, a fieldbender from Karaj Robat, she had crafted a security system to hide the sword at the monastery. Many forces in the world could use that weapon for evil things. And the system had been successful.

Until last night.

As she rushed through the streets, many waved to her. She forced herself to slow down, to smile back at them. Part of the burden of being a leader was to never let others see your stress. If the people of DunDegore saw the fear she felt inside, rumors would spread like wildfire. She stopped to shake hands with one of her flock, Mrs. Jonstone. She ruffled the hair of the woman's son and pretended that everything was right with the world. Inside, she wanted to run.

Eventually she reached her destination. The front doors to the local fieldbender guild were tall and imposing: twenty-foot tall thick slates of metal-reinforced wood. Two guards armed with swords stood outside. Three months ago, the Sword of Kassandra had been recovered during an archeology dig. Ever since, the fieldbenders had become suspicious of strangers, heavily restricting admittance. Both guards recognized Torch Karehn as she approached and pushed the doors open for her.

Inside, away from the public eye, her composure melted. She leaned against a wall and stared down at her hands. They shook. She clenched them and took deep breaths until the shaking stopped.

The main foyer was empty. Most initiates would be in classes at this time of the morning. The man she needed to see would be on the second floor. She raced up the wide stone steps before her, no longer caring who saw the panic in her face. The fieldbenders could keep secrets.

She stopped in front of an open door. Inside, young men and women wearing the white robes of initiates stood in a circle, hands extended inwards. In the middle of the circle, purple energy swirled and twisted creating ornate shapes. This was Akashic energy, the foundation of the fieldbenders' abilities. One of the initiates, a young man with brown hair, saw her. His eyes went wide in surprise. He lowered his hands and left the circle. The other initiates tightened the circle without hesitation to cover his absence.

"What are you doing here?" Instantly, he seemed to remember decorum. He bowed respectfully. "Apologies, mistress. I…"

Torch Karen grabbed his forearms. "We have no time for niceties, Mikhel. I need to speak to you." She looked over Mikhel's shoulder at the others. "Alone. Where can we ensure we'll not be overheard?"

"This way," Mikhel said. "There's an empty classroom next door."

Once inside the empty room, Torch Karehn sat on a bench and clasped her hands together tightly.

Mikhel remained standing. "Should I set up a shield?"

"No need. I'll be brief. We have a disaster. Listen closely. I won't have time to repeat this, and I need you to speak with your leaders."

"You could speak with them directly."

She shook her head. "I don't have time to deal with inter-denominational politics. That's why I came to you. I know you. Trust you. As soon as I leave here, I have to head to the Aerie and make preparations in case the worst happens."

"What do you mean?"

Torch Karehn bit her lip. "Something happened at the monastery last night. We were attacked. The Sword of Kassandra was stolen."

Mikhel sat down now. "But how? Sirion…"

"Sirion is dead." She covered her mouth. "That's the first time I've said it aloud. Whatever hit the monastery last night proved too powerful for him. What they did to his body…"

"Damnation." Mikhel ran a hand through his hair. "We have to let the Sage know."

Torch Karehn shook her head. "You know that's not an option. Because of what happened with Defksquar, the Sage has distanced himself. He no longer trusts the fieldbenders."

"But surely he'll want to know. Defksquar isn't even in Karaj Robat anymore. Rumor has it he's deep undercover somewhere."

"Wherever he is, he's working for Karaj Robat. Contacting the Sage is not an option. I've known the Sage for a very long time. When his mind is made up, nothing can sway him. Believe me. I've tried. Now, I need you to focus, Mikhel. After I set up defenses at the Aerie, I'll contact Elmontrazar. He left a nizarian device that allows communication across great distances. I'm going to ask him to send reinforcements. Speak with your leaders. Tell them to prepare."

"Prepare for what?"

Torch Karen stood, her expression steely. "You know what the Sword is capable of. In the wrong hands…"

She could not bring herself to finish the sentence. From the expression on Mikhel's face she didn't need to.

Mikhel's face paled. "I guess a part of me always knew this was going to happen. When I first went south to Karaj Robat and told them about the Sword, something told me things were only going to get worse. How much time do we have?"

Torch Karehn's lower lip trembled. "We may already be too late."

Chapter Two

Far to the southeast of DunDegore, in the country of Shirza, Tadgh Dooley ran barefoot through the woods. He was an hour into his daily morning run. Sweat poured from every inch of his body, soaking through his sleeveless white tunic. Menphis kept pace beside him easily, his breath slow and steady. His white tunic looked as clean and pristine as it had when they began the run.

"Ready to try again?" Menphis asked.

Tadgh groaned. "Starting to hate you a little bit."

"Do it anyway."

Still running, Tadgh flipped a switch in his mind and released the feline demon inside him. Thick orange fur sprouted all over his body. His muscles grew thicker, his limbs stretching to make him several inches taller. His senses shifted as well. Most colors disappeared, the world becoming a wash of blues and greens. As his werecat form solidified, his peripheral vision expanded. The woods grew brighter as his eyes took in more light, but objects in the distance faded. He guessed it was a by-product of cats being hunters. They needed to focus on their immediate surroundings.

His three-foot long tail pushed out of his pants...and then he tripped over his own feet.

He crashed, head-first, into the dirt. Menphis stopped beside him, lowering a hand to help Tadgh back to his feet. Tadgh gripped Menphis' hand, taking care that his thick black claws did not cut into his friend.

"I'm never going to get this." Tadgh brushed dirt and small green leaves from the front of his tunic. "We've been practicing this for weeks, and I still fall every time. It's not possible to switch forms mid-run."

Menphis passed Tadgh a metal flask of water. "You said the same thing about learning the iron fist technique. And yet I seem to remember you knocking a chip off the stone yesterday."

Tadgh looked down at his hands. "I also remember feeling like I'd shattered every bone in my hand. And getting blood all over everything. I don't know how you do it, make your skin so hard it doesn't break. For me, that rarely works even in cat form."

"It's not about making your skin hard. It's about making your mind harder than the stone. And you've come a long way. You've only been training for a few months now. In a few years…"

"A few years?"

Menphis raised an eyebrow. "Yes. A few years. Did you really expect to master elmire ahk in a matter of months? Don't answer that. Of course you did. I swear, you have less patience that a tuft in heat. Come on. We're only half way through the run. I want to see you try the mid-run transformation at least three more times."

"And they say I'm a monster." Tadgh looked at his reflection in the shiny metal of the flask. There were no mirrors at the monastery. This was one of the few ways he could see what he looked like in cat form. Upon close inspection, he could still identify his features beneath the fur, but the shape of his face had changed. His nose and jaw broadened, jutting out like a cougar. His ears were larger and more pointed.

Shifting back to human form, he took a long drink from the flask and passed it back to Menphis. Then he took a deep breath and continued the run.

For Tadgh, the last three months had been a haze of pain and exhaustion. After the demon Bes bound the cat-spirit to him, Tadgh grew stronger, but he had never been an athlete. It had taken him months before he could finish a day's training without falling on his face from exhaustion. Menphis was solely in charge of his training. For various reasons, Tadgh didn't train with the other acolytes. One reason was his age. Tadgh was significantly older than the others. Most boys joined the monastery between the ages of ten and fourteen. Tadgh was seventeen. And there was the issue with his special abilities.

Although he had little contact with the other members of the monastery, his time with Menphis had created a real camaraderie between them. Tadgh now counted Menphis as his best friend, the best friend he could ever remember having.

The morning run would be followed by combat training with Menphis. Later in the afternoon, he would meet with Instructor Mal, the head of the monastery, for private meditation instruction. In the last few weeks, Tadgh had learned to focus his mind even when his body screamed in pain. As a result, the Akashic bolts he could hurl now were larger and more powerful than ever.

Despite the difficulty of training, in many ways his life was less complicated than ever before. Three months ago, he had arrived at the monastery, wounded, near death, with a head injury that caused temporary amnesia. He went to visit the Sage, an expert in the city of GardenKeep, to discover how he ended up on Maghe Sihre. That led him on an adventure that almost killed him, one in which he had committed an unspeakable act. These days, the most adventure he saw was daily practice. And that suited him just fine.

Three more times he attempted the mid-run transformation. Each time he failed. By the time they returned to the monastery, he was filthy and exhausted.

Menphis smacked Tadgh on the shoulder. "You did well today. You might not see the progress, but I do. Clean yourself up and get ready for weapons training."

Tadgh headed back to his room, stripped off his tunic and leather pants and gave himself a sponge bath using water in a ceramic basin.

"What I wouldn't give for a shower." He sniffed under his arms. "Ick. And some deodorant. If I hurry, I can climb to the tower. It's always cooler up there. It will be a nice break before Menphis starts the torture again.

He left his room feeling slightly cleaner than before and wearing a fresh set of clothes. The training pavilion was steps away from his room. Younger acolytes ran through the last stages of their morning training. Turning right, he walked up a steep set of cracked stone steps to the top of the inner wall.

He stepped through a stone archway and walked up a spiral staircase to the top of a tower. This was one of the four pinecone-shaped towers of the monastery's central square, one at each corner. At the center of the square, above Instructor Mal's office, a fifth tower rose higher and more slender than the others. The monastery was a near mirror image of Angkor Wat, a Cambodian temple back on Earth. It was another hint of shared, common history between the two planets.

The main hint was that the predominant speicies here looked human. They called themselves sirian, a name derived from their planet, Maghe Sihre. Their physiological differences were minor: slight variations in skin pigmentation and swirls in their irises.

'It still bothers me,' he thought. 'This is an alien planet. Maybe I didn't technically graduate high school because of the whole turning into a werecat thing, but I know enough about biology to realize people here should look completely different. The fact that they don't implies some sort of intelligence may be behind the creation of both species. I'm not sure I'm comfortable with that.'

It was nearly noon. The deep orange sun in the clouded sky above was noticeably larger than the one Earth orbited. It rose later and later each day. Summer was nearly over. The days were cooling and the nights grew longer. Thankfully, at the monastery that also meant more time sleeping. Without the benefit of watches or alarm clocks, the Brothers scheduled their day around the sun.

Below, he saw Menphis arrive in the training pavilion. Reluctantly, Tadgh left the tower.

***

Tadgh lowered his center of gravity and tightened his grip on his quarterstaff. A thick blindfold covered his eyes, completely blocking his sight.

"A warrior cannot rely on his sight," Menphis said. Tadgh followed Menphis' voice as his mentor circled around him. "Your job today is to hit me. Nothing more."

Tadgh focused on his hearing. The cat spirit improved his auditory acuity in the same way it altered his other senses. He heard the soft whoosh of bare feet across dirt, the steady in and out of Menphis' breath, and the wind in the trees. He followed Menphis' path and struck out with his quarterstaff.

Menphis knocked the attack aside. "Pay attention."

"I am." Tadgh shook his head. "I thought I knew where you were."

"That's your problem. Too much thinking. You're trying to think about what I'm going to do, trying to think about how to counter it. If you ever want to beat me, you need to stop thinking and learn how to feel."

"I swear if you say 'use the force' I will tell Mirelda you're in love with her."

Menphis swung the quarterstaff again. At the last second, Tadgh anticipated where the blow would land and brought up his own staff to block the attack.

"Better," Menphis said. "And I told you if you mentioned this *Star Wars* thing one more time I'd make you do thirty laps around the monastery. Now stop talking and fight."

For several minutes, conversation stopped. Tadgh focused on his hearing and quieted his mind. He reached out with his awareness, trying to sense Menphis' location. Time and again, he jabbed and missed. Tadgh blocked most of Menphis' swings, but several times he wasn't fast enough. One of Menphis' attacks hit Tadgh in the leg, and he fell to the ground.

Tadgh ripped the blindfold from his head and threw it at the ground. "This is pointless. There's no way I can hit you. You're stronger than I am, and you've studied kung fu for years."

"I'm not sure what this kung fu thing is, but that's not why you can't hit me." Menphis reached down and picked up the blindfold. "Your biggest obstacle is your lack of faith. You keep telling me what is and what isn't possible. You know what's impossible? Saying a wish aloud and having it come true. But somehow you manage to do that?"

Tadgh pounded the dirt in frustration. "That's different and you know it."

"Hmm." Menphis looked over his shoulder and waved at one of the younger acolytes. "Feelix, come here."

The young boy, no more than twelve, approached Menphis and bowed deeply. "Yes, Prelate. How can I assist you?"

"This acolyte needs a new sparring partner. Prelate Fin tells me you show some promise with the staff." Menphis looked down at Tadgh who still sat on the ground. "Here's your chance Tadgh. Prove to me it is simply a matter of training. Acolyte Feelix has been with us for only two months. If you can hit him with your staff even once we'll stop training for the day."

"Are you kidding?" Tadgh got to his feet and looked at Feelix. "I can't fight him. He's just a kid!"

"Oooh." Menphis grinned and nodded. "Then perhaps you should go easy on him. Start now."

Feelix immediately fell into a warrior stance, quarterstaff ready. Reluctantly, Tadgh faced off and prepared for attack. The young boy surprised him, moving his weapon so quickly and accurately, he bypassed Tadgh's defenses, striking him in the face. The edge of the wood sliced at Tadgh's cheek, drawing blood.

"Oops! Sorry." Feelix went red in the face. "I didn't mean to do that. I'm still learning."

"You're…learning?" Tadgh bit his lip and glared at Menphis who stood nearby, quietly laughing. "You're enjoying this, aren't you?"

Menphis nodded. "Immensely. Watch out."

Tadgh turned back to see Feelix attacking again. This time Tadgh swung his staff, easily blocking the blow and attempted to push back, to turn the tide of battle to the offensive. Every time he tried to push past Feelix's defenses, the young boy drove him back. After repeated failures, he rolled out of attack range and threw his staff in the dirt.

"Oh come on! How can this kid be beating me?"

Menphis stared at the staff on the ground. "That is the question, isn't it? Pick up your staff."

Tadgh grunted and did as ordered. "We both know I'm stronger than this. If I was in cat form, I could beat this kid and you at the same time."

"You think so?" Menphis looked at the blindfold still in his hands. "The reason we train, Tadgh, is we rarely choose the time and place we do battle. Our enemies rarely wait for us to be at our strongest before attacking. One day, perhaps you will not be able to get into cat form and you will have to defend yourself. You rely too much on your abilities."

"What does that even mean? How can anyone rely too much on their abilities?"

"I'll show you." Menphis passed his staff to Feelix and secured the blindfold over his own eyes. "You believe your cat form will make this a fair fight. So transform. But if you can't hit me, I want your word you will lose this non-productive attitude and focus on your training."

"And if I win?"

Menphis shook his head. "You won't. Attack when you're ready."

Tadgh looked around. Everyone in the training pavilion had stopped and turned to face him.

Tadgh flipped the switch in his mind and, once again, assumed his feline form. 'Who does he think he is? Menphis is no match for me. I'm going to gut him. Tear out his...' Tadgh shook the thoughts away, and cleared his mind. 'That's not me thinking. That's the demon. I can't get angry, or I'll lose control.'

He spun his staff in a figure-eight pattern searching for

a crack in Menphis' defenses. Before he could strike, Menphis went low to the ground and spun his staff directly at Tadgh's ankles. Tadgh tried to jump but was too slow. He fell on his back. He quickly rolled away as Menphis brought his quarterstaff down in the spot where Tadgh had fallen. If he hadn't been so quick, the blow would have struck Tadgh in the head.

'He's not holding back.' Tadgh growled, a low throaty sound. 'Good. Neither will I.' He leapt at Menphis, claws out ready to slash across his chest. Menphis, still close to the ground, punched up with an open palm. The blow hit Tadgh square in the chest and sent him flying back several feet. Tadgh charged again. This time Menphis leaped up, and smashed the staff down on Tadgh's shoulder. Once again, Tadgh fell in the dirt.

"Enough!" Tadgh threw up his hands in surrender. "I give. Damn it. That hurt. You almost took my arm off."

Menphis removed the blindfold, his eyes bright and a smile firmly on his lips. "Doubtful. The way you heal, you won't even have a bruise by dinner. You're getting better, Tadgh, but it's not your body that needs extra training. As soon as you realize what's holding you back, you will achieve amazing things." Menphis helped Tadgh to his feet. They had gathered the attention of the entire monastery. "Okay, everyone. The show's over. Back to your own studies."

Most of the acolytes did as instructed. One group, however, continued to stare at Tadgh from the edge of the pavilion. Tadgh, embarrassed, switched back to human form and stared at his feet. When he looked up, he found Menphis studying him.

"Give them time," Menphis said. "They're just children. They fear the unknown."

Tadgh sighed. "But they should be afraid of me, shouldn't they? They know what I am. Fod sel-onde. Any time I make a wish, it comes true. You know, when I first learned what I could do, I thought I'd won the lottery."

"Then you learned the cost."

Tadgh nodded. "The first time I used my wish power, I attracted the attention of a demon. Bes made me a werecat…and a murderer. The next time I used my power, I teleported here. After that jerk Oshu kidnapped me, I used it again to learn how to throw that purple energy around."

"Akashic energy."

"Whatever. Yay, I have super powers, but it hasn't worked out well for everyone else, has it? The last time I used my ability I wished an entire army out of existence. I killed thousands of people."

"You also prevented an invasion that would have destroyed our country."

Tadgh shrugged. "If you say so. To make matters worse, each time I wish aloud, I tear at the seams of the Void. That's why those kids are looking at me like that. Dispayre is the biggest of bad guys and, thanks to me, it's more than likely he'll get free."

Menphis pinched his nose and closed his eyes. "Stop being an idiot. You didn't know what you were doing. As soon as you realized your wish power weakened the Void, you promised to stop using it. And you have."

"Well, it helps having a group of homicidal fieldbenders out there ready to kill me if I use my power again. Kind of a strong motivator."

"Only the gods are infallible, Tadgh. Remember your lessons."

"I know, I know." Tadgh nodded but couldn't allow himself to agree with Menphis. With his power, he could destroy the world. He needed to be infallible.

The one power he never discussed around Menphis was the one he may or may not have used on Menphis' cousin, Shonn. Shonn who said he was in love with Tadgh. With a touch, Tadgh could enchant anyone, making them completely devoted to him. Bes told him it made him a perfect predator. His victims did not want to fight. Because of his power, there was no way for Tadgh to know if Shonn's love was real or not.

Menphis folded his arms across his chest. "Like I said, give them time. When they get to know you as well as I have, they will change their minds. Walk with me. There's something I've been meaning to tell you. It's important."

Before Menphis could continue, a familiar figure came running toward them. His name was Beilaugh, a recent addition to the monastery. He was formerly a servant, enslaved by the army Tadgh had destroyed with a wish. After all his employers' demise, Beilaugh sought help from the local monastery. Tadgh, out of guilt, put in a good word for Beilaugh. Now, he did the job Shonn used to.

"Come quick," Beilaugh said. "Instructor Mal called for you. We have a visitor."

"But nobody knows I'm here." Tadgh looked over at Menphis. "I swear I haven't used my power. Only the Sage and your cousin know where I am. Do you think it's one of them?"

Beilaugh shook his head. "Not for you. It's a woman. She's here to see Menphis. Instructor Mal says you both need to come, but he didn't say why."

Menphis frowned. "Does this woman have a name?"

"Yes." Beilaugh looked at the ground. "But Instructor Mal told me not to tell you her name or you might not come."

"Damn it." Menphis rubbed the back of his neck and shook his head.

Tadgh held up his hands. "Wait! I know that look. That's the ex-girlfriend look."

Menphis said nothing.

"Seriously? I was right! You think this woman is your ex-girlfriend. This I have to see. I was starting to think you were made of stone or something."

Menphis flicked his quarterstaff and hit Tadgh in the elbow.

"Hey!" Tadgh rubbed the wound.

"Stop whining. You're a fast healer, remember? Besides, it is probably not her. I haven't seen her in years. Most likely, it's someone from my home town."

Tadgh grinned. "Back home we call that denial. Lead the way, Beilaugh. Something tells me today is about to get very interesting."

Chapter Three

In the border town of Gateway, the Sage stood on a rooftop, his attention fixed on the streets below. His dark brown skin drank in the heat of the noonday sun, a welcome relief after a cold, damp morning. Below, a tall figure walked methodically through the streets, head lowered and covered with a cowl. A small man cloaked with invisibility followed the figure. The Sage could see through the illusion, however. His eyes saw a broader spectrum of light than normal people. It was very useful on a planet with limited electronic surveillance. It was one of the few things he missed about life on Earth. That and chocolate.

He sent a telepathic message to the invisible man. *'Hurry, Gnocko. You're losing him.'*

'I can see that,' came the annoyed response. *'I'm only three feet tall, you bastard. How did you expect me to follow the blasted trofast through the streets?'*

'Well, I couldn't very well send Eiodeesh. She has a way of sticking out. Wait. He turned down an alley. Take your next left.'

As Gnocko followed the figure on the streets, the Sage ran to catch up. He gracefully leapt the thirty-foot gap between rooftops, landing in a roll. Teleporting would have been faster, but he couldn't risk using his powers. Their quarry could sense changes in the reality field. Thankfully, Gnocko's invisibility was a natural skill. His people, the frie stavs, bent light and shadow as easily as sirians took breath.

For the last month, the Sage and his employees had been investigating rumors of a new general sent by the Quadumvirate, rulers of the country of Dispayre. Still intent on invasion, the Quadumvirate sent a replacement for Lord Vyken. The possibility of an army being rebuilt inside Shirza was enough to pull the Sage away from his home in GardenKeep to this city at the western edge of Shirza.

Looking over the edge of the roof, the Sage searched for signs of the cloaked figure. He couldn't find him.

'Damn. Do you have him, Gnocko?'

'Yes. See that red door on the right? I saw him go inside. You might want to get down here.'

The Sage nodded and jumped off the roof, landing with a thud on the dirt floor of the alley. After brushing the dust off the lapels of his white suit, he bent down and put his ear to the door. From inside came a murmur of voices.

"How many are inside?" Gnocko spoke aloud as he dispelled the sheath of invisibility around his body. A three-foot tall man with light orange skin appeared. His eyes were covered with thick welding glasses. Gnocko's people lived in a subterranean country, far to the north, known as the Badlands. His eyes were extremely sensitive to sunlight. He wore a new set of nizarian armor the Sage had commissioned for him. It helped Gnocko deal with the surface temperatures that were significantly lower than his home country.

"Can't be sure. I hear at least five" The Sage tried the door knob. "Locked. Could break it open, but we'd lose our element of surprise. Care to slip inside for a peek?"

"Sure. Send the little guy after the trofast. We need to discuss my pay scale."

The Sage watched as Gnocko altered his molecular density, becoming as translucent as a ghost. It was a skill the Sage envied, a perfect evolutionary ability for a subterranean race. The frie stavs were miners and, as such, often dealt with cave-ins. The ability to phase through solid stone lowered their mortality rates. Gnocko poked his head through the door for a moment and quickly retrieved it.

"Looks clean. Want me to open the door or keep spying?"

"Open the door. I think spy time is over. We wanted to follow him to his contacts. I think we found them. To be on the safe side, go back to mindspeak when we're inside."

Gnocko stepped completely through the door. A moment later, there was a soft click and the door opened. Gnocko stood at the top of a set of wooden steps that led down to a dark cellar. The sound of voices came from below.

'Cloak up,' the Sage sent to Gnocko. *'Get me details on the people below.'*

'I thought you said spying time was over.'

The Sage gave Gnocko a silent, steady look. *'You're being difficult again.'*

'You're big and powerful. Can't you just blast them all?'

'I'd prefer not to kill them. We need them alive.'

Gnocko held up his hands in surrender and, once again, turned invisible. The illusion did not affect the sound of his footsteps, however. The Sage clearly heard each of his tiny feet on the wood stairs as he stepped down into the basement. So, apparently, did the people downstairs.

The murmur of voices stopped. Gnocko froze in place.

"What was that?" came a gruff manly voice from below.

"Just the rats again," another man said. "You going to jump every time you hear them?"

The murmur of voices began again and Gnocko continued down the steps.

Shortly after, Gnocko sent him a message. *'Only five. Four soldier-types in leather armor and our friend the dem straki.'*

'Keep your eyes on them. Show me what you see.'

The Sage closed his eyes and delved further into Gnocko's mind. He took over the frie stav's senses. In his mind's eye, it was as if he stood in the basement himself. Four bearded soldiers, each with light blond hair, stood beside a wooden table pointing at something on the table top. Gnocko's perspective was too low to the ground for the Sage to make out what that something was. The fifth figure stood off at a distance. He removed his cowl to reveal his familiar face: wide jaw, flat nose and mauve-colored eyes. His skin was a darker mauve with evidence of recent scarring.

'Damn,' the Sage thought. *'It really is him.'*

'Told you so. What are you going to do?'

'Watch and learn. This is how it's done.'

The Sage flicked his wrist and a circle of yellow energy appeared beneath him. The disks of light were his method of teleportation. They allowed for instantaneous travel around Maghe Sihre.

He fell through the teleportation field and landed in the basement. The soldiers turned quickly, swords drawn. The Sage rushed forward punching one in the throat with his right hand while simultaneously kicking a second in the solar plexus. Both men dropped to the ground in pain. The third soldier swung his sword at the Sage who grabbed the blade with his hands, stopping it mid-swing. He tore the sword from the soldier's grip and brought the hilt down on the head of the forth soldier. As the forth soldier fell, the Sage swung the weapon and hit the third soldier in the head with the hilt.

It had only taken a second, but all four soldiers were either unconscious or on the floor, groaning in pain. Only the fifth man remained standing, his hands crackling with purple energy.

Gnocko stepped forward and dropped his invisibility. "Show off."

The Sage shrugged. "I like to make an entrance."

"I'm not sure I like this new sense of humor." Gnocko lowered his lips in a scowl.

"I don't know what you're talking about. I've always been funny." But the Sage knew that was a lie. For a long time, there had been no reason to smile. The love of his life, a woman named Echo, had died in his arms, killed by the leader of a group of evil sorcerers. Despite all his power, he couldn't keep her alive. After an unfortunate chain of events trapped him in a dark dimension and prevented him from returning to Earth, he fled to this planet, Maghe Sihre. He'd rebuilt his life. Many years later, he met another young man from Earth, Tadgh Dooley, and everything changed. Inexplicably, Echo was back from the dead. She had some connection to Tadgh, leading him to evidence of a massive invasion. Without her, the invasion may have succeeded. But if she was alive, why didn't she come to him? So far, every attempt to track her down had been fruitless. However, when the shock faded, it was replaced by something else. Hope.

A soldier attempted to get back to his feet. The Sage stepped on his back, pushing him back down to the floor. "Ein, my old friend. Been awhile. I suppose you should thank me."

"Thank you?" The trofast growled. The energy surrounding his fists grew brighter. "Why the hell would I thank you?"

"Well, if it wasn't for me you would be dead."

"You invaded my home and teleported me into the middle of the Badlands. I wandered for days without food or water. If I hadn't run into a band of nomadic moduners...."

"And if you'd stayed, the fod sel-onde would have killed you the same way he did the rest of your army. You're lucky his power didn't extend that far. So, like I said, you should thank me."

"That's not going to happen." Ein glared at the Sage. After a moment, he dispelled the Akashic energy around his hands and folded his arms across his chest. "Obviously you aren't here to kill me. What do you want?"

"Information."

Another soldier tried to stand. Gnocko held a knife to the man's throat, stopping him.

"Stop, you fool," Ein said to the soldier. "This is the Sage. Swords won't do anything to him." Turning back to the Sage, Ein squared his shoulders. "You have to know I'm not going to tell you anything."

The Sage took a step forward. "And you have to know I can send you back to the Badlands if you don't. You know me. Remember what I did to the last army that sprang up in my country? What could possess you to try again?"

Surprisingly, Ein began to laugh. "Oh, you truly have no idea, do you? I thought the Sage was supposed to be all-knowing. We're not trying to raise an army. We already have. And this time we have something scarier than you."

"We beat your whole army last time," Gnocko said. "In less than an hour. What's scarier than the Sage?"

Ein leaned forward. "A hermadur."

"I knew it!" Gnocko stomped his foot.

The Sage's eyes went wide. "Seriously? You knew a hermadur was in town and didn't say anything?"

Gnocko threw back his head and sighed. "Of course not! But I knew this adventure thing was going to be the death of me. So that's it, right? We're dropping this? You can't expect to compete with a monster like that."

"Stop being such a drama queen." The Sage rolled his eyes. "And for future reference, telling the enemy we're completely out-powered is not really the best strategy. So, Ein, you're working with a hermadur. Let's discuss your working arrangements."

"Stop talking!" One of the soldiers got to his feet and lunged at Ein. The trofast shot a bolt of Akashic energy at the soldier, knocking him back several feet.

"On second thought, maybe he's lying." Gnocko took off his welding glasses revealing small white eyes flecked with red. "There hasn't been a hermadur on Maghe Sihre since StarFall."

Ein sighed, a satisfied look on his face. "You asked. I told. I couldn't care less if you believe me or not. But whatever you think you can do to stop this, you're already too late. The hermadur is here in Gateway, the first of many. You got lucky last time. You had your pet fod sel-onde at your side. Tadgh Dooley will not be there for you this time."

The Sage hesitated. "Tadgh died at the fortress."

"Did he, now?" The expression on the trofast's face suggested Ein knew it was a lie.

"You must have heard that. The process of destroying the army was too much for him."

Ein laughed again. "We know exactly where Tadgh is and where he'll be heading."

The Sage frowned. "What do you mean where he'll be heading?"

Ein glanced away quickly as if realizing he'd said too much. "That is one piece of the puzzle I will not be sharing with you. Send me back to the Badlands. Kill me if you want. Like I said, there are scarier things in this city than you. Only a fool would cross a hermadur."

The Sage looked at Gnocko. "Are you thinking what I'm thinking?"

Gnocko shrugged. "Well, he did give you permission."

The smile fell of Ein's face disappeared as the teleportation field opened beneath his feet. He fell down through the field of energy, his screams cutting off quickly. Before the soldiers could react, the Sage opened similar portals beneath them, sending each of the men away.

"Were did you send them?" Gnocko sheathed the dagger still in his hands and began to search the room.

"Mogul tower."

Gnocko raised an eyebrow. "That old ruin in the middle of the desert. Why?"

"Because it's the perfect prison. Only way in or out is teleportation. Ein knows more than he's telling. Perhaps spending a night in the Badlands will make him more talkative. We need to track down details on this hermadur. If there really is one in town, we need to find out where it is."

"That had to be a lie." Gnocko opened a sack beside the table and rummaged through the contents. "You can't believe there's an actual demon running lose in Gateway." He removed a strange weapon from the sac: two small sickles joined together by a length of chain. "Well, would you look at this. Climbing gear. I haven't seen these since I left home."

"Back home we call those kusari-gama. They're a weapon. Very deadly."

"A weapon, huh?" Gnocko closed the sac finding nothing else of interest. "I think I'll keep these."

The Sage looked at the map on the table. "Look at this.

It's a map of the entire continent. My guess is each of these red marks represents troop placements. See where they're focused?"

Gnocko climbed up on one of the wooden stools beside the table to get a clear view of the tabletop. He studied the map for a moment before letting out a long, low whistle.

"Yes," the Sage said. "They have troops outside every capital city on the continent and agents in every major city." He leaned further over the table, his fingers tracing lines between troop placements. "Strange. The only place they don't seem to be gathering is DunDegore."

"Do you think they found the Sword?"

The Sage shook his head. "Something doesn't make sense. If they knew the Sword of Kassandra was on the island, they would send troops to recover it. We're missing a piece of the puzzle here." The Sage gathered the map, carefully folding it up. "Finding the hermadur is our best chance to learn what's really going on here. I need to take this to the local authorities. This should be enough to convince them to lend me the help I asked for weeks ago. In the mean time, head back to the hotel. Fill Eiodeesh in on what we've learned. We'll start searching for the hermadur later today. Hopefully, by then, we'll have extra ears to the ground."

Gnocko stepped off the chair. "What about the boy? Ein said they know where Tadgh is. Won't they go after him again?"

"Possibly. But he's surrounded by elmire ahk. As long as he doesn't leave the monastery, he's as safe there as anywhere on the planet. Still…" The Sage stroked his chin. "I'll teleport back to GardenKeep. Barnes is probably bored to tears anyway. I grounded him because he wanted to do something incredibly stupid. He hasn't had a mission in weeks. I'll send him and Pwella out to the monastery to warn Tadgh. That's the best I can do right now. Talking to the council here is going to take hours, and we need to search for the hermadur before nightfall."

"Good point," Gnocko said. "Facing a demon is bad enough. I'd rather do it when they're weakened by the sun. You go ahead. I'll walk back to the hotel. I'm still not used to all this open air and sunlight, but it's better than being stuck in that horrid room."

The Sage opened another portal and stepped through it into his study back in GardenKeep. The room was usually reserved for quiet reading and visiting dignitaries. Plush white furniture sat in the center of the room. Three of the four walls were lined with overflowing bookshelves. Floor-to-ceiling windows made up the fourth wall providing a quaint view of his city.

He went to the top of the stairs and yelled down to the main floor. "I'm back, Pwella."

A woman wearing a white servant's uniform appeared below. She had a kind, plump face and eyes that danced with joy. As she walked up the stairs, she wiped her flour-covered hands on her apron. When she reached the top floor, the smile slowly slid from her face.

The Sage hung his head. "What did Barnes do now?"

"Don't be mad."

"Among the stupidest sayings in any language is 'don't be mad.' It pretty much guarantees I'm going to be furious about whatever comes out of your mouth next. So spit it out already. I promise nothing."

Pwella hid her hands behind her back. "Remember how you told him not to look into the fieldbender situation anymore?"

"See? What did I tell you? I'm already angry. Where is he?"

Pwella blushed. "A group of fieldbenders from Karaj Robat arrived a few hours ago. He arranged for them to stay at that hotel you like, the one Gnocko and Eiodeesh usually stay in. He's there now, talking to them. I mentioned having them stay here. Barnes said there were too many."

"He was probably worried I'd attack anyone I saw from

Karaj Robat." The Sage chewed on the inside of his lip, trying to piece together a story from the small amount of information. Latimer, head of the fieldbender guild in Karaj Robat, had been sending him messages for weeks, all of which the Sage had dutifully ignored. They hadn't communicated since Latimer chose to ally himself with Defksquar, the man responsible for ending life on Earth. Well, life on Earth as it had been. "The fieldbenders are obviously not here on official business. Otherwise they would be staying in the parliamentary buildings. How many were here?"

Pwella shook her head. "Sorry, sir. I didn't count. It was a tad overwhelming. My guess would be at least twenty."

Unbuttoning his white jacket, the Sage laid it carefully over the back of a nearby chair. He knew he didn't really have time to spend on this current predicament. The hermadur was a pressing matter. However, he also realized twenty fieldbenders from Karaj Robat in his hometown was something equally important. He went to a nearby closet and pulled out a red ceremonial cloak, a small one that hung just past his waist.

"I'll head to them immediately," he said. "I haven't walked the streets of GardenKeep for awhile now. The fresh air might do me good."

He walked down two sets of stairs and out the stone front door. Once outside, he inhaled deeply and felt some of the tension of the day dissipate. The air smelt salty and much cleaner than the air in Gateway. GardenKeep was one of the major shipping ports in the country of Shirza. Although the docks were several blocks away, the humidity covered the entire city.

The streets were crowded. People rushed about their daily lives, completely unaware of the dangerous currents running in the world.

'I envy them sometimes,' he thought. He turned left, away from the docks and toward the edge of town. Ever since the incident with Lord Vyken and the sudden return of the Sword of Kassandra, everything in my life has been one drama after another. First Tadgh used his power and destroyed an army. Then I sent Eiodeesh and Gnocko to Te Vark and look how that turned out. My life is beginning to remind me of the way things were when I left Earth. That can't be a good thing.'

Nearby two young girls played with their dolls in the front doorstep of a bakery. A new family had recently taken ownership of the store. At the sight of him, the girls squealed in fear and ran inside. Their mother came outside to see what the source of the commotion was. Seeing the Sage, she slammed the door shut and turned the "Open" sign over to "Closed."

"Ah. Yes," the Sage said. "This is why I don't walk through the streets more often. According to rumor I'm either a graunskyeg or a child-eating demon. Oh well, I'll only make matters worse if I teleport in the middle of the street. Might as well keep going."

No other children screamed in fear as he walked toward the edge of town. However, many people gave him a wide berth. A very wide berth.

Twenty minutes later, he arrived at a non-descript five-storey hotel. A faded sign hung over the door, the name – The Silver Cross – barely legible. The Sage walked through the front door and stopped at the front desk.

"Long time, Tobeith."

The man behind the counter, Tobeith, was thin and greasy. His eyes moved too quickly and the Sage found his hands freakishly small. A former thief, the Sage had procured his services several times in the past. He did not speak. He simply nodded toward the stairs.

"Thank you. Always nice talking with you." The Sage took the stairs to the top floor. He knocked on the door to room four. A moment later, a man with long brown hair opened the door.

"You're back." The man looked over his shoulder. This was Barnes, a second-generation servant who had served under the Sage for years. "Please don't kill him. Or me. At least hear what he has to say first. "

"Occasionally I'm known to have patience." The Sage looked over Barnes' shoulder and saw a man wearing an elaborate black robe. His face was turned away, but the Sage recognized him. This was Eschandel, a high-ranking member of the fieldbender council in Karaj Robat. He was there at the last meeting the Sage attended. "But it's limited. Where are the others?"

"Around." Eschandel turned around. The Sage gazed at the man's ice-blue eyes and slender features. He looked older than the last time they'd spoken. More world-weary. "We've rented the top two floors." The man rubbed the back of his neck and looked at the floor. "Look, I owe you an apology. A big one. We should have listened to you."

"Yes." The Sage stepped past Barnes and entered the room. His servant closed the door behind him. "You should have." For a moment, the Sage hesitated, an uncomfortable thought forming in his mind. "But who can tell? Even if you had listened, Latimer wouldn't have. Anyway, your support may not have been enough to stop Defksquar. Why are you here, Eschandel?"

"We have to talk." Eschandel pointed to a table and chairs. After all three men sat down, Eschandel folded his hands together and placed them before him on the table. "After Defksquar used the Verdenstab to remake the world you came from, Earth, I left the council. I couldn't stay there with that sanctimonious idiot. Dealing with Sirion was bad enough. Defksquar was impossible."

The Sage grunted. "That's an understatement. You know my history with him. After he destroyed my world, I left Earth and traveled back in time hoping to alter events here, tweak them in a way to lessen the damage. I wish I could go back there, see if I was successful. But I'm trapped. I can never return to Earth, so there's no way of knowing if I succeeded or not."

"I can help with that." Eschandel passed the Sage a

small diamond-shaped crystal. "One of the apostates is a seer. She's been monitoring your planet, trying to gather any information possible. Everything she knows is on this nizarian memory chip."

"Apostates?" The Sage turned the crystal over in his hands. Part of him ached to read the information now, but he remembered his time constraints. He put the crystal in one of his pockets and turned his focus back to Eschandel. "Is that seriously what you're calling yourselves?"

Eschandel shrugged. "Believe it or not, we've been too busy running to put the name to a committee. That's the name Latimer gave us. We've forsaken the council in favor of something else."

The Sage raised an eyebrow and waited.

"Well, isn't it obvious?" Eschandel asked. "We've chosen you. I always knew what Defksquar planned to do. I can't pretend to be innocent. But as soon as it happened, I realized I couldn't live with myself if I supported him. I left. And I wasn't alone. Thirty-three of us made the voyage by boat from Karaj Robat to GardenKeep. We all agreed on one thing. It's time to start a new fieldbender guild with a new leader, one with the integrity and the power to stand up to the corruption in Karaj Robat."

Barnes poked the Sage in the side. "See? I told you you'd want to hear this."

Eyes wide, the Sage shook his head. "Let me get this straight. You and thirty-two others came here because you want me to start up a new fieldbending guild?"

Eschandel held up his hand, palm outward, and nodded. "Wait. Before you say no, listen to me. I can't begin to understand the fieldbending required to travel back through time. I don't even know if it's truly possible to change the past. But it is our duty to take control of our future. Defksquar is single-minded and reckless. He's so determined to fight the armies of Dispayre that he doesn't care how his actions affect others. In my mind, he's as bad as the Quadumvirate. If you don't want to lead us, I understand. I'll take over leadership. But I'm not strong enough for this. I don't have the world experience or the skill in fieldbending. You do. Without you, the Apostates can't succeed. We'll try. We'll fight. But we can't win."

Touching his lip, the Sage inhaled and exhaled slowly.

Eschandel reached out and grabbed the Sage's hand, pleading. "The Activation brought you to Maghe Sihre. If the Activation had never happened, how could you travel back in time to prevent it? What happened on Earth was monstrous. But you're here now. This world needs you." He looked over the Sage's shoulder at the door. "We need you."

"What you're suggesting could end in disaster." The Sage stopped and closed his eyes. "Or it could be the best thing to happen in years. I've felt marginalized since I left the fieldbending guild. I've tried to keep up the fight on my own with a few trusted allies. But things are spiraling out of control. As soon as I leave here I have to track down a hermadur in Gateway."

"What?" Eschandel pulled his hand off the Sages so quickly he nearly fell out of his chair. "Is the Void weakened? Is that…."

The Sage held up a hand, stopping Eschandel mid-sentence. "We don't know. Maybe it came from the Void. Maybe some idiot dem straki conjured it from a hell dimension. I'll know more later today." He lowered his hand and smiled. "I'll do it. I'll help you start a new fieldbending guild here in GardenKeep. I can't imagine changing the world with thirty-three people, but that's more allies than I had yesterday." The smile slid from his face. "Where the hell are we going to put you all?"

Barnes exchanged a quick glance with Eschandel. "We were discussing that when you arrived. There's one place that's sizable and close. Lord Vyken's fortress just outside the city."

The Sage grunted. "You want me to set up the guild there? The same fortress Tadgh almost destroyed a few months ago?"

Barnes smiled and learned forward. "It is large enough. And even though you technically don't have legal rights to the property, you do have clout with the local royal family. Seems to me, they think you're solely responsible for ending the invasion. Maybe they'll give you the fortress."

Eschandel leaned back in his chair. "And if not, you have a ridiculous amount of money. I'm sure you could buy the property."

The Sage threw back his head and laughed. "Yes, I suppose I could. Moving the fieldbenders there would be poetic. And there's no way they could all fit in my house. Having them all in one location will send a very strong message to the other guilds." He clasped Barnes' forearm. "This sounds like an excellent plan. You're in luck. I'm not going to kill either one of you today."

Standing, the Sage opened a portal. "Barnes, I leave everything in your capable hands. Draft a letter to the royal families. Let them know I want the property and be very specific about why I want it. Having a guild here will bring prestige to the city. Also more tax revenue. They'll like that part. I have to head back to Gateway. I'll check in with you tomorrow."

Then he stepped through the portal, heading back to Gateway.

In all the excitement, he had forgotten to instruct Barnes to send a warning to Tadgh.

Chapter Four

Tadgh and Menphis followed Beilaugh past the training pavilion toward Instructor Mal's private quarters.

"How have you been, Beilaugh?" Tadgh asked. "I haven't seen you in days."

"Oh, you know how it is." The former slave smiled and held out his dirty hands. "Mirelda keeps me pretty busy. Especially now that it's almost harvest. Can't find most of the local herbs in the winter. She has me scrounging in the dirt all hours of the day building up a stockpile." He half glanced at the brand on his left arm, a large "D" that showed he had once been property of the armies of Dispayre. "Every time I start complaining I remember the old days. Mirelda is demanding, but she is nothing like the slave trainers."

When they reached Instructor Mal's office, Beilaugh bowed to them and left. A woman with dark brown skin and short black hair stood beside the door, glaring at them as they approached. She wore well-polished leather armor, a sword sheathed at her waist. A clean-shaven young man, not much older than Tadgh, stood beside her. Blond curly hair hung down to his shoulders. He wore a simple outfit of unbleached woven flax. Both were strangers to Tadgh. The man looked at Tadgh with an odd, unreadable expression on his face. When he realized Tadgh was watching him, the man looked away.

Menphis approached the woman. "Are you the one looking for me?"

The woman shook her head. "The mistress is inside." She ran her eyes up and down Menphis. His thick chest and biceps were barely concealed by his white tunic. His strawberry-blond hair was cut short, a sharp contrast to his lightly tanned skin. "You look like him."

Menphis inhaled sharply and looked away uncomfortably.

"Care to clue me in? Who does he look like?" Tadgh

asked.

The woman turned to Tadgh but said nothing.

"Forgive Bethel," said the man beside her. He smiled and Tadgh noticed the way his blue eyes sparkled. "You know how temple guards are. Always on the lookout for something to stab."

"Who are you?" Tadgh asked.

The man bowed slightly. "Samar Fesh, sir. You can safely ignore me. I'm just the carriage driver."

Tadgh narrowed his eyes. Though Samar's lips were smiling, his eyes displayed a different emotion.

"Come." Menphis grabbed Tadgh by the arm and pulled him away. "Let's get this over with so we can go back to training."

The scent of jasmine and sandalwood permeated the air inside. Several low benches lined the other walls. Long open windows let in fresh air and light. Dozens of knee-high white pillar candles, currently unlit, were positioned around the room. Instructor Mal stood behind a desk built of reddish wood.

Next to Mal stood a beautiful, full-figured woman with soft, elegant features and auburn hair. Simply standing there with her arms crossed was enough to make her seem like the only person in the room. She wore a crimson coat laced down to her waist that flowed freely like a skirt to the floor. Beneath the coat was a blue velvet dress. Wrapped around her waist, worn like a belt, was a weighted chain. Although it appeared ornamental, Tadgh recognized it could easily be used as a weapon.

"She's crazy hot." Tadgh elbowed Menphis. "Dude, I'm still totally gay, but if that's your ex-girlfriend I'm going to high-five you as soon as we're outside."

Menphis scowled and walked toward the desk. Tadgh followed, several steps behind, grinning at his friend's discomfort.

"I came as quickly as I could." Menphis kept his eyes on Instructor Mal, looking at the woman only out of the corner of his eyes. "It's good to see you Tamara. You look well."

"As do you." For a moment her eyes lit up. Then her expression faded as if she recalled an unpleasant memory. When she spoke again, her voice was more subdued. "I know we promised never to see each other again, but I had nowhere else to turn. No one else I could trust."

Now Menphis turned to fully look at Tamara. "What is this about?"

Tadgh heard something in Menphis' voice that forced the smile from his lips.

"You know there is only one reason I would ever come to you," Tamara said. "It's about your son."

"What!" Tadgh punched Menphis in the arm. "You have a freaking son? How am I just learning about this now?"

Menphis raised a hand to hush Tadgh. "The situation is…difficult. You wouldn't understand."

"Really? We have tons of absent fathers where I come from."

Tamara turned her attention to Tadgh. Her eyes narrowed. "And where exactly do you come from? Your energy signature is…odd."

Tadgh clamped his mouth shut. 'Damn. She's an elmire ahk. No one is supposed to know I'm from another planet. One of these days I'll learn to stop talking. I hope.'

Instructor Mal cleared his throat, drawing the attention away from Tadgh and back to him. "Tamara, this is Tadgh Dooley. He will accompany you and Menphis on your journey. I'm sure you will have time to discuss his past at length on the road."

"We're leaving the monastery?" Menphis turned to look at Tadgh. "Sir, are you sure that's wise given Tadgh's…situation?"

Instructor Mal nodded. "It's precisely because of his situation that I'm sending him with you. His training needs to continue. The journey there and back may take a month.

He can't afford that much time without your tutelage. Aside from that, he has certain characteristics that will make your task much easier." He turned toward Tamara. "Young Tadgh is also a fod sel-onde."

Menphis blanched. "Instructor, you said that was a secret. Are you sure…" He stopped and covered his mouth with his right hand. He turned to look Tamara in the eyes. "He said 'also.' Our son is fod sel-onde?"

Tamara reached out and touched Menphis' cheek. "His name is Grandwyn. He turned eight last month. And yes, he is fod sel-onde. I tried to convince him to keep it a secret. I told him people would hurt him if they knew. He has your eyes and your hair but he has my stubbornness. I should have known he wouldn't listen. Once he makes up his mind, nothing can stop him."

Instructor Mal walked around the desk and sat down on the edge. "Perhaps you should start from the beginning Tamara. Tell Menphis what happened."

"Of course." Tamara folded her hands together. "My life has changed much since we last met. I'm now head of the temple in FleshPrayer."

Menphis looked at her, wide eyed. "That's…impressive."

Tamara smiled. "I'm the youngest Instructor since StarFall. I wasn't at the temple when Grandwyn left. I was in South Point with Councilor Randall. She and her family are dealing with matters that require my full attention. As you know, part of my duty as Instructor of the Sisterhood of Flesh is to act as social worker for the royal families. It was far from home, but Councilor Randall is a woman of some influence. You've heard of her, of course."

Menphis shook his head. "I don't follow politics much."

Tamara laughed. "And I'm a virgin. You're a member of the Brotherhood of Tyche. You may have the common folk fooled into thinking you're simple healers, but I know the truth. The Brotherhood of Tyche is much more concerned with espionage and information trading than medicine."

Instructor Mal cleared his throat. "We try not to focus on rumor here at the monastery. Councilor Randall is head of the committee investigating the strange events at the fort outside GardenKeep. You remember. The one where an army planning a coup suddenly disappeared."

Tadgh tensed and took an involuntary step back. A quick, subtle look from Instructor Mal signaled him to calm himself.

"I have…heard of the event," Menphis said. "But I know little of the details. Contrary to what you may think, Tamara, much of what happens at the monastery is no more than it seems. We train. We align our spirits with our physical bodies, much as you do. Elmire ahk at my level are rarely involved in…other things. You were saying something about Councilor Randall?"

"After working with the Sage for months, she completed her investigation. As you may have heard, it is believed a fod sel-onde is behind the destruction. She needed to ensure someone that powerful was no longer a threat. Thankfully, she found no evidence the poor creature is still alive. So she headed to the capital, South Point, to share her findings."

"Why do you call him a poor creature?" Tadgh spoke without thinking. 'Idiot. I'm not supposed to be drawing attention to myself. Why did I ask that question?'

"Power, of all sorts, can change you." Tamara wet her lips and spoke softly. "I've seen it all too often at the temple and in the parliament buildings. Real power can make you forget who you are, who use used to be. Can you imagine being burdened with the power of that fod sel-onde? The ability to wipe out hundreds of lives in the blink of an eye is something no mortal should posses. One would assume the power would eat at his soul, eventually turning him into something callous. Monstrous. Any faction on the planet would want to capture him, use him for their own end. That's why I fear…"

She stopped and shook her head. "I am getting ahead of myself. Councilor Randal left for South Point. I went with her. While I was gone, Grandwyn stole some coin from my room and ran away."

"Wasn't anyone from the temple watching him?" Menphis asked.

Tamara sighed deeply. "Of course I left someone to watch over Grandwyn. I'm not an idiot. Business often takes me away from him. He has a full-time nanny, and all the exits to the temple are under guard. But Grandwyn is too smart for his own good. We don't know how he did it, but he escaped. My sources tell me he snuck aboard a delivery carriage. By the time anyone realized he was gone, he was already in the next town.

"Who is your source?"

"Fricka." Tamara closed her eyes and touched her forehead and chest, an action that Tadgh perceived to be religious.

Menphis repeated her action. "You spoke with the goddess herself?"

Tamara nodded. "From time to time, Fricka graces me with her attention. When I learned that Grandwyn had run away, I turned to her for guidance. Grandwyn told no one he was leaving. All he left was this note."

She pulled a piece of paper from the folds of her dress, unfurled it and read from it aloud. "'Mother, I know you will be angry. I'm sorry. But I don't want to live this way anymore. I'm turning myself over to the fieldbenders. Hopefully they will train me. Maybe you're wrong. Maybe I'm not fod sel-onde. If I am, we both know what will happen. Either way, I will not have to lie anymore. I would say not to follow me, but I know you will. By the time you read this it will be too late. I hope to see you after my training is complete. Love Grandwyn."

Tadgh scratched his jaw. "How old is this kid, again? I thought you said he was eight. When I was that age I could barely read and write."

"As I said, he is a gifted child." Tamara folded the letter and replaced it in its hiding place. "Very bright. But also very foolish. If he reveals himself to the fieldbenders, they will put him on trial. They will find him guilty of being a fod selonde and order his death. Not even my position will be able to stop them. You know how those people are. How sanctimonious they can be. We have to get Grandwyn back by force. I cannot use any official channels or I risk shaming the temple."

"So you know where he is?" Menphis asked. "Karaj Robat?"

"No." Tamara stared at the ground. "Even further away. He's gone to the island of DunDegore. He left two weeks ago and arrived early this morning. He checked into a hotel. Fricka gave the directions."

"Is that all she did?" Tadgh shook his head. "I mean, if she really is a goddess, couldn't she have zapped you over to DunDegore?"

Menphis punched Tadgh in the arm. "We serve the gods. Not the other way around."

"No," Tamara said. Her eyes grew distant. "He's right. I noticed something...odd in the way Fricka spoke with me. My intuition tells me something is preventing her from taking more direct action."

"What could prevent a god from taking action?" Menphis asked.

"Precisely," Instructor Mal said. "There may be more happening on the Island of DunDegore than we suspect. Before you head home, I need you to speak with the head of the monastery there. Anything that concerns the gods should be a concern to mortals as well."

Tamara touched her forehead again. "If I know Grandwyn, he'll head to the fieldbenders tomorrow. We have to move quickly. His trial and execution will be fast. We don't have much time."

Menphis covered his mouth again with a trembling hand. "This is a lot to take in. I'll help. Of course I'll help. What do you need me to do?"

Tamara's shoulders relaxed. "I have a carriage out front. I know your school prefers walking, but this is a matter of some urgency. I could not acquire a nizarian flying ship and, honestly, doing so would have been too high profile. We need to enter the city quietly if we hope to steal Grandwyn away."

"And after?" Menphis forced his hand away from his face. "You won't be able to take him back with you."

Tamara closed her eyes. "Probably not. But we'll deal with one problem at a time. When can you be ready to leave?"

Menphis glanced over a Tadgh, his eyes pleading with a vulnerability Tadgh had never seen there before.

"I'm ready now," Tadgh said. "Doesn't Tyche tell us all a traveler needs is his staff and a few coins?"

Menphis bit his lip and nodded. "Okay. We leave now. Take us to your coach."

Chapter Five

Grandwyn spent the night lying awake. Loud music came up through the floors from the tavern below. Moans and cries filled the upper floors, sounds he associated with things adults did with each other behind closed doors.

In the morning when he woke, dread, like he'd never felt before, settled into his stomach, an overwhelming sensation that something bad was about to happen. For the first time, he had doubts about turning himself over to the fieldbenders. What if his mother was right? What if he was fod sel-onde? Would the fieldbenders kill him immediately, or would he be granted a trial?

The brochure he carried with him had a map of the island. He used it to navigate the narrow streets and find the fieldbender guild. Guards stood at either side of the door, staring back at him. Grandwyn flushed, his nerves overwhelming him. Lowering his head, he walked past them.

'This is stupid.' He walked right past the guild and turned his gaze to the candy shop across the street. 'What's wrong with me? I've come this far. I can't go home now.'

He wandered the streets for several blocks until he came to a large public square. Tall stone buildings surrounded an open area filled with artists and jugglers. Ornate stone fountains sprayed fresh water into shallow pools. Most of the people milling about had maps in their hands as they pointed up at various buildings or sat at the edge of the fountains. Grandwyn saw a café nearby. Although most of the tables inside were occupied, he found an empty table on the patio. He sat and placed a hand over his stomach, trying to calm his nerves.

'I've never felt this way,' he thought. 'Back in FleshPrayer, I so sure this was the right thing. But now...?'

A young woman with blond hair in a ponytail approach him, smiling. She wore a simple serving uniform: white shirt and pants with pink strips. She placed a menu on the table.

"Good morning. My name's Jessica. Are you here by yourself?"

Grandwyn nodded. "My parent's told me to wait for them here. I got hungry, and they wanted to look at more stupid statues."

Jessica laughed, believing his lie. "Take your time with the menu. I'll be back in a bit." As she walked back inside the restaurant, Grandwyn opened the menu absently but didn't read it. Truth is, he couldn't imagine eating anything right now. Not with his stomach in knots. He looked around the square, but his eyes were constantly drawn back in the direction of the fieldbender guild.

Somewhere in the distance, a woman screamed.

Grandwyn glanced up but saw no sign of disturbance. He tried to convince himself it was nothing, that he shouldn't overreact. Things happen in big cities all the time. But a tiny voice inside whispered to him that something was not right. He refolded the menu and stood, his eyes searching the crowd for danger.

"Looking for your mother, little man?" Jessica had returned with a glass of ice water.

Grandwyn shook his head. "I heard something. A scream."

She put the glass on the table. "Nothing to worry about. Most likely someone saw a rat. They come up from the sewers sometimes. If there is any trouble the city guard will look into it. Did you want to order something, or did you want to wait until your mother gets here?"

"I haven't really…"

Another scream filled the air. This time it was a man's.

"Oh dear." Jessica touched Grandwyn's arm. The look on her face was no longer condescending. "Why don't you come inside with me?"

"What is it?"

Jessica shook her head, now pushing Grandwyn toward the interior of the café. "Sometimes people get upset when their on vacation. Fights happen. Couples that love each other sometimes start yelling. Sometimes they do more."

"I don't think that's what this is." Grandwyn stopped, slipping away from the server's arms. He looked up at her and noticed how narrow her eyes were as she scanned the crowd. "You feel it to don't you? I can see it in your face. Something is very wrong."

"Probably nothing to worry about." Jessica smiled down at him, but there was an odd expression on her face." Come inside. I'll get you some ice cream while you wait for your…."

She stopped midsentence and screamed, a sound more terrifying and chilling than anything Grandwyn had ever heard. Grandwyn tried to turn, to see what had made her scream, but she pulled at him, dragging him inside the café. Once inside, she turned and bolted the glass door. She knelt down and looked Grandwyn in the eyes.

"I need you to go down to the basement. There's a spot under the stairs where you'll be safe."

"I don't understand." Grandwyn frowned. Outside, more people were screaming now. Someone pounded on the café door. Grandwyn tried to look outside, but the server had positioned her body to block his view.

"Neither do I." Jessica pointed toward an open door. "Please, go through there and close the door. Will you do that for me?"

Grandwyn walked backwards toward the basement door, trying to look through the glass door outside. There were several people at the door now, all banging to be let in. He saw one of them, a man in the white robes of an acolyte, look over his shoulder. Whatever he saw made him forget about the café. He took off running.

Standing at the top of the stairs, Grandwyn looked into the basement. He didn't want to head down there. He had always hated basements. They were dark and creepy. He watched as Jessica spoke rapidly with a group of others in the same uniform she wore. One went to the door, apparently to open it. The others pulled her back. Then

Jessica ran off, only to come back later with several large knives. She handed the blades out to her coworkers before looking over to see Grandwyn, who still stood in the doorway.

She came to him and pushed him inside. "You'll be safe down there. No matter what you hear up here, don't make a sound. And don't come up. I'll come for you when it's safe." Then she pulled the door closed. There was a clicking sound followed by footsteps leading away. Grandwyn tried the doorknob. It wouldn't move.

"She locked me in here." He pressed his ear to the wood of the door, listening. He heard the crash of glass breaking, followed by people screaming. The shrieks lasted a long time. Then silence. A stream of blood seeped through the crack beneath the door.

Grandwyn back away. As quietly as he could, he walked down the wooden steps to the basement and found a place to hide.

Chapter Six

Tadgh pushed aside the orange curtain that covered the carriage window and looked out on the highway. Large sections of high grass and wild flowers stood between the road and the trees in the distance. He couldn't stop smiling.

'Can't believe this is the first time I've left the monastery since returning from GardenKeep,' he thought. 'I've seen the maps but they're hard to read. I really should have wished for the ability to read this messed up language instead of just to speak it. This world, Maghe Sihre, is so large, and I've only seen such a small part of it. I would love to see the Great Castles in the north or some of the other races. I've never seen a valgt'til, but I hear they're common in other countries. Most things I've seen here could easily exist back on Earth.'

The journey to DunDegore would take ten days by carriage. Yesterday, they had left the monastery almost immediately. They traveled for hours before stopping in the city of Beauty Tree shortly after sunset. Thick clouds of incense and perfume drifted out from every doorway and window. Tadgh had kept his eyes glued to the ground as they left the carriage. Revelers walked around nearly naked, kissing and touching each other. Most of the activity was between men and women, but Tadgh had seen one tangle of flesh with men only. He tried not to be judgmental, to remind himself that this was a different culture, but he was brought up Catholic. There were limits.

In the morning, after breakfast and a very rushed session of exercise, they got back into the carriage. The plan was to travel all day until they reached the town of Tryst where they would stop for the second night.

Menphis sat beside Tadgh, eyes closed in mediation. Tamara sat across from him. Her eyes stared out the window, but the expression on her face suggested she was not seeing the scenery. Her mind was somewhere else. In her hands she held a small stuffed animal. From the way she held it, Tadgh assumed it belonged to her son. Bethel sat across from Tadgh, reading a book. For the second day in a row, it appeared no one would be talking to each other. Hoping to break the awkward silence, Tadgh asked a question.

"So, how did you guys meet?"

Menphis cleared his throat. Tamara glanced at Tadgh briefly before returning to look out the window. She surprised him a moment later when she spoke.

"I was new to my title," she said. "Like all priestesses, I was schooled at the temple since childhood. However, we do not take our vows until we turn eighteen. Menphis was one of the first men I saw."

Tadgh bit his lip. "I know I'm going to regret this, but what do you mean by saw? I know very little about your order. How is your branch of elmire ahk different than ours?"

"What a curious thing to say." Tamara leaned forward. "You are obviously not from Shirza. As a member of the Sisterhood of Flesh, I dedicate my life to Fricka, goddess of sex and fertility. You are a member of the Brotherhood of Tyche, the god of travelers. You spend your lives spying…"

Menphis interjected. "We're not spies."

Tamara waved away the interruption. "We spend our lives focused on making life better for people. We assist women seeking to become pregnant, offer family counseling services, and we heal through sexual activity." Tamara leaned in closer, studying Tadgh's face. "Those eyes…they are unlike any eye I've ever seen, even on a fod sel-onde. Where are you from?"

Menphis came to his rescue. "I met Tamara when I was sixteen. You know I joined the monastery early, at ten. What you don't know is, I ran away once. It wasn't long after Shonn's father, my uncle, died. I was home at the time. Summer vacation. Everything changed for me that day. Maybe it was the look in Shonn's eyes. That was the first time his abilities manifested, first time he realized he was fod sel-onde. He saw the death before it actually happened. A vision. He knew something bad was going to happen and felt powerless to stop it. I started questioning things. I knew becoming a Brother of Tyche meant I would never have a family. A part of me wanted to experience certain things. So I went to Fricka's temple in FleshPrayer."

"You went there at sixteen? Is that allowed?"

Menphis frowned. "Of course. I was well into my manhood. Every adult is capable of prayer. The temple understood my pain. My confusion. Many Brothers weaken during their studies. It distracts them, slows down their advancement. Our vows are not for chastity, only to put the monastery ahead of everything. Even family. Tamara was the first and only woman I have…known."

Tadgh inhaled and looked back and forth between Tamara and Menphis. "Oh. So you weren't boyfriend and girlfriend? It was just a one-time thing?"

Tamara shook her head. "We spent significant time together. Weeks."

Tadgh elbowed Menphis. "Damn. That must have got expensive."

Bethel slapped Tadgh across the face. "Mistress is not a whore. She is not something to be bought. Her actions are divine will. You will show respect."

Tamara sat the stuffed animal on her lap and placed a gentle hand on Bethel's shoulder, calming her. "Enough. It is obvious Tadgh knows nothing of our ways. Other cultures are not like our own. It is you who needs to show respect."

Bethel lowered her head. "Of course. Sorry, mistress." She looked up, her eyes focused on Tadgh. "Forgive me. I acted in haste."

Tadgh touched his face. "No. I'm the one who needs to apologize. What I said was disrespectful. My big mouth is going to be the death of me some day."

"Yes, it will." Menphis glowered at him. "It seems we need to spend a little less time on the combat floor and a little more on social etiquette training."

"You are correct about one thing, Tadgh." Tamara folded her hands together in her lap. "Spending that much time together is not common. In fact, it is forbidden. My superiors reprimanded me after Menphis left. Priestesses must not form a connection with the worshippers. We are a vessel, a medium for others to experience the divinity of the holy mother. Nothing more. Any interference with that channel is discouraged."

Tadgh turned to Bethel. "Please don't hit me but I have another question."

Bethel nodded, but the cold expression in her eyes warned Tadgh to phrase his question carefully.

"No disrespect intended," Tadgh said, "but didn't you take precautions against…you know…"

Tamara touched her forehead and breast. "We did. Every time. But a child was conceived nonetheless. The temple interprets that as a sign of divine will. This child was meant to live. The Sisterhood has intimate knowledge of pregnancy. I could have ended it, of course, but that was never a consideration for me."

Menphis shifted uncomfortably beside him. "This conversation is becoming increasingly uncomfortable. Do we have to speak of this?"

"I have nothing to be ashamed of." Tamara touched Menphis' kneed. "Neither do you. Tadgh, as a member of the Sisterhood of the Flesh, I regularly meet with women who have an undesired pregnancy. We commune with the unborn child and ask if it is willing to incarnate later to another mother. If it is, the child's spirit leaves and the pregnancy ends. If not, the mother knows the child is meant to be. We do not terminate the pregnancy by using herbs or surgical devices like they do in the north. We have a conversation. That is all."

Tadgh scratched his jaw. "I think I understand that. Did Menphis know? Did you tell him you were having his child?"

Menphis looked out the window, keeping his eyes away

from everyone. "She told me. She is a woman of honor and duty. I was just a boy, younger than you, but I knew my duty as well. The child did not belong to me or to Tamara. He belongs to the monastery. I would never be a part of his life."

"Never?"

Bethel sighed in annoyance. "Why are the pretty ones always so dumb? The only way Menphis could have remained in the boy's life was to leave the Brotherhood of Tyche and become a servant of the Sisterhood."

Tadgh's eyes went wide. "Wait. Menphis almost became a sexy monk?"

Menphis reached over and flicked Tadgh's ear with his middle finger. "Remember that thing about your mouth being the death of you? Only women can join the Sisterhood. If I'd stayed, I could have become a member of the guard like Bethel. And I think that is enough of this conversation. Drop it."

"Sure." Tadgh felt like a piece of dog turd. He'd made his best friend angry. "Let's change the subject. Before we went to see Instructor Mal, you were going to tell me something."

"You have horrible timing." All of Menphis' anger deflated, replaced by something completely different. "Instructor Mal has heard from my cousin, Shonn. He sent word from Castle Nizaria. For obvious reasons, it has me a little…emotional."

Tadgh felt himself blush. "Oh. Is he…I mean, is he okay?"

"He is fine." Menphis touched his chest, a sign that he was praying to Tyche for guidance. "He studies with the neurotechs to improve his control over his abilities. Apparently he is making progress, and his teachers have high expectations for him. He…he said to tell you he thinks of you often."

Tadgh nodded his head rapidly. He blinked. His mouth was too dry to say anything. He'd fallen in love with Shonn at first glance. At first, it appeared the feeling was mutual. Then Tadgh learned about his ability to control people's minds with a touch. From that point on, he couldn't be sure if Shonn's feelings were real or something Tadgh had forced him to feel. Plagued by doubt, Tadgh ended the relationship.

"For the love of Tyche," Menphis said. "I'm a simple man, Tadgh. I don't know what to make of you and my cousin. He was never…different…until he met you. Whether you are to blame or not is…"

"He didn't leave because of me." Tadgh looked over. Thankfully both Tamara and Bethel were doing an excellent job of appearing fascinated with the world outside. "Whether he was gay – that's the word we use – before he met me, I don't know. But he has always been different. He went to the nizarians because he's fod sel-onde. All his life he's been afraid the authorities would kill him if they learned what he is. Perhaps the nizarians can help him get control of his abilities."

"I know that. I'm partially responsible for him leaving, too. Because I was reckless and got myself captured, Shonn allowed the Sage to alter him, strengthen his abilities. If I'd only…." Menphis took a deep breath and smiled shallowly. "Perhaps we should work on having less explosive conversations in public."

"No, please continue," Bethel said. "We have a long journey and your drama is more entertaining than watching the trees."

They travelled in silence for awhile. Tadgh focused on the beauty of the day and the bright blue sky. The nearest forest – or hunts as they were called here – were far in the distance. The land in-between was populated with farms growing grains and leafy green vegetables. He saw livestock that resembled white-skinned deer. He wanted to ask about them, but remembered he was supposed to be pretending to be a native of the planet. If he asked what they were, he risked drawing too much attention to himself.

Occasionally, Tamara stroked the fur on the stuffed animal. Sometimes she smiled as she did so. Other times, her face was heavy and drawn with sorrow. After a long period of silence, she leaned toward Menphis.

"There is a wound in your aura. I don't mean to pry, but I can help you with that."

Menphis stared at the floor. "You're welcome to try, but don't get your hopes up. None of the brothers have been able to remove it."

"What happened?"

Menphis' shoulders tensed. He said nothing.

"He doesn't like to talk about it," Tadgh said. "You heard Menphis say he was imprisoned? A few months ago, he had an encounter with a graunskyeg. Menphis was under its control for awhile."

"A graunskyeg?" Bethel's voice was filled with skepticism. "Really?"

Menphis glared at the dark-skinned girl. "Trust me. They are real. It wasn't one of the lesser ones. This one was well-fed. Ancient and strong. Pray you never meet one."

The conversation turned to travel. Tamara's position often had her traveling around the country. She spoke of museums in the southern port town of Pulse and the view of the mountains in Renunciation. Neither Tadgh nor Menphis had seen either location. Tadgh drank in every detail.

"I've missed going on vacation," Tadgh said. "When I was kid we went somewhere every summer, but I was too young to appreciate it. We even went to England once, but it's all a blur."

Menphis glared at Tadgh then, with a deep sigh, slowly looked away.

Tamara frowned. "I've not heard of this place. Where is this city?"

'Stupid,' Tadgh thought. He stared out the window trying to think of something to say. Menphis saved him.

"Tadgh suffered a brain injury," Menphis said. "When he came to the monastery, he'd lost significant portions of his memory. Prelate Leif and Instructor Mal have worked with him, trying to help him remember. Sometimes he says bizarre things. We even had to re-teach him how to read."

Relief flooded Tadgh. Menphis had given him the perfect excuse for his ignorance of everyday things. And it was partially true. When he first arrived at the monastery, many of his memories were blocked. The effect was only temporary, however. He now remembered everything. Even the things he wished he could forget.

Tamara studied Tadgh, her eyes tracing the lines of his face. He felt a surge of energy surround his body. He recognized this. She was sending portions of her own energy into his aura. This was how the elmire ahk healed others. He wasn't used to someone doing this without his permission. The energy dissipated, and she slid back in her chair.

"I sense a great tragedy." Tamara rubbed her forehead. "Sometimes the mind forgets things that will cause severe pain. You have my sympathies. Has your reading improved?"

Tadgh shrugged. "A little. I haven't had much chance to practice, though. Training and meditation takes up most of the day. The majority of our teaching is oral so there hasn't been much opportunity to practice."

Bethel smiled. "You're in luck. I happen to be a collector of books. Mostly almanacs with details on local culture and history. I'll be happy to lend you a few while we travel. There's not much else we can do on the road."

Tadgh nodded. "That would be fantastic." Maybe now he would learn more about this strange world.

Chapter Seven

The streets in Gateway were crowded as the Sage left the city guard headquarters. The afternoon sun burned brighter and hotter than it had in weeks. The beautiful weather drove people out into the streets to enjoy the last days of summer. The Sage enjoyed being in a city where few people knew him. A group of children ran past him, laughing as they chased a purple butterfly. Vendors shouted at him, trying to coerce him to buy smoked meat on sticks or chilled fruit.

Leaving the crowded streets behind, he climbed a flight of stairs to the top floor of a small house he'd rented in town. He knocked on the door. A moment later, a woman answered the door. She was seven feet tall and wore armor. Her light mauve skin was marked with occasional green spots and sporadic black lines. Her thick hair was long and braided. Like Ein, she was a trofast, but she was a no friend of the Quadumvirate.

"You're back." She looked over the Sages shoulder as if searching the shadows. Then she stepped aside, letting him in. They stood in a comfortable, carpeted sitting room, the first section of the two-bedroom suite. "How did the meeting with the head of the guard go?"

"Better than expected." The Sage sat on a plush red couch beneath a large window that overlooked the city. "He's dedicated twenty men to the search for other soldiers. They're starting a sweep of the docks first. That's where most travelers stay. I should have reports by the end of the day. I know I've said it before, but I'm truly grateful you are here. I know your last mission was a little…tense."

"Tense!" Gnocko burst into the room from the adjoining bathroom. "You sent us to Te Vark. We were chased by a horde of bandits armed with nizarian weapons! We barely escaped with our lives."

The Sage shrugged. "Like I said. Tense. It wasn't like you faced down a squadron of Umbral Knights. It could have been worse."

Gnocko grunted and walked back into the bathroom.

"Ignore him." Eiodeesh sat in a wooden chair and picked a large battle-axe off the nearby table. As she spoke, she drew a small cube over the blade. Subtle blue light seeped from the cube, sharpening the edge. "Between you and me, I think he's finally starting to enjoy it. He would never admit it, but if you look in his eyes, you can tell it's all bluster now."

"Is not!" Gnocko shouted from the bathroom.

Eiodeesh rolled her eyes and continued sharpening her weapon.

Gnocko returned from the bathroom running a hand through his damp hair. "Ick. I hate having to wash in water. It's unnatural. Give me a pool of lava any day. Now that's a real clean." He climbed up on the couch beside the Sage and looked out the window. Because of his size, it was the only way he could look out the window. "Heat and ash, this is a step up from the hotel Eiodeesh and I stayed in when we stopped here. You can see the stadium from here and the university. All we could see was the backside of an aqueduct tunnel."

The Sage smiled. "I have connections. When were you last here?"

"A few months back. Just before we met you." Eiodeesh unhooked her battleaxe from her waist and leaned it against the wall. "After Gnocko escaped from the graunskyegs and I found him, we went to Marlax first. That's where we learned about you. We stopped here on the way to GardenKeep."

Gnocko grunted and stepped off the couch. "Seems like a lifetime ago. So much has changed in a few months. Never in my life did I expect to be chasing down a blasted hermadur with a trofast and a..." He looked over at the Sage. "What are you anyway? You're obviously not a sirian."

"Obviously," the Sage said. "But that is a mystery for another day."

"What's a hermadur, exactly?" Eiodeesh looked back and forth between the others, a look of confusion on her face. "You keep using the word, but I'm not familiar with the term."

The Sage folded his hands. "In simplest terms, a hermadur is a demon. An extra-dimensional creature from a section of the Void. Humanoid creatures, eight feet tall, usually seen in blood-red armor with wings of fire. I haven't seen one in over a century and that was on an elemental plane. I've never seen one here on Maghe Sihre before. Were you able to confirm there's a hermadur in town?"

Gnocko grumbled. "Unfortunately, yes."

"Any firsthand accounts?" the Sage asked. "Did anyone actually see the hermadur?"

Gnocko cocked his head to the side. "Of course they aren't firsthand accounts. The people we spoke to are still alive. But, we think we've found out where it lives."

Eiodeesh removed a heavily-folded piece of paper from her pocket and spread it out over a nearby table. It was a detailed map of the city, meticulously drawn in pen. Points of interest were marked with circles and stars. The others gathered around to see it better.

"We're here," Eiodeesh said pointing at a square near the center of town. "I spent a few hours in a pub listening for rumors. Anything out of the ordinary. Apparently, there's a sudden increase in the number of northerners in the area I've circled here."

"Probably not a coincidence." The Sage touched his lips. "The soldiers with Ein were all northerners. Shouldn't be that hard to track them down. Not many people with blond hair and beards this far south.

"Exactly." Eiodeesh pointed at a section marked with a star. "And this is where I think the hermadur is."

"Really?" The Sage glanced over at her. "Why?"

Gnocko grunted. "Because the voices in her head told

her that's where it is."

"For the last time the voices aren't in my head." Eiodeesh swiped a large hand at Gnocko, but he ducked away from it easily. "Tiny man here knows all trofast have rudimentary telepathic powers. If I focus, I can hear surface thoughts. Once people have been drinking, they tend to let their guard down so pubs are the perfect spots to gather information. There has been strange activity around this warehouse for the last few weeks. Weird smells. Unusual sounds at all hours of the night. People are spooked. I figure it's as good a place to start as any."

"So we have a hermadur and an unknown number of soldiers," Gnocko said. We need a plan. Which do which do we hit first?"

The Sage touched his fingertips to his lips, deep in thought. "I think we need to split up."

Gnocko threw his hands in the air. "Seriously? When is that ever a good idea?"

"Now." The Sage continued to stroke his lips, a far off expression on his face. "Gnocko, I need you and Eiodeesh to check out this place where the soldiers have been living. I need whatever information you can find."

"And what about you?" Gnocko asked. "You're not thinking of taking on this hermadur by yourself. Surely you can't be serious."

"Of course I'm serious. And don't call me Shirley."

Gnocko and Eiodeesh exchanged a confused look.

The Sage sighed. "I wish that boy Tadgh was here. At least he would understand that joke. Look, if there really is a hermadur at the warehouse, I'm the only one here equipped to fight it. And if it comes down to a battle, I'm better off alone. That way I won't have to worry about your safety. Trust me. I'm more than capable of taking care of myself."

***

The three friends went their separate ways. The Sage thought about teleporting but decided against it. Demons could sense alterations in the reality field, and his teleportation disks sent large ripples. Most likely, the rumors of a hermadur were exaggerated. It was much more likely there was a fieldbender or dem straki in town who specialized in illusions. Normally, the veils between realities were too strong for demons to cross over. Still, just in case, he decided to walk.

The warehouse was on the far side of Gateway. He took the most linear path, directly through the center of town. He walked past city hall and tall stone monuments to the royal families. Young people filled the center square. Some sat at the edge of fountains. Others ate sugar ice or walked arm in arm.

'Reminds me of Rome,' he thought. 'Echo and I used to walk the streets at night with a bottle of wine. She loved watching the street artists in Piazza Navona.'

Thinking of Echo brought back multiple waves of emotion: love, loss and sorrow. When he arrived on Maghe Sihre, the first thing the Sage did was travel back through time. Although her death had happened only recently on Earth, for him, three hundred years had passed. In all that time, he'd known the company of several women but had never allowed himself to love another. He'd come close with Torch Karehn, but they ended their relationship more than a decade ago. He'd never spoken of Echo to her, but she knew there was someone, or something, holding him back, making him unable to give himself over to her fully. Karehn demanded nothing less than all of him. He could not blame her for that.

Past the city center, the streets slowly emptied of people. Women in drab dresses swept the stoops and door-ways of surrounding houses. Above, a couple yelled at each other. Nearby, a baby cried. The sounds of life made the Sage uncomfortable.

'Look at these people. Blissfully unaware of the danger. A hermadur in this place could kill every living thing in Gateway. I pray the rumors are wrong.'

He crouched in an alley across the street from the

warehouse. Dozens of servants in gray uniforms unloaded boxes from horse-drawn carriages and carried them inside. The building was a long rectangle with the short side facing the street. Guards in black leather armor stood equally spaced along the perimeter of the warehouse. Two of them stood in front of the main entrance, their hands resting on the hilts of their swords.

He watched the activity for a break in the workflow. He needed to get inside but didn't want to blast his way through. This task needed stealth, not power. Hermadur or not, whoever led these men might run if it looked like the situation here was unwinnable. If there truly was a demon in Gateway, he needed to see it with his own eyes.

Finally, the carts were empty and the servants left the entranceway. When only the guards remained, the Sage made his move.

Taking two smooth pieces of stone from his pocket, he hurled them as hard as he could at the two nearest guards. Even back on Earth, he'd never cared for guns. Why bother? His strength allowed him to throw projectiles as fast as any arrow.

Each stone hit a guard in the throat with deadly accuracy. Unable to shout for help, each collapsed to his knees, clutching his throat. The Sage ran to the first guard, propping him up against the wall to make it appear, from a distance, as if he was sleeping. After doing the same to the other guard, he slipped through the door and entered the warehouse.

He crept along the rows of crates until he heard voices. Crouching down, he looked over the edge of the boxes and searched for the speaker.

'Well I'll be damned,' he thought. 'It really is a hermadur.'

Red metallic armor covered the creature's entire body, glistening like fresh-spilled blood. Translucent yellow wings that flickered like flames hung from its back. In its hands was a long sword constructed of light. It took a moment for the Sage to see to whom the hermadur was speaking. A second figure stepped forward and began speaking. An orange house cat with glowing green eyes.

'Hmm.' The Sage frowned. 'I wasn't expecting that. House cats aren't common in this part of Maghe Sihre. Let alone talking ones. Hmm. A talking cat. Why is that so familiar?' He settled into a crouch to listen to their conversation.

"And I told you to stop worrying," the cat said. "The boy is on his way. He'll be in Gateway tomorrow."

"You don't know that." The hermadur's voice crackled like burning embers.

"But I do. My plans always work."

"Not always. You lost him once before. The operation in DunDegore is underway. The graunskyeg are in play. We need him there immediately."

The cat grew until he was the size of a lion. "I said he'll be there. I have more invested in that worm than you do. This whole thing was my plan, remember? I'm the one who found Grandwyn. I'm the one who snuck into his tiny brain and convinced him to run away to DunDegore. I made it impossible for the boy not to head to DunDegore. All you have to do when he gets there is make sure he picks up the Sword of Kassandra."

"He will, Bes, but you're missing the point." The hermadur's wings flashed. "The others are worried. You have a history of...failure."

'Bes.' The Sage stroked his jaw. 'I know that name. The boy....' Suddenly the pieces of the puzzle clicked together. 'They mean Tadgh. That's the cat demon that turned him into a werecat, the thing that almost killed him. It must have tracked him here from Earth.'

Bes grew again, this time becoming as large as a horse. "Say that one more time. I dare you."

The hermadur took a step back and lowered his head.

"Better." Bes shrank back to the size of a normal house cat. "Just remember, once the boy does his thing with the

Sword of Kassandra, he leaves with me."

"Lord Dispayre could have uses for him. He may not want...."

"I don't care what Dispayre or the Quadumvirate want. My lords demand him, and I answer to them, not you. We're only working with you because it currently serves our interest. We are not allies. A creature like this comes along once in a millennium. The power of a djinn in a human body ...the possibilities are endless."

'The power of a...' The Sage felt his body grow cold. 'What were they talking about? Isn't Tadgh a fod sel-onde?'

The hermadur took a step forward. "Exactly my point. When the djinn died on Earth, a portion of its power settled into a human host, the closest person it could find who was fueled by a monstrous rage. A need for revenge. It settled in Tadgh and gave him the ability to make his wishes come true. We need to understand how it happened. How it works. Dispayre will send his generals, the Quadumvirate, to invade the Kaz. They will slaughter hundreds of djinns if it means transferring their abilities to more malleable hosts."

The Sage covered his mouth. Numb. 'How could I be so stupid? Tadgh has part of my father's power. I should have known. I should have felt it. No. I did feel it. The first time he used his wish ability on Maghe Sihre, I felt the power of the djinn. I just didn't want to believe it. That means Tadgh was hospitalized the same day I killed my father, the same day we destroyed the Council of Peacocks headquarters in Thessaloniki. After that, he used his wish power to teleport to this planet. This is too much. Too much coincidence. And I don't believe in coincidence.'

On the opposite side of the warehouse, past Bes and the hermadur, something stirred in the shadows. At first, the Sage only caught a glimpse of blue fabric. A face appeared. He fell to his knees; tears poured from his eyes. He wanted to run to her, to touch her. Make sure she was real. After all this time he couldn't believe what he was seeing.

Echo.

She put a finger to her lips, motioning for him to remain silent. It took everything he had to control his body, to stop himself from moving.

"How?" he mouthed the word, hoping she would understand.

She turned away and looked down, a pained expression on her face. Finally, she shook her head. She touched her ear and pointed at Bes. The Sage turned his attention back to the conversation. He caught Bes in midsentence.

"...most of the city is dead now. Teric and the others sleep during the day, but the army of graunskyegs they created continues to feed. Soon they will be strong enough for the next step. All we need is for Tadgh to hold the Sword of Kassandra and use his power to reopen the Void."

"And you're sure he'll do it?"

"I'm sure he won't have a choice."

The Sage had heard enough. It was time for him to make his move. He glanced over at Echo, to make sure she was still there. Seeing her eyes and her pale skin made his heart melt. He had many questions.

Echo's eyes went wide. She lifted her hand in warning.

Something struck the Sage in the head from behind. His world went black.

***

Echo watched as the Sage tumbled to the floor. The sound alerted the hermadur who raced to find the Sage's unconscious body. The cat demon, Bes, sniffed at the unconscious body and whispered something to the hermadur.

Behind her, Echo felt the shadows swirl. Her companion stepped out of the shadow portal. He had pale skin and snow-white hair that hung to his shoulders. He wore black robes. Around his waist was a leather belt and a sheath, but there was no sign of a sword.

"What the hell were you thinking?" he asked. "He's not supposed to know you're alive. Not yet. The incident with Grandwyn this morning was bad enough. Now you risked everything...."

Echo punched him in the shoulder. "Shut up! Just shut up. You didn't have to do that to him Tempertin."

"Yes, I did. If he attacked those two right now he would win. And then he would come after you. I brought you back for a reason. You have a role to play, but it's not time for that yet. Come. We need to leave here before he regains consciousness."

Echo looked back as guards dragged the Sage's body away. Hanging her head, she followed Tempertin into the shadows.

Chapter Eight

Grandwyn's eyes fluttered open. For a moment, lying there in the dark, he forgot where he was. He pushed himself off the dirt floor and looked around. He saw wooden shelves lined with food: dried meat, vegetables in wooden crates, and jars of preservatives. There were no windows. The only light came from a faint nizarian light fixture at the top of the stairs.

'I'm in a basement.' He jumped to his feet, completely awake now. Suddenly, he remembered everything. The screams. The moans. The smell of blood.

After the server locked him in the basement, Grandwyn had retreated to the bottom of the stairs. He heard someone – something – pound on the door. There was a low growl like a wild animal with a mouth full of meat and blood. Every instinct told him to be quiet. He was so terrified he nearly wet his pants. But his mother had taught him to be strong. So he was.

He had pressed his back against the wall and covered his ears, trying to block out the sound. But he could clearly hear wet chewing and the tearing of flesh. He had no idea what was happening. Was it rabid dogs? As far as he knew, there were no dangerous animals on the isle of DunDegore. Maybe it was crazy people. He'd seen a few of them, homeless on the streets of FleshPrayer. Mother always said they could be dangerous. Not knowing what it was made it worse.

The screams had died down long ago, but he'd been too afraid to try the door again. He had lain there until, surprisingly, he'd fallen asleep.

'Don't know how long I slept for,' he thought. He brushed the dirt from his pants. In his mind he heard his mother chastising him for getting dirty. She always hated when he ruined his clothes. 'I can't stay down here forever. Maybe everything's over now. The city guard probably stopped whatever it was by now. The only one who knows I'm down here is that server and she's probably…gone.'

At his core, he knew the server was dead, or at least so injured she couldn't reach him. That was the only reason she wouldn't have opened the door. Unless….

'What if it's some sort of joke? Adults do this sort of thing, don't they? Play jokes on each other. Maybe they're up there waiting to see how long I stay down here.'

He knew it was unlikely. The screams had sounded so real. But he would never know for sure unless he checked. He crept up the stairs, the wood creaking under his feet with each step. When he reached the top, he turned the door knob. It was still locked. But that couldn't stop him.

'I can use my power,' he thought. 'Open the door from the other side. It will be easy.'

He put his ear to the door and listened. Nothing.

Grandwyn focused on the doorknob. In his mind's eye, he could see the internal gears and tumblers. He felt the power flow out of him and, with a click, the lock disengaged. He turned the knob and let the door swing open.

When he saw the bodies he screamed. His hands flew to his mouth to cover the sound.

He'd never seen a dead body before. Now, there were so many. Splatters of blood covered every surface of the café. He glanced at one of their faces and quickly turned away.

"I'm not weak." It helped to speak aloud. The silence made everything too scary. Grandwyn looked at his hands. Purple light flickered around them again. "I can fight them. Shoot them with this energy. Mother would want me to be strong."

He crossed the café floor, carefully stepping around the bodies. Whenever possible, he tried to avoid stepping in the pools of blood. That was significantly more difficult. The glass door that led to the patio was shattered. Small shards of glass lay around the metal frame. They made a strange scrunching sound beneath his feet as he walked outside.

When he reached the patio, he watched the sun slowly sinking below the rooftops. It was late afternoon. In a few more hours it would be night.

'I'm not sure what's going on, but I don't want to be out on the street in the dark.'

He looked up and down the street. Blood covered every surface he saw. Store windows were smashed in. Shopping bags filled with souvenirs lay abandoned in the street. A single shoe lay at the edge of a fountain. He saw no sign of its owner. In fact, there was no sign of anyone.

"Where is everybody?" Turning in a circle he realized the entire city square was empty. He'd heard so many screams, he assumed that whatever had attacked the people in the café had attacked these people too. But if so... "Where are all the bodies?"

Grandwyn walked back toward the fieldbender guild. The only sound he heard was his footsteps echoing between the buildings and the wind whooshing above. The further he walked, the more nervous he became. The streets were covered in blood, but there were no bodies.

'It's like someone dragged the bodies away,' he thought. 'Or they got up and walked away. But that's crazy. Graunskyegs aren't real. There's no such thing as monsters.'

A loud bang echoed from a nearby alley. Grandwyn, acting on instinct, pointed at the sound and fired Akashic energy from his hand. A second later, a large black rat jumped out of a metal garbage can. Grandwyn watched as it ran away. When nothing else moved, he lowered his hands and extinguished the power.

He reached the front doors of the fieldbender guild and found them open. The wood was charred as if recently burned. A solitary arm, still holding a sword, lay nearby.

'Whatever happened, whoever did this, they got in the fieldbender guild too. If that place isn't safe, where is?'

A scream echoed from somewhere in the distance.

"Not again." He heard the pounding of feet but it was impossible to tell which direction it came from. It was loud, as if hundreds of people were running. Then he heard the moans, a sound that chilled him to the core. He turned in a circle trying to determine where the sound was coming from. He felt something brush past him, so fast his eyes couldn't see it. When he looked back at the front doors to the guild, the arm was gone. The sword remained.

He started to shake. Grandwyn knew he was no longer alone. He couldn't see them, but he knew something was with him. Watching him. The moans grew louder. But now he could tell from which direction they came. He ran in the opposite direction, his feet slapping loudly against the stone streets. He turned a corner and almost ran into a woman.

Relief flowed through him. She was middle-aged, older than his mother, and skinny. Her clothes were torn and her eyes were wide and glassy.

Grandwyn smiled up at her, happy to see someone else.

The woman shook her head, mumbled something incoherent, and ran away.

"Hey!" Grandwyn ran after her, but her long legs outdistanced him quickly. Soon she was several blocks ahead of him. Exhausted, he slowed but continued to walk in her direction. Aside from the rat, she was the only other living thing he'd seen. She was his only hope.

The woman, turned a corner and moved out of Grandwyn's line of sight. A moment later, he heard a horrible high-pitched scream. And the moaning started again. Grandwyn stopped. He listened as the woman called for help. Her voice cut off mid-scream.

The sun sank completely behind the houses now, and the shadows grew longer.

A feeling grew in Grandwyn. He wasn't old enough to put a name to it, but he thought it might be what adults call panic. He ran as fast as he could away from the moans. However, he wasn't watching where he was going. He turn-ed a corner into an alley. The far end was blocked by a tall wire fence. The docks were on the other side it. The water looked crisp, brightly lit by the setting sun.

All the boats were gone.

"There's no way off the island. If all the boats are gone, I'm stuck here."

He turned around to leave the alley but discovered he was no longer alone. Dozens of figures stood at the alley's entrance, staring at him. He couldn't make out their features in the shadows, but they were definitely people. They didn't move. They just stared at him.

For a moment he thought of calling out to them. Maybe they were here to rescue him. But the way they stood there, staring at him, not moving, made him want to scream. These were not his friends. They were not here to help him.

One of the figures took a step toward Grandwyn. The others began to moan.

Grandwyn screamed. He knew he should fight back, that he should do something, but the way the figures walked slowly, unhurriedly toward him froze him in place. He felt like prey. Like he was watching an animal about to pounce on its meal.

He turned back to the fence, looking for a way to climb it when he saw another figure on the other side of the metal. This one was close enough for him to see. It was a brown-haired man in the white robes of an initiate.

"You're a fieldbender?" Grandwyn said.

The man nodded and glanced past Grandwyn at the approaching crowd. "Stand back. I'll cut through the fence."

Grandwyn moved back a few feet and looked at the far end of the alley. The shadowy figures were moving faster now; not running, but walking very quickly

There was a flash of light and Grandwyn covered his eyes. He turned to look back at the fence and saw the bottom half had been melted away. The fieldbender's hands glowed with a thin sheath of flame.

"Move!" The fieldbender said. "They move quicker than you think."

Grandwyn rushed through the hole in the fence. As soon as he reached the other side, the fieldbender pointed at the fence again. A wall of flames appeared reaching high in to the air.

"It won't hold for long," he said. "But it should give us a few minutes. What's your name, kid?"

"Grandwyn. My name's Grandwyn. Who are you?"

"My name's Mikhel." The fieldbender put a hand on Grandwyn's shoulder and pushed him forward. "Run now. Talk later. The graunskyegs will be stronger when the sun sets."

Grandwyn ran with Mikhel through the streets of DunDegore. When the fieldbender finally said the word, graunskyeg, some of Grandwyn's panic left him. As scary as the monsters were, at least he knew what they were. And he was no longer alone.

Chapter Nine

At the end of their second day of travel, Tadgh and the others arrived in Tryst, an industrial town just off the highway. Thick black smoke hung in the air above them. Tamara informed them the pollution came from a coal-powered factory at the edge of town that produced metal framework for carriages. She directed them to an inn she was familiar with. While she booked rooms, Samar parked the carriage and tended to the horses. Supper was several hours off so, after checking into their rooms, Menphis and Tadgh sparred with quarterstaffs behind the stables. Once again, Tadgh wore a blindfold.

Hearing someone approach, Tadgh removed his blindfold. Bethel, still in her armor, walked toward them.

"Nice moves," she said. "Almost like you're dancing instead of fighting. Since you insisted on getting sweaty, mistress says you are to change for supper. She's had clothes delivered to your room. A servant will be there to collect your dirty clothes. They'll be laundered overnight so they'll be clean when we leave tomorrow."

Tadgh and Menphis went to their room. Laid out on each bed was a black tunic embroidered with gold and green thread. Matching pants and shoes were included. They washed up with warm water from a basin in the room. As they dressed for dinner, Tadgh turned to Menphis.

"Thanks for the save back there. I can't believe I mentioned England. I was an idiot."

Menphis smirked. "No more than usual. The books will be good for you. The more you know about our country the less strange you will seem. Tamara is very bright. I suggest you watch your words more closely from now on."

After dressing, they walked downstairs to the hotel's restaurant. Elegant candles lit each table. The restaurant was nearly empty. The few people there were impeccably dressed, even the children. Waiters carried metal plates filled with steaming meat and bottles of wine.

"I'm glad I changed," Tadgh said. "This place looks posh."

Menphis frowned. "I don't think I know this word. What does 'posh' mean?"

"You know, posh. Fancy." Tadgh searched for Tamara and Bethel, but it appeared the women were not downstairs yet. They walked to the bar and ordered drinks. Halfway through their second pint, Tadgh grew quiet for a moment.

"What?" Menphis asked.

"Can I ask you a question? A serious one?"

Menphis took a deep breath, shrugged, and finished the rest of his beverage in one gulp.

"Do you ever regret not staying to help raise your son?"

Menphis opened his eyes. "Never. Well, sometimes. Maybe. I don't even know what he looks like. The sound of his voice. I know he exists and sometimes that's enough. I know, rationally, I couldn't have stayed. Even if I left the monastery, Tamara never would. We could never have been a real family. So I left." Menphis motioned the barkeep for another drink. "If it's all the same to you, I'd rather not talk about it."

Bethel walked into the pub. She, too, had changed, no longer wearing her well-polished armor. Instead, she wore a sleeveless white jerkin over a red shirt with matching red pants. Seeing Menphis and Tadgh, she joined them at the bar.

"I'm surprised to see you both drinking," she said. "Isn't alcohol bad for meditation?"

Menphis and Tadgh exchanged a knowing glance and smiled.

"Ancient Elmire Ahk secret," Tadgh said. Menphis laughed. "Where's Tamara?"

"Mistress will be down in a moment. The local government learned she was in town and insisted on welcoming her officially." Bethel waved to the barkeep who brought over a glass of ale for her.

Tadgh glanced around the pub. "Strange."

Bethel sipped her drink. "What is?"

"It's probably nothing." Tadgh shrugged. "I'm just surprised this place is so empty."

Menphis looked past the bar out a large window that opened to the city. "We're getting closer to the border. Soon we'll be in Gateway which lies on the southern bank of a great river. On the northern bank is Celtica. You'll notice the further west we go, the more…cautious people tend to be. We're still far from the Realm of Dispayre and the frontline of battle. However, it is not unheard of to see strange things in the night. Wild creatures like the tuft."

"What's that?"

Bethel held her hands out approximately four feet above the ground. "Bipedal reptile, stands this big. Hunts weak prey at the edge of foramen and drinks their blood. Usually they only attack livestock, but occasionally they wander into the city."

"Ick." Tadgh turned away from the window. "Lovely."

"We're a long way from the war." Bethel drank deeply from her cup. "If we walked west for three weeks, we'd be at the shores of the Bay of Ancients. The Realm of Dispayre is on the other side of the Bay. It would take a week to sail the bay by boat. So, like I said, we're far enough away."

"Are you trying to convince me or yourself?" Tadgh asked.

Bethel smiled. "Perhaps a little of both."

Tamara walked in wearing a simple white and blue dress, the weighted chain still wrapped around her waist. After a server led them to a table, Tamara ordered appetizers of dried grilled vegetables. The food arrived at the table shortly followed by a plate of steaming meat Tadgh could not identify. Whatever it was, it was juicy and flavorful without being overly gamey.

As they ate, Tadgh glanced over at the bar. Samar, still wearing his simple outfit of unbleached woven flax, sat in a dim corner, drinking alone. For a moment, Tadgh felt sorry for him. Samar spent his entire day alone atop the carriage and the entire evening by himself. He thought briefly of going to say hello but quickly pushed the thought from his mind.

Midway through the meal, they ran out of wine. Seeing no servers around, Tadgh went to the bar to order more for the table. While he waited, he glanced over at Samar.

The blond man stared back at Tadgh, a strange look in his eye. Tadgh shivered and took an involuntary step back. Seeming to realize the effect he had on Tadgh, Samar smiled and bowed his head.

"Apologies. I didn't mean to stare. It is just…you are very attractive."

That was the last thing Tadgh expected the man to say. "Um, what?"

"Perhaps I misread you." Samar waved to the bartender who brought over another glass of beer for the driver. "However, I think you and I have something in common."

Tadgh looked around to see if anyone else could hear their conversation.

Samar laughed. "Ah. A bashful one. No need. You've seen what happens in the streets in this country. Shirza is a good place for people like you and me."

"You're really gay?" Tadgh sat down in the seat next to Samar. "Sorry. Weird to just ask like that but I haven't really met anyone like me since I came here."

Samar reached over and touched Tadgh's forearm. His hands were large, his fingers calloused. Tadgh pulled his arm back with a jolt.

"Jumpy." Samar took a drink of beer and turned away from Tadgh. "Or perhaps I am not your type."

"No. I mean, yes. I mean…" Tadgh took a deep breath. "Sure, you are sexy with the big muscles and dreamy eyes. And maybe blond hair is my kryptonite. It's just…my love life has been a complete mess lately. I'm not sure I'm interested in romance."

"Well, it wasn't romance I was interested in. I had

something else in mind."

Tadgh blushed and rose from his seat. "On that note, I think I'll be getting back to the others."

When he reached the table, Tamara looked up at him. "Are they bringing the wine over?"

Tadgh hit his forehead with the heel of his hand. "Duh. I knew I forgot something."

Menphis looked back and forth between Tadgh and Samar sitting at the bar. Then, with a sigh, he returned to his food.

After supper, everyone retired to their rooms. Menphis sat on the floor, meditating while Tadgh read one of the books Bethel gave him by candlelight. He'd been an avid reader back on Earth, but he had yet to become proficient at reading the Sirian language. The process was slow and painful, but he was improving. He read about the political families in Southpoint, and the merging of the royal family and the military. To Tadgh, the subject matter wasn't important. He was happy to be reading again.

Hours later, Menphis said it was time for bed. Tadgh extinguished the candle but found himself unable to sleep. Getting out of bed, he put on his dress clothes again and left the room. He wandered the halls of the hotel until he found a staircase that led to the roof. When he reached the top, he found wooden chairs and benches lined with cushions that looked out over the city. Small, lit candles floated inside bowls of water. Fresh flowers bloomed in a rooftop garden.

He sat on a bench and stared up at the star-filled sky. Both of Maghe Sihre's moons were visible: one was nearly full above him, the other a sliver sinking below the horizon. The streets below were full of revelers. Music from taverns filtered out into the street. Tadgh felt something in his chest loosen and his head felt lighter. He sniffed the air. In his cat form, his sense of smell was stronger, but even in his human form, each of his senses were enhanced. He could detect three types of perfume coming from an open window directly beneath him. He could hear the whishing of robes from people on the sidewalks. From somewhere nearby, he heard the sound of chanting.

He smiled and realized why he felt so relaxed. For the first time in months, he was alone: just him and his thoughts on this strange world. He spent so much time trying to hide his special abilities that he never truly enjoyed them. He thought about shifting into feline form and running along the rooftops. As he unbuttoned his tunic, he looked around to ensure he was alone.

Samar stood at the top of the stairs.

"Don't let me stop you." He crossed his arms and stared at Tadgh. "Please continue with whatever you were planning on doing."

Tadgh backed away. "You always sneak up on people like that? Look, can you do me a favor and tone down the flirting. My heart belongs to someone else."

"I wasn't really interested in your heart," Samar said with a smirk.

Tadgh made a gagging sound. "My heart is kinda attached to the parts of me you seem to be interested in."

Samar shrugged. "If you say so." He looked up at the sky. "Do you remember the legend of the two moons?"

Tadgh shook his head. "Must be one of the things I forgot."

"The full one, of course, is Boaz, the strong one. The other is Jachin, the foundation. They are the sister-wives of the sun god, Baal. Legend says they once fought for his attention. The battle caused earthquakes and floods all over the world. One day they realized Baal's love was big enough for both of them. Time spent with one moon did not diminish his love for the other. Now they share. Each has a time to shine, a time to be dependent, and a time to be free. Each has a moment to be full and a moment to be empty."

Tadgh gagged. "That has got to be the lamest pick up attempt ever. You're using astronomy to make a pass at me? I'm not an idiot. The two moons just have different orbits. Boaz looks larger, so I'm assuming its either the larger moon or closer to the planet. Jachin is about fourteen days behind Boaz' cycle. It will be full in about two weeks."

Tadgh stopped, realizing something. 'Boaz moves in twenty-eight day cycles just like the moon back home. That's quite the coincidence.' Unless, of course, it wasn't a coincidence. He thought back to the legends of the Beherskers that Shonn had told him. Perhaps there was more to the moon than he thought.

Samar laughed. "You can't blame a guy for trying. There is something about you, Tadgh. My eyes like to look at you. If your situation ever becomes less complicated, keep me in mind. However, I will not pressure you anymore." He extended his hand to be shaken. "Friends?"

Tadgh shook his hand. "Friends. Just keep your Jachin in your pants, if you catch my drift."

Samar stared back up at the night sky. "You seem to know a bit about the cycle of planets. The average person does not speak of orbits and moon cycles. Perhaps you trained with a fieldbender. They know a great deal about astrology. Do you know anything of the other planets?"

Tadgh scratched his head, hoping it looked like he was searching his memory. "It's all a little foggy. Can you refresh my memory?"

Samar pointed at a bluish light low on the horizon. "That is the next closest planet. Icimount. We believe it to be an uninhabited ice planet. My sister back in Norshire was a fieldbender. She's much older than me. She used to sneak me into the guild and let me use their telescopes. Told me all about the five planets in our system. Even hinted that there could be other planets out there with life on them. Can you believe that?"

Tadgh smirked. "Life on other planets? I think I can believe that."

Something in the tone of his voice must have hinted he was hiding something. Samar stared at Tadgh with a very pointed expression on his face. He looked very closely at Tadgh's eyes.

Tadgh looked away. "How far away is your hometown?"

Samar stared at Tadgh for a moment more before shaking his head as if to dismiss his thoughts. "I'm from Loard, the capital city of Norshire. It's at the northern edge of the continent not far from the ice caps."

"That sounds very far away." Tadgh thought back to the maps he'd seen of the planet.

"Not far enough." Samar's shoulders slumped. "My family was poor with too many mouths to feed. My father sold me into slavery when he discovered I preferred the company of boys. He said there was no sense feeding me if I wasn't going to carry on the family name. I was twelve, the last time I saw him. I spent the next four years owned by the royal family. They took me with them when they traveled south to a conference at Castle Grygar. I realized it was my one shot at freedom. So I ran. While they sat in meetings with Prince Grygar, I slipped out of the castle and ran. Several months later, I found myself here, in Shirza. That was two years ago. I've worked at the temple ever since."

Tadgh felt sick to his stomach. "You were a slave? They still have that sort of thing here?"

"Not here. Slavery is outlawed across the south. But it's alive and well back in Norshire."

A bright light flashed horizontally across the sky.

"Whoa! What the…?" Tadgh pointed at the object as it disappeared in the distance. "Did you see that? What was that?"

Samar laughed. "You really did lose your memory. It's just a Pharocai."

"A pharo-what?"

Samar yawned and stretched lazily. "A Pharocai. A nizarian flying ship. You remember the nizarians, right?"

Tadgh shrugged his head. "Not really. I've heard of them, but I've never seen one. What do they look like?"

"I haven't seen one in years, but they used to visit the royal family often." Samar leaned forward, resting his elbows on his legs. "They have these great big eyes, black as the…"

Tadgh threw his hand over Samar's mouth. "Shh."

Samar looked up at him, his eyes clouding over with confusion.

Tadgh pointed at the rooftop across the street. A familiar shape stalked in the night: an orange house cat with eyes that glowed as bright as lasers. It was the first cat he'd seen since arriving on Maghe Sihre. But, of course, this was not truly a cat.

"Bes." Tadgh mouthed the name. Although it looked like a cat, he knew it was truly a shape-shifting demon, the same creature who had made him a werecat. The same one who had turned him into a monster. "How did he find me?"

Samar pulled Tadgh's hand from off his mouth. "Does that creature frighten you?"

Tadgh ducked down and motioned for silence. Crouched, he watched as Bes lifted his head, seemingly trying to sniff the air. Tracking something. Whether it was the pollution from burning coal or too much perfume in the air, it seemed the demon could not pinpoint Tadgh's location.

Bes jumped to the next roof and disappeared into the night.

"You're acting very peculiar," Samar said. "Is it your head injury?"

"I wish. We need to go. Now. That was not an animal. We are all in grave danger.

***

"Absolutely not." Menphis, hair tousled from lying down, rubbed the sleep from his eyes.

Tadgh grunted. "We have to tell them. It's a demon, and it's following us."

"You don't know that."

Tadgh punched the wall. "What? You think the creature that cursed me and nearly killed me just happened to be in the neighbourhood? Stopped in for a pint? Stop being stupid."

Menphis raised an eyebrow. He no longer looked sleepy.

"Sorry. Prelate." Tadgh stuck his hands beneath his armpits to avoid hitting anything else. "I know you're supposed to be my superior, and I'm supposed to follow your every command…"

"Supposed to?"

Tadgh grunted. "We don't have time for this. You don't know what demon thing is capable of. We have to warn Tamara. Great Caesar's ghost, she's the mother of your child."

"Who is Caesar?"

"Um, that's just a saying from back home."

Menphis stood and straightened his clothing. "I know who Tamara is. She's an elmire ahk. She can take care of herself."

"Not if she doesn't know she needs to. Look, I know I'm supposed to keep my history a secret, but aren't there some things more important than that?"

There was a knock at the door.

"Damn it." Menphis ran his fingers through his hair. "That will be her. Keep your mouth shut, Tadgh."

"Nuh-uh." Tadgh squared his shoulders. "Reprimand me all you want later. I'm going to tell them. You know you can't stop me. And you also know you shouldn't."

Menphis muttered under his breath before giving a half-hearted shrug.

Tadgh opened the door. Tamara, Bethel, and Samar stood outside, looks of confusion on each of their faces.

"Come in," Tadgh said. "I have some explaining to do. We have a bit of a problem."

"What kind of problem?" Tamara asked.

"The demon kind."

Chapter Ten

Grandwyn pushed aside a wispy blue curtain and looked out the window. A light rain fell on the streets of DunDegore. He stood in a room on the third floor of a house not far from the docks. They'd been here for only a few minutes but Grandwyn already felt much safer than he had out in the open. He searched for signs of activity outside but nothing moved. Whatever had been chasing them was gone.

"Were those really graunskyeg?" Grandwyn glanced over his shoulder at Mikhel. The fieldbender sat at a small table slicing bread for a quick meal. "You don't have to lie to me. I'm young, not stupid."

Mikhel smiled. "I think you might be too smart for your own good. Yes, kid. I'm afraid those really were graunskyegs. You should probably move away from the window. Best not to give away our position. Come over here and have something to eat."

Grandwyn let the curtain fall back into place and joined Mikhel at the table. "What is this place?"

"My home." Mikhel put a piece of bread on a white plate and passed it to Grandwyn. "Well, my parents' house actually. These days I live at the fieldbender guild."

"Where are your parents now?"

Mikhel bit his lower lip. After a moment, he shook his head. "I want to believe they're safe somewhere, but it's not very likely. Both worked by the docks selling junk to tourists. I went there after the guild was attacked, but the area was completely overrun. Thousands of graunskyegs." Mikhel looked toward the window. "As far as I know, you and I are the only survivors."

Grandwyn's eyes went wide. "But the pamphlets said there are over 100,000 people on DunDegore. And that's not including the tourists. They can't all be…gone."

"Yes they can." Mikhel turned away from the window

and opened a mason jar of jam. "Here. It's my mother's specialty. Blastberries and sea current. You must be starving."

Grandwyn picked up a knife and spread the jam over the bread. He took a slow bite, trying to be polite. The jam was so delicious, however, he ate the rest of the slice ravenously. When it was gone, he looked longingly at his empty plate.

Mikhel laughed and started cutting another piece of bread. "Well, you've got a healthy appetite. That makes you a normal boy."

'But I'm not,' Grandwyn thought. Something must have registered on his face because Mikhel gave him a long, slow look.

"You don't live on the island, do you? Who were you here with?"

"Just myself."

"Really?" Mikhel spread jam over a slice of bread for himself. "Aren't you a little young to be traveling by yourself?"

"That's what everybody says." Grandwyn looked down at his shoes. A small patch of blood had soaked into the seams. "My mother told me there was no such thing as graunskyegs. Did she lie to me?"

Mikhel hung his head. "No. We all thought there was no such thing as the living dead. It appears we were all wrong." He leaned forward and touched Grandwyn's hand. "You're one tough kid. I don't know how I would deal with this if I was your age. We're safe here for now. I placed a ward over the door. Nothing short of fieldbending will open it. These graunskyegs are still weak. They haven't fed enough to have that kind of power yet. We'll be fine."

"If I ask you a question, do you promise to tell me the truth?" Grandwyn asked.

Mikhel nodded.

"My mom never let me read stories with graunskyegs in them. She said it was bad for me. Would interfere with my sleeping or something. But I read them anyway. All the kids did. If graunskyegs feed, they get stronger and stronger. The weak ones barely remember anything from their life. They can't speak, they move slowly, and all they do is kill and eat. But the strong ones are smart. They can do things that fieldbenders can do. And they can plan. If there really is an army of smart graunskyegs out there, will this place still be protected?"

Mikhel placed his elbows on the table and leaned forward. "No. If there are that many strong graunskyegs, I can't think of any place on Maghe Sihre that will be safe."

"Oh." Grandwyn's mind tumbled with thoughts. "You said we may be the last two people alive on the island. If the graunskyegs have eaten everyone else, it may already be too late. Shouldn't we be doing something? Send a warning to the mainland or try to destroy the monsters?"

Mikhel grunted, a sound that started like a laugh but had no humor to it. "I think you're missing the point. We're just two people. Sure, I'm a fieldbender, but I'm only an initiate. I don't have that much power. And you're just a kid. What can…?"

"I'm not just a kid."

Mikhel raised an eyebrow. "Well, you look like one."

Grandwyn held his breath. Eyes on the ground, he pushed his chair back and walked a few feet away from the table. He lifted his hands and called on his abilities. His hands glowed purple with Akashic energy. He looked up at Mikhel and saw a look of horror settle on the fieldbender's face.

"Please don't kill me," Grandwyn said.

"Mother of stone. You're fod sel-onde." Mikhel covered his mouth with his hand and stared at Grandwyn.

"I didn't do this!" Grandwyn threw his hands down. A nearby plate fell to the floor. "Oops. Sorry. That was me though. Sometimes I can move things with my mind. But I swear I didn't bring the graunskyegs here."

Mikhel ran to Grandwyn and put a comforting hand on

his shoulder. "I know, kid. I know. This wasn't you. This…" He looked over Grandwyn's shoulder, out toward the street. "This is probably my fault. Our fault, really. We knew how dangerous it was. We should have protected it more."

"What are you talking about? Did you make these graunskyegs?" Grandwyn knew that only powerful field-bending could raise the dead and turn them into the monsters. It made sense that the fieldbenders could be responsible.

"No. We didn't create them. We found something. A very powerful object. It was too dangerous to keep in the city so we moved it to the monastery just outside of town. We thought it was safe there. We were wrong."

"And this object created the graunskyegs?"

Mikhel nodded. "Yes. But not all of them. Yesterday I learned the object had been stolen, so I went to the monastery to investigate. Not long after I got there, a powerful demon with orange fur and green eyes appeared. It did not come alone. Five portals appeared around the perimeter of the monastery. From each portal stepped a greater graunskyeg with squadrons of lesser ones. They swarmed over the monastery, but they didn't eat the ones they killed. They brought them back to the demon who used the object to create new ones. The change happened so quickly. A matter of minutes."

"Did you see it happen?"

Mikhel started shaking. "Are you sure you want to hear this?"

"I can't be a child right now. I haven't felt like one since I found out I had powers. I know you're supposed to kill me but…"

"Shh," Mikhel interrupted. "Stop saying that. I'm not going to kill you. We have more pressing issues right now than you being fod sel-onde. Fine. I'll tell you what I saw. When the graunskyegs swarmed the monastery, I hid. Maybe it was cowardly, but I knew we couldn't defeat them. And I knew someone had to tell people what had happened, to warn them. In the literature, creating a graunskyeg, even a lesser one, should take weeks. The process of binding void energy to a corpse is complex fieldbending. Yet I watched the demon create a graunskyeg in minutes. It was like the Sword of…I mean the object…opened a portal between worlds and filled each dead body with pure, intelligent void. It was horrifying. The moment I could get away safely, I ran back to town. I was too late. Most of the city was infested by the time I got here."

Grandwyn thought about what Mikhel had said. It seemed unbelievable, like something from one of the stories he liked to read. But those things outside were not part of a story. They were real. And scary.

"So what can you do?" Mikhel asked.

"Do?"

"Well, you're a fod sel-onde. You obviously have multiple abilities, which is rare. I've seen you conjure Akashic energy and move things with your mind. Anything else?"

Grandwyn nodded. "Just this." Holding his hand out in front of him, he closed his eyes and called on his power. His fingers tingled as his skin grew cold and damp. When he opened his eyes, a sphere of translucent ice hung in the air.

Mikhel kneeled and studied the object. "It's beautiful."

Grandwyn blushed. "First time I did this was after I broke one of my mother's vases. She likes roses. Keeps them all over the house. She was so angry. I wanted to make something pretty, something she could use to put her roses in. But it didn't work. It's solid and pretty strong but only lasts a few minutes before it melts. Still, I like making things."

Mikhel touched the ice globe. "I've never seen anything like it. Most fieldbenders focus on Akashic energy or fire. They make more sense for the battlefield." Grabbing the globe with both hands, he moved it away from Grandwyn and sat it down on the table. "I never knew fod sel-onde were capable of such things. All you ever hear about is the bad ones, like the one that killed all those people outside of GardenKeep a few months ago, or the one that killed Prince Grygar's wife. I think you should be proud of your abilities, Grandwyn."

Once again, Grandwyn blushed. "So what's the plan?"

Mikhel rubbed his forehead. "I honestly don't know. There are too many graunskyegs for us to fight even if you are fod sel-onde. I'd like to get off the island. If we found a boat, we could sail to Karaj Robat and alert the army. But all the boats are gone. Something put massive holes in the bottoms and sides, sinking them."

"But there will be more boats tomorrow, right?"

"Thundering lord." Mikhel gripped the edge of the table, his knuckles white. "Tomorrow, a whole new group of tourists arrive. We can't let them land or…"

"Or the graunskyegs will have more food." Grandwyn shivered and looked back at the window. Suddenly, he didn't feel quite so safe.

"That was probably the plan all along. DunDegore is completely cut off from the outside world. And it's filled with people. The demon brought those graunskyegs here for the sole purpose of feeding them just enough to make them strong. I don't know how, but we need to get off this island and warn someone. I hate to think of what thousands of greater graunskyegs could do if they were let loose on the continent. The loss of life…"

Grandwyn went to Mikhel and hugged him. "I'm really scared. But I'll help you. I'll do whatever I can to stop those monsters. My mom would want me to."

Mikhel patted Grandwyn on the head. "You're an amazing kid. Your mom must be so proud of you. Now, let's get you another slice of bread. You look like you're starving. Then we'll try to get some sleep. Tomorrow is going to be a big day."

Chapter Eleven

As the carriage drove through the streets of Gateway, Tadgh realized he could summarize the city in one word: seedy. Although the architecture was similar to Tryst, the buildings were in disrepair. The paint on business signs was faded. Garbage piled up unattended along the sides of buildings. The people walked with their heads down. The city guards kept their hands on the hilts of their swords, their eyes constantly scanning the crowd.

Tamara dropped Tadgh and Menphis off at the market to gather supplies while she and the others secured their rooms for the night. When the carriage drove off, Tadgh turned to his friend.

"See? She took the news better than expected."

"Well, she didn't try to kill you on the spot. That's something." Menphis leaned on his quarterstaff and shook his head. "I still think it was a mistake telling her you're from another planet...and the extent of your abilities. People in power would kill to have someone with your talents under their control."

"Don't you trust her?"

Menphis glanced over his shoulder and sighed. "Sometimes we can't afford to trust anyone."

They walked past numerous people who carried fishing poles. Several also had still-damp nets filled with fish that looked similar to the silvery-green ones he'd seen for sale in the markets. Tadgh had learned on the road that Gateway stood on the border of two countries: Shirza to the south and Celtica to the north. The Shirza River ran between them, a major trading route that flowed northeast to the Gulf of Baptism.

Tadgh walked past a cart selling red and yellow globe-shaped fruits. He remembered how sweet they were but could not remember their name.

"Grab one if you like," Menphis said. "They don't keep

well on the road unless their packed with ice. When we leave tomorrow it's back to standard supplies for lunch."

Tadgh groaned. "Super. Can't wait for all the dried meat and nuts. You know what your world needs? Fast food. On my world, they have these things called rest stations along the highway where you can stop and use the toilet and get food. Nobody travels with food. Well, except maybe my grandmother but…"

"Hmm," Menphis said.

Tadgh cocked his head to the side. "What?"

"I believe that is the first time you've mentioned your family. Do you miss them?"

For a moment, a dark wave of sorrow fell over Tadgh. "Ah. I try not to think about them. The last time I saw my parents was at the hospital. It's not a pleasant memory. Forgetting them gets easier each day. I haven't seen my grandmother since Easter. She's an old hippie, close to retirement. My dad was her only son. She spoiled me." A sinking feeling settled in Tadgh's but. "Damn. I'm never going to see her again, am I?"

"Never say never." Menphis waved to the fruit merchant. He passed over a coin in exchange for a cloth bag filled with fruit. "Stranger things have happened. You should know that."

Tadgh spun around. He clenched his staff tighter.

At the edge of the market, a figure ducked quickly back into a doorway.

"Took you long enough," Menphis said with a smile. "She's been on us since Tamara left."

"She who?"

Menphis passed the bag of fruit to Tadgh. "Whoever she is, she's good. Always just out of sight. Don't panic yet. This might have nothing to do with Bes. Gateway has a thriving thieves' guild. Could be nothing more than a pickpocket. Why don't we ask our friend why she's shadowing us? Follow me. If I remember the city correctly, there's a place nearby where we can set a trap.

Menphis led them deep into the city. Past the city gates and the market, the bustle gave way to the relative tranquility of a residential area. Tadgh saw tanned red-haired children playing with a bleached-leather ball. The game seemed similar to one he'd played as a child back on Earth, four corners. Every day it seemed he saw more and more evidence of common ancestry between the two planets.

Now that he knew he was being followed, Tadgh didn't need to turn around. He could smell their pursuer. Her scent was familiar but he could not place it.

Menphis pointed ahead and to the right. "It's just over this way. My uncle and his wife used to live in that house over there. Third from the right."

"You mean…"

Menphis shook his head. "Not Shonn's parents. My father had many brothers. Shonn grew up in Tarkon with me, remember? Behind the houses, there is an open area that leads to the entertainment district. Our shadow will be forced into the open or she will lose us. Either way it's a win."

Tadgh nodded. "You remember how far I can jump?"

Menphis turned and winked. "I'm counting on it."

As they walked past the houses, Tadgh smelled sweet pastries in the air. It reminded him of apple pie. Immediately past the houses, the scent was replaced by dew-damp grass and wood smoke. They walked into the field in silence. Up ahead, he heard the sound of cheering and music. Behind them, was the faint sound of a horse plodding along cobblestone streets.

"Ready?" Menphis asked.

Tadgh nodded, switched to feline form, and jumped. Before his training at the monastery, he had been able to jump to the roof of two-story buildings in feline form. Now, he could jump that far even in human form. He leapt with ferocity and struck their shadow in the chest. The woman fell on her back with a grunt of shock. Tadgh grappled her, pinning her to the ground.

"Move and I eat you," he said. Whether it was the tone of his voice or the furry-clawed fist at her throat, the woman stayed still. Only then did he look at her. She was beautiful and wore an elegant blue dress. She had brown hair and eyes that looked like his.

"Wait," he said. "I know you."

"Of course you do, you idiot." The woman pushed Tadgh off of her. "It's me. Andy. Is it okay if I move or do you still want to eat me? Wait. Don't answer that."

Menphis approached now. "This is Andy? The woman you met at the fortress? The one the Sage knows?"

"Yes," the woman said brushing the dirt from her dress. "Guilty as charged."

Tadgh studied the woman carefully. "He didn't talk about you. But when the Sage found out you were the one who helped me, he had a total meltdown. Who are you? And why are you following me? Again."

Tadgh's words seemed to affect Andy. Her eyes filled with tears and her voice shook slightly. "The Sage and I have a complicated history. Who I am doesn't matter right now. The important thing is the Sage is in trouble and you're the only one who can help him. He's been captured."

"And that's our problem how?" Menphis asked.

Andy clenched her fists. "I'm sorry. And here I thought you wanted to save your son."

"What do you know about my son?" Menphis lifted his quarterstaff into attack position. "Speak or…."

"Woah!" Tadgh stepped between the two of them and switched back to human form. "Relax big guy. You wouldn't hit a girl would you?"

Andy pressed her foot into the crook behind Tadgh's knee, driving him to the ground. "Sexist pig. I'm not a girl. I'm a woman, and I don't need you to protect me. What I need is for both of you to calm down and let me speak. We're running out of time and so is Grandwyn."

Menphis reached down and helped Tadgh back to his feet. "The woman is correct about one thing, Tadgh. You would do best to never turn your back on someone just because she is a woman. Remember, Tamara is also an elmire ahk, stronger and more powerful than I am."

"Point taken." Tadgh rubbed his leg. "She's wearing a pretty dress. I didn't think she'd get all Charlie's Angels on me. I won't make that mistake again. I think you should answer his question, though. What do you know about his son?"

Andy looked around, studying the shadows. "I can't talk long. He's going to punish me for speaking with you, but I can't let the Sage stay where he is. It's my fault he was captured. Tadgh, this whole situation has been arranged by Bes."

Tadgh felt his face go numb. "Slow down. I don't understand."

"I don't have time to slow down." Andy jumped as a section of shadow seemed to grow. She looked up at the sky and relaxed visibly when she realized it was simply the sun sliding behind a cloud. "Bes needs you on the island of DunDegore. He wants you to use your wish power to finish opening the Void. He needed a reason to draw you there, a trap you would never suspect until it was too late. He manipulated Menphis' son, Grandwyn, filling him with the suicidal desire to turn himself over to the fieldbender guild on DunDegore. He knew Menphis would go to rescue him just as he knew you would go with him."

Menphis' face grew red with anger. "Grandwyn is bait? The demon is using my son as bait?"

Andy shrugged. "In a sense. Tadgh, when you get to DunDegore, the forces Bes works with will hand you a very powerful item. It's called the Sword of Kassandra. We...I need you to take that sword and give it to me. This is incredibly important. The Sword of Kassandra cannot stay in their possession anymore."

Tadgh shook his head. "How am I supposed to get the sword away from them? I can't fight Bes. The last time I tried, he nearly killed me. The only reason I'm alive is I used my wish power to teleport to another planet. I don't think that trick will work a second time."

Andy grabbed Tadgh's hand and squeezed it lightly. "I don't need to you to fight Bes. Take the sword and run."

"What about my son?"

Andy released Tadgh's hand and looked up at Menphis. "He's safe. For now. Look, there's something you need to know. DunDegore has been overrun with…"

She stopped. The shadows around them grew larger. This time the movement of the sun and clouds was not responsible for the darkness.

Menphis and Tadgh raised their weapons. A figure appeared in the shadows but did not approach. The unnatural darkness made it impossible to distinguish any of the person's features, but it seemed to be a man.

"Who is that?" Tadgh asked.

Andy walked toward the shadows. "I can't tell you. I wish I could but…Go to the Sage. Tadgh, you have his scent. You can track him. He's in the warehouse district under heavy guard. Saving him will help you save Grandwyn. Tadgh, remember what I said about the sword."

Andy jumped into the darkness. The shadows spun away like water through an open drain. Both she and the strange man were gone.

Menphis grabbed Tadgh's arm. "We don't have time for this. The Sage got himself into this. He can get himself out. We have nothing to gain by doing this."

Tadgh's eyes went wide as he realized something. "Yes we do. She said saving the Sage will help save Grandwyn. Think about it. What can the Sage do for us?"

Menphis frowned, a blank expression on his face. Then his eyes lit up. "Of course! We need to find the Sage quickly. Lead the way."

Chapter Twelve

Menphis shook his head and rubbed the back of his neck. "Are you sure this is the way?"

Tadgh tried to remain calm. "You know, where I'm from repeatedly asking the same question is generally seen as annoying. How should I know? I've never tried anything like this before." Tadgh became aware of his enhanced olfactory abilities months ago, back when armed soldiers attacked the monastery. That first time, he'd smelt blood and been able to follow Shonn's scent. But this was different. He hadn't seen the Sage in months and only had a vague recollection of what the Sage smelled like. It helped that his scent was peculiar – like sulfur and cinnamon – but this was still a challenge.

Tadgh led them through the streets of Gateway. They passed through the colorful and noisy entertainment district. Jugglers and musicians lined the street performing for passers-by. Storefronts advertised live theaters and other delights. On the outer edge of the district was a darker, seedier section. The air was thick with something that looked like tobacco smoke but smelled like nothing Tadgh had ever experienced before. Men and women loitered in the streets, their eyes dull and their faces expressionless.

Tadgh plugged his nose. "What is that stench?"

Menphis sniffed the air. "Oh. That. It's Leivox. An herb from the counties of Ctar. Some people smoke it recreationally. Its chemical makeup causes…unusual experiences. Best not to inhale too much."

"Got it." Tadgh covered his nose and took shallow breaths until they left the area. The Sage's scent grew stronger. He opened his mouth slightly, having learned that for some reason his sense of smell was more acute that way. "He definitely came this way. I think we're getting close."

Several minutes later, they crouched at the edge of an alley that ran between two detached houses. Across the street was a two-story building constructed of stone and mortar: a warehouse. There were many windows, but all were covered with wooden shutters to keep the light out. The building was unguarded. No sound came from inside.

"I don't like this," Menphis said. "This place feels…wrong. Something unnatural was here."

Tadgh opened his mouth further and inhaled. "The Sage is in there, but he's not alone. There's tons of scents in there. I'd guess at least twenty. Maybe more."

"Fantastic." Menphis touched his chest and closed his eyes. "Well, they say the gods favor the bold. Let's hope they also favor the reckless and insane."

They walked to the front door. Tadgh pressed his ear against the metal. He heard the rustle of movement inside. Tadgh pulled the handle and found it locked.

"I could try pulling the door off the hinges," he said.

Menphis pulled Tadgh's hand off the handle. "Not if there are twenty men in there, you can't. I'd prefer to avoid a full-on confrontation if we can avoid it. We know nothing about their level of training."

Tadgh smiled and winked at Menphis. "Wimp." He pointed at the roof. "I can get to the roof in cat form. Look for a way in. How about you? Can you jump that high?"

Menphis narrowed his eyes as he studied the edge of the roof. "Doubtful. I'm sure Instructor Mal could, but not me. Besides, I can't land as softly as you do. If I jumped up there it would sound like stone smashing against the roof. I think I saw a smaller door around the side. I'll check it."

Tadgh flipped a switch in his mind and shifted to his feline form. The rush of strength was intoxicating. Orange fur sprouted from every part of his body. He grew taller, his muscles longer and leaner. His pants stretched but did not rip. His eyes changed as well, becoming green with enlarged, slanted irises. Colors disappeared, replaced by a more predatory vision of yellows and greens. Thick black claws sprouted from his finger nails and a long tail grew from his tailbone.

"God I've missed this." Stepping back from the door, he took a running jump and soared up to the roof nearly thirty feet above, landing soundlessly. He listened for any sign he'd been detected. Hearing nothing, he walked to a narrow stone chimney set near the back of the roof. Leaning over the hole, he focused on his hearing. He heard two distinct voices. They spoke quietly making it difficult to hear any specific words. He leaned closer. Finally, he heard one of the men raise his voice ever so slightly.

"...bloody super...rat...I tell you..."

"...you're not...basement...Creeps me out."

"Humph. He...."

'Too garbled,' he thought. 'I'll have to find a better vantage point if I want to learn anything useful.' Nearby, he saw a skylight that looked down on a dark office. A wooden desk covered with papers lay directly beneath the window. A quick search revealed the window only opened from the inside. Using the claw on his right index finger, he carefully cut a fist-sized circle in the window. When he was done, the glass dropped. It landed behind the desk. And shattered.

Below, the office door opened and a figure stepped into the room. Tadgh threw himself back out of view.

'Clearly, wasn't thinking that one through.' Tadgh waited a moment then crept to the edge of the skylight. A quick glance at the room told him it was empty again. He slipped his hand through the open hole and unlocked the window. 'I should count my blessings they didn't look up. You know what would be super useful? Being able to teleport like the Sage. And I could. All it would take is to say the wish aloud. But I can't. I promised I'd never use that power again. The risk of damaging the barriers around the Void is too high.'

He lowered himself through the window and landed on the paper-covered desk. He went to the door. The voices were much clearer now.

"It wasn't my bloody imagination," the first voice said. "Do you honestly mean you heard nothing? Are you drunk?"

"Not as much as I'd like to be," the second voice said. "Look, we just checked the room. It's empty. If you want to go check again, be my guest. Personally, I think you're just letting the stories go to your head."

Silence.

"Do you think it's really possible? Could there really be that many of them on the island?"

"We're not paid to think. Nothing good ever came from people like us thinking."

Tadgh glanced around the room. Thumb-sized insects with ant-like bodies crawled up and down the walls. Along one wall was a small bed covered with green sheets.

The door leading out of the room was slightly ajar. As he approached it, the floorboards under his feet groaned.

The voices outside stopped again.

'Never easy, is it?' Tadgh thought.

Tadgh flung open the door and pounced. His hand grabbed one surprised guard by the throat. Tadgh extended his willpower into the touch, dominating the man's mind. The second guard drew his sword and stabbed it through Tadgh's chest. Thankfully, the blade was not silver, the only metal that seemed to affect Tadgh since his change. The wound was painful and bled, but not very much. The first guard, now under Tadgh's control, flashed into action. Pulling out his own sword, the possessed guard stabbed his colleague. The wounded man gurgled something. As his body crumpled, the man's eyes dimmed. Tadgh helped lower him silently to the floor.

Tadgh looked down at his hands. Blood stained his fur. The cat demon purred in delight. It urged him to lick the blood before killing the other man. It whispered inside his mind that killing was fun. He did his best to ignore it.

"Where's the Sage?" Tadgh couldn't look at his mind-controlled slave. He found the adoration disturbing.

"In the basement, sire. I can bring you to him if you want."

Tadgh frowned. "Any chance you could just bring him here? How likely is that?"

The guard hesitated. "He's wearing a power dampener, chained to the floor. Twelve men are guarding him. The Sage is very powerful and he's heard what we have planned. I don't think the Ramir will let him go."

"What's a power dampener?"

The guard blinked. "It a device. It dampens powers. You know, it's kind of all in the name."

Tadgh punched guard lightly in the chest. "I guessed that part. I'm not an idiot. Well, not normally. What I meant was how does it work? Can I get it off the Sage?"

The guard bowed his head. "Of course, sire. My mistake. It's a nizarian device, a thick collar that adjusts to fit any neck size. It's used in prisons to incapacitate field-benders and fod sel-onde. I'm not sure how it actually works but it prevents people from manipulating the reality field. I think the Ramir is the only one with the key to remove it."

Tadgh groaned. "Of course." Tadgh glanced down at the cold, empty eyes of the dead guard on the floor then turned his attention to the enchanted guard. "I don't want to kill you. I've murdered enough people in my life. So do me a favor. See that bed over there? Sit there. Don't move no matter what you hear. Deal?"

"I'll do anything for you, sire." The guard smiled, his eyes glistening with joyful tears. "Anything to make you…"

"Yeah yeah yeah. Just move it, okay?" A sour taste grew in Tadgh's mouth, and he felt queasy. He was not comfortable violating others and hoped he never would be.

He left the office and walked down a dimly lit hallway. Paint peeled from the walls. Dark stains like wet oil and dried blood covered the floor. He could smell something vile and putrid in the wall. 'Ick. Rats. Just another thing this world has in common with Earth. Why can't they share coffee in common? Or deodorant. I miss people wearing deodorant.'

Searching the rest of the top floor, Tadgh found a large room filled with beds. In each of them slept a man in leather armor. A sword rested on a trunk at the foot of each bed.

'Soldiers. They look ready for action. Smart thing for me to do is kill them while they're sleeping. I could take one of those swords, stab them in the...' Tadgh pounded a fist against his head, trying to knock the thoughts out. 'No no no! Stop it! I'm not a monster. I refuse to be a monster.'

As quietly as he could, he crushed the doorknob and pushed the twisted metal inwards. He hoped it would be enough to damage the mechanics and prevent the door from opening easily. At least he would hear it if they attempted to knock the door down.

He found a set of metal steps leading down to the main floor of the warehouse. From below, he heard voices: talking, laughing. The air brought the scents of five men. From the slur in their voices, he assumed they had been drinking. One look at the stairs told him not to trust them. They looked old and rusted. Moving down the steps would make too much noise. He jumped, landing in a crouch at the bottom.

The blocked windows kept the floor of the warehouse dark. Wooden crates piled one atop the other creating a labyrinth of wide paths. He followed the sound of voices to an open area and crouched at the edge of the shadows. Before him, four men in brown leather armor played cards at a round table. A pile of money lay between them. On the opposite side of the table, another man busied himself with a woman. Her back was pressed to the wall, skirt lifted. The woman's eyes were bored and listless.

'Classy,' Tadgh thought. 'Must be love.'

One of the men at the table stood, and threw his cards on the table. His movement gave Tadgh a shock. He was not really a man at all. Or, at least, he wasn't sirian. His skin was mauve with green markings, his body monstrously large and muscular. He appeared to be the same race as Eiodeesh, a woman he'd briefly met at the Sage's.

'A trofast,' he thought. 'Wait. The guard said the Ramir wouldn't be pleased. That's a military term used by the forces of Dispayre, a high-ranking member of the dem straki. That means he has magic.'

Which also meant Tadgh was vulnerable. Since becoming a werecat, few things could damage Tadgh: one was silver, the other magic.

Tadgh's ears caught a soft sound from the right. He crouched down further and watched as a door to the outside opened and a soldier walked into the warehouse. Before the door closed, another figure appeared in the shadows. Menphis. He grappled the guard from behind, a hand pressed over the man's mouth. With a sharp jerking motion, Menphis twisted the guard's neck, killing him.

The trofast grunted in pain and held his head. He drew a dagger from a sheath at his waist.

"What is it?" One of the men playing cards got to his feet. "Is it the Sage?"

The trofast closed his eyes and touched his forehead. "No. He's still unconscious. We're not alone. I sense the thoughts of two others in the warehouse."

'Damn,' Tadgh thought. 'I forgot they were telepathic. He realized it was time to put caution aside. 'So much for avoiding confrontation. I need to cause a distraction, or they're going to overwhelm us.'

He focused on the weakest target to cause a panic. He shot a bolt of Akashic energy, hitting the back of the man preoccupied with the woman. The energy struck him in the shoulder, and he collapsed. The woman screamed and ran away.

Tadgh leapt. Spinning his quarterstaff, he smacked it into the head of the man beside the trofast. Unprepared for the assault, the man dropped to his knees. Menphis raced forward, moving faster than a sirian should be able to. It was a trick the Brotherhood of Tyche taught their advanced students. Menphis' quarterstaff spun with deadly precision. He jabbed at one man's knee. It popped and the man tumbled. Menphis brought the staff down on the man's head. The guard did not get up.

Tadgh turned his attention to the trofast. He shot another bolt of Akashic energy at his chest, but it never made a contact. The dem straki quickly erected an energy shield. Tadgh shot another bolt of energy at the ceiling. Instinct made the trofast look up. Dust and wood splinters fell into his eyes causing temporary blindness.

'Now's my chance.' Tadgh leapt at him. His claws slashed easily through the leather armor, shredding the flesh beneath. The trofast roared in pain but Tadgh did not stop. Putting his hand against the trofast's head, Tadgh shot another burst of Akashic energy.

The dem straki dropped, suddenly still. Dead. Blood dripped from its ear. Most of its flesh was cracked and blackened.

Tadgh looked down at what he'd down, sickened. 'What have I done? Why didn't I just turn him? Damn. Can't think of that now. Have to focus on the fight.'

Menphis deflected a dagger strike with his quarterstaff and punched another man in the chest. The soldier shuddered, coughed up blood, and dropped.

Tadgh looked behind Menphis as a stream of men poured out of the basement.

"Sometimes I hate my life."

He leapt past Menphis, swinging his staff like a baseball bat at the first guard. His cat form enhanced his reflexes and reaction time. It allowed him to dodge two sets of swords that struck at him. Unfortunately, five swords were swinging at him. Three of them sliced him, drawing blood. The pain fueled the demon inside him, the thing that wanted him to kill, that wanted to violate. He knew survival depended on giving that demon full reign.

He grabbed one guard by the neck and threw him, hurtling him into a stack of crates. Tadgh jumped straight up to avoid another flurry of sword attacks. Mid-air, he shot down with his Akashic bolts, hitting several soldiers in their sword arms. They dropped their weapons, howling in pain. When he landed, Tadgh spun his quarterstaff through a series of practiced movements, hitting several others. However, the soldier's armor protected them from much of the blunt force. It kept them back, but it didn't incapacitate them.

"Incoming!" Menphis shouted in warning. Tadgh looked around and saw another group of guards appeared, this one armed with crossbows.

"See?" Tadgh said. "I told you this would be fun."

"You have a strange idea of fun." Menphis ducked behind a set of wooden crates to avoid being struck with bolts form the crossbows.

Tadgh leapt up again, this time landing atop a set of nearby crates, and started shooting Akashic energy at soldiers. These men had no magic to protect them and, thankfully, Akashic energy moved much faster than bolts from a crossbow. Tadgh's weapon did not need to be reloaded. In a few moments, all the guards lay wounded and moaning on the floor.

Jumping down beside Menphis, Tadgh helped his friend back to his feet. "We have to move quickly. Most of those men are only wounded. They'll recover. It's probably best if we're not here when they do."

"Did you find the Sage?"

Tadgh nodded. "He's in the basement. I'm guessing we can get to it with those stairs. It's the direction the guards came from."

Moving past the moaning wounded, Tadgh and Menphis went down the stairs into a basement lit by nizarian lights. Hallways led in three directions. There were dozens of closed metal doors lining each corridor. A single guard stood below. His eyes went wide as Tadgh approached. He backed away and drew his sword.

Tadgh approached the man. "Where?"

The guard held Tadgh's eyes for a moment. He tightened his grip on the sword and blinked quickly.

Tadgh waited.

The guard dropped his sword and pointed to an open door down the hall to the right.

Tadgh flipped the switch in his mind and relaxed his control. Slowly, the blood-covered fur retreated, his claws disappeared, and he became human again. At least in appearance.

They found the Sage, unconscious and chained to the floor. He looked older than the last time Tadgh had seen him. His hair had hints of gray. He was not alone. Two others were chained to the floor: one, a small orange-skinned man, the other a large trofast woman. The man was unconscious, wearing a black metal collar identical to the one on the Sage. There was no collar around the woman. She smiled up at them, her eyes bright with recognition.

"Well," Menphis said. "Guess it's three for the price of one. Nice to see you, Eiodeesh."

"Seems almost poetic," she said. "Weren't you the one being rescued last time?"

Menphis shivered. "Don't remind me."

Tadgh picked up the chains and tugged at them. "Ugh. We're not out of this yet. These are pretty thick. We'll need to find the key." He smacked his head. "Duh. The Ramir is supposed to have the key on him. It should also work on those collars, so you can get your powers back. I'll be right back."

"I'll wait here," Eiodeesh said.

Tadgh smiled and raced up the stairs. Now that they'd rescued the Sage, he could teleport them to the island of DunDegore. It would save them a week of traveling which meant they were more likely than ever to rescue Grandwyn. It also meant Eiodeesh and Gnocko might help them with the mission. Suddenly he felt a bit better about his odds on DunDegore.

Chapter Thirteen

The Sage opened his eyes. An unexpected face stared down at him. He nearly screamed in shock.

"Jeesh," Tadgh Dooley said as he backed away from the Sage. "Am I that hideous?"

The Sage shook his head and pushed himself up to a seated position. He was in a basement. A deactivated power dampener lay on the floor beside him. Nearby, Gnocko and Eiodeesh spoke with Menphis Bannmerci, another familiar face.

"No, Tadgh. I just wasn't expecting to see you." The Sage shook his head. "There's something I need to tell you, but it will have to wait. How did you get here?"

Tadgh helped the Sage to his feet. "I followed your scent. Well, actually it started with Andy. You know, the woman in the blue dress. She appeared out of nowhere like last time and asked me to rescue you. She said it was her fault you were captured. Does that make sense?"

"None of this makes sense." The Sage touched the back of his head. Something had struck him hard enough to knock him unconscious. That scared him. Although he appeared human, his body was not truly flesh and blood anymore. Like the djinn, his body was constructed of solidified thermal energy, what legends called 'smokeless fire.' The fire gave him enhanced strength and near immortality. The last time he'd been struck this hard was fighting his adopted father, the djinn. Whatever or whomever had hit him, one thing was clear: the Sage was no longer the most powerful person playing this game.

"Is this place secure?" the Sage asked.

Tadgh looked up at the ceiling. "Secure-ish. When I got here, I found a group of sleeping soldiers on the top floor. After we freed you, Menphis and I went to check on them. They broke out. Took most of the injured with them."

"Which means they're somewhere out in the city. We need to inform the city guards about this." The Sage flicked his wrist. Nothing happened. "Looks like my powers haven't completely returned yet."

"You had us worried," Tadgh said. "After we took off the power dampeners, Gnocko woke up immediately. You were unconscious for nearly an hour. Is that normal?"

"I've never had one on before." The Sage ran his fingers along his neck where the collar had been. The skin still felt numb. Because his body was more energy than matter, the dampening collar affected him more profoundly than it would a fieldbender. "While we wait for my powers to come back, tell me everything."

The Sage listened as Tadgh relayed the story of Menphis' son, the trip to Gateway, and the rescue. He also learned that Tadgh had seen Bes the night before.

"I saw him as well," the Sage said. "Bes was here in this warehouse earlier."

"Bes was here?" Tadgh said the words extremely slowly. His eyes grew distant as he looked around the room. "But that doesn't make sense. What would he be doing here?"

The Sage put a comforting hand on Tadgh's shoulder. "Like I said, there's something I need to tell you. I found out where you got your power and why Bes is so interested in you. I'll tell you everything. I promise. But first I need to check in with Gnocko and Eiodeesh."

"Sure." Tadgh nodded, his face wrinkled in confusion.

When the Sage walked over to the others, Eiodeesh embraced him quickly.

"How did you end up here?" the Sage asked.

Gnocko and Eiodeesh exchanged a look. Gnocko rubbed the back of his neck and spoke. "The armies aren't our only concern. Did Tadgh tell you why he and Menphis are in town?"

The Sage nodded.

"It's all connected," Menphis said. "Somehow, the soldiers that captured you knew about my son. They knew we were heading to DunDegore to rescue him. What's going on?"

"We'll figure that out," Eiodeesh said. "I promise you, my friend, we'll do everything in our power to protect your boy. But we have a bigger problem right now."

The Sage lifted an eyebrow. "Don't tell me. There's worse news."

Gnocko groaned. "Isn't there always worse news when you're around? No offense."

Eiodeesh smacked Gnocko playfully upside the head. "Not worse news, but more pressing. We found the living quarters of a few soldiers in town. Mercenaries from Norshire have been moving to Shirza for months now. That means this operation started not long after the defeat of Lord Vyken's army outside GardenKeep. Plans previously set in motion are finally being executed. When we were spying on the soldiers, we were a little too aggressive."

"We?" Gnocko glared up at her.

Eiodeesh shrugged. "Fine. I was a little too aggressive. I heard something that sounded important. I came out of hiding and rushed the man to get more information. Unfortunately, we were outnumbered and captured. But not before I learned what I needed to. There is a spy traveling with Tadgh's group."

"What?" Tadgh's voice was loud, angry. "Who?" His face fell and his shoulders slumped. "Never mind. I know who it is."

"You do?" Menphis asked.

"Isn't it obvious?" Tadgh clenched his fists, but his eyes held more sorrow than anger. "Samar."

"The carriage driver?" Menphis scratched his head. "Doesn't it make more sense that it's Bethel? I mean, she's a soldier. She's closer to Tamara than anyone. She would also have much greater access to Grandwyn."

"But Samar has more access to me." Tadgh covered his face with his hands and turned away.

The Sage exhaled slowly. "I take it you and this Samar

have grown close."

Tadgh nodded, his face still buried in his hands. "Not as close as he'd like. But he's been trying. Really hard. He's also from up north. He told me he was a slave with the royal family of Norshire before he ran away to Shirza." Tadgh threw his hands to his side. "Damn! We have to act fast. If you're right and there are more soldiers around the city, won't they realize something has happened to this warehouse?"

"They might," Eiodeesh said. "And if the spy thinks he may be compromised…."

Menphis tightened his grip on his quarterstaff. "Tamara. We have to get to her."

Menphis started for the stairs but Eiodeesh stopped him.

"No need to run," the Sage said. "My powers have returned. I can teleport, remember? I'll get you to your baby momma."

Tadgh grunted. "Did you actually just say baby momma?"

The Sage shrugged. "I may have watched the occasional Jerry Springer back in the day. Listen, we have to be smart about this. We don't know what this spy is capable of. So here's what we're going to do."

***

Tadgh crouched behind a bale of hay in the loft of the hotel's stables looking down at Tamara's carriage. Nearby, the horses were penned in, their heads lowered as if asleep. Menphis knelt beside Tadgh, a silent ball of tension waiting to explode.

"What's taking so long?" Menphis asked.

"Dude, you have to breathe."

"I am breathing."

Tadgh elbowed his friend. "You know what I mean. We have the situation under control. The Sage is on the rooftop watching the back entrance. Eiodeesh is in the front lobby and Gnocko is in the suite with Tamara and Bethel doing his invisibility thing. Nothing is going to happen to her."

Menphis said nothing.

Something became clear to Tadgh. "You still have feelings for her, don't you?"

The tension drained from Menphis' body. "I can't have feelings for her. And she can't have feelings for me. We just can't."

"Man. And I thought my love life was complicated."

Menphis chuckled and elbowed Tadgh back. "Your love life is complicated. How do you think my cousin is going to react when he hears you've been making out with another man?"

"Have not! Samar did not get anywhere close to touchy-feely land with me." Tadgh listened for a moment as Menphis quietly laughed. When he spoke again, his voice was a whisper. "But if I'm honest? Part of me wanted him to."

"Really?" Menphis looked over at him, a startled look on his face.

"Can you blame me? Studly McBigChest seemed really interested in me. And have you seen his eyes? All blue and seducy. For awhile, I thought maybe Shonn was interested in me too, but I'll never be completely sure if I didn't use my power to make him feel that way. There's no way I used my abilities on Samar. His interest was real." Tadgh stopped and looked down at his hands. "Or at least I thought it was real.""

"Why did you call him Studly McBigChest?"

Tadgh waived the question away. "You wouldn't understand. You've never seen Buffy."

A sound startled Tadgh, and he placed a finger over his lips, signaling for silence. A few moments later, Samar entered the stables with a basket of apple-like fruit. He walked to one of the horses and held up a piece of fruit for the horses to eat.

'Target acquired,' Tadgh thought. *'Repeat target acquired.*

Can you hear me?'

'Loud and clear,' a voice said in his head. It was the Sage, communicating telepathically. The sensation was unnerving, like an unseen person whispering in his ear. *'I won't risk teleporting. If he's a fieldbender, he'd sense the shift in the reality field. We're on our way. You know what to do.'*

'Understood.' Tadgh flipped the switch in his mind, shifting into werecat form. When the transformation was complete, he looked over at Menphis. Both men nodded and jumped over the side of the loft. Menphis landed nearest the door, blocking the exit. Tadgh landed closer to Samar and struck outwards with his staff.

Samar moved faster than expected. He dodged Tadgh's attack. Then he did something Tadgh could never have expected.

Samar pulled out a gun.

Tadgh looked at it for a moment, so startled by the appearance of the futuristic weapon, he forgot to react for a moment. Samar's lips parted, and his eyes glossed over and softened. Then the blond man turned and fired the gun at Menphis.

A bolt of blue energy shot from the gun and struck Menphis in the chest. The elmire ahk flew out the door of the stable and landed on his back. He did not get up.

"No!" Tadgh screamed and swung his quarterstaff at Samar. Once again, the carriage driver evaded the blow. Then, in another strange move, he threw his gun aside and attacked Tadgh with his hands. It didn't take long for Tadgh to realize he was in trouble. Samar was a far better fighter than Tadgh. If he'd been in human form, Samar would have bested him quickly. But Tadgh realized something else. He didn't have to beat Samar. He only had to keep him busy.

Tadgh leapt away from Samar's attacks and landed on the roof of the carriage. "Why are you doing this?"

Samar took a step toward Tadgh. Then, his jaw set in determination, he looked over at Menphis, who still lay on his back. Thrusting his chest out, he picked up his gun and pointed it at Tadgh.

Like a ghost, Gnocko rose up through the ground behind Samar. The carriage driver sensed something behind him and turned around…which opened him for Eiodeesh's attack. She charged him, one armored shoulder hitting him in the torso, driving him to the ground. Samar twisted his body, trying to find the leverage to get back to his feet. He was no match for Eiodeesh's strength.

Tadgh jumped down, landing beside Samar. Anger broiling inside him, he curled his furred hand around Samar's throat.

"Don't." A hand touched Tadgh gently on the forearm. Immediately, all his anger drained from his body. Turning, he saw Tamara beside him, a look of gentle compassion on her face. "We need him to find my son."

Tadgh withdrew his hand and switched back to human form. Standing, he saw the Sage and Bethel helping Menphis to his feet. Relief flooded Tadgh's body as he realized his friend was not dead.

Gnocko picked up Samar's gun, studying it carefully. "And here I'd hoped to never see one of these again. Nizarian weapons. Nasty business." He held up the weapon for Tadgh, showing him a series of buttons. "Three settings: stun, kill, laser welding. Surprisingly, our spy had his weapon on stun."

"Why?" Eiodeesh asked the man pinned beneath her.

"Oh, dear," Tamara said as she looked between Tadgh and Samar. "Why is nothing ever simple?" She took her hands off Tadgh and touched Samar's forehead. His eyes went wide for a moment, then closed, a peaceful expression on his face. "Bring him to my room, Eiodeesh. It's time for Samar to answer some questions."

Chapter Fourteen

Tadgh was exhausted from an eventful day. He was also starving. He couldn't remember the last time he'd had a real meal. Samar, still unconscious was tied to a chair in Tamara's hotel room. Outside in the hallway, the Sage discussed the situation with the head of the city guard. Gnocko and Eiodeesh were busy going through Samar's belongings looking for clues. Menphis lay on a couch nearby, while Tamara used her abilities to heal him. Bethel stood behind Samar, her hand resting on the hilt of her sword

"I thought the weapon was set to stun," Tadgh asked.

"It was," Tamara answered. "It disrupted his nervous system. Left untreated, Menphis would make a full recovery in a day or so. Unfortunately, we need him at full strength now."

"I'm fine," Menphis grumbled. He tried to push past Tamara. She fixed her eyes on him and mumbled something Tadgh could not hear. Whatever it was, Menphis relented and lowered himself back to the couch.

"What did you do to Samar?" Tadgh took a step closer to Samar. The man's clothing had been loosened as they searched him for other weapons. His tunic had been unbuttoned, giving Tadgh a clear view of his chiseled abs and firm chest. "He looks…peaceful."

Tamara stood and came to stand beside Tadgh. "He is. I often use this in couples therapy. Sometimes people are so consumed by their anger they stop hearing each other. I've simply taken away his anger, the same way I took away yours."

"But you didn't put me to sleep."

Tamara sighed. "You're anger wasn't as powerful as his." Surprisingly, Tamara touched Tadgh's cheek. She pulled him toward her in a tight embrace. "I am so sorry, Tadgh."

"For what?"

"For what you have to do."

Tadgh pulled away from the embrace and stared at Tamara. "I don't understand."

Tamara straightened her clothing and looked Tadgh in the eyes. "Anything we can learn from Samar might help save my son's life. When I took away his anger, I caught a glimpse of his mind. Samar is a very broken man. He once told me he was a slave."

"He told me the same thing."

"Well, he lied." Tamara reached out and smoothed hair away from Samar's forehead. "Or shifted the truth. He was sold into slavery, but not to the royal family. Maybe it is different where you are from, but here each country has two governments. The one the people know about and a secret one known only to those in power. That is who bought Samar. For years, they tortured him, shattering his mind and body until he was little more than a tool. The perfect spy. When he was ready, they sent him to Shirza to infiltrate our power structures. He's served me for almost two years, yet never once did I suspect what he was."

Tamara glanced at Bethel. A look passed between them and Bethel removed her hand from the hilt of her sword. She walked away to the back of the room, out of earshot.

"And that brings us to our current dilemma," Tamara said. "While your school of elmire ahk focuses on conditioning the body, mine studies human emotion and sexuality. Because of my relationship with Fricka, I have some degree of control over other people's emotions. I can heighten them, lessen them. In some cases, I can even create emotions where there were none before. Sensing emotion is a sixth sense for me. Do you see the problem?"

Tadgh shook his head.

Tamara crossed her arms, making her expression steely, removed. "I read people's intentions like you hear sound or taste food. But not with Samar. Whatever they did to him, he is so completely broken my abilities do not work on him. In many ways, he doesn't know what he thinks or feels about anything. Except one thing. On that he is very clear. And since he refuses to talk, there is only one solution to learn what he knows."

Tadgh glanced back at her. For a moment, he didn't understand what she was talking about. Then it hit him.

"You want me to do it," he said. "Use my ability on him, to make him fall in love with me so that he'll answer my questions."

"No, Tadgh. You can't make him fall in love with you." She sighed and, reaching out, grasped his hand. "I told you there is only one thing Samar is sure about. And that is you. He truly does have feelings for you. It's why he didn't kill Menphis. I saw it when I was inside his mind. He knows all about you. That you come from another planet. That powerful people used you, turned you into a monster. He knows you've killed people, and that you are ashamed of what you've become. Can't you see? When he looks at you, he sees someone he can relate to. A soul mate. Yet despite all that, if you simply ask him to help, he won't tell you anything. Not because he doesn't want to, but because he can't. His conditioning was too thorough."

Tadgh backed away. Walking to the window, he glanced over at Bethel. She refused to meet his gaze, which suggested she was all too aware of what Tamara was asking of him. He looked out across the city suddenly feeling alone and cold.

A few moments later, Tamara came to stand behind him. Tadgh spoke to her reflection in the window rather than turn to face her.

"If I touch him, everything he feels about me will become a lie," he said. "You don't know what you're asking me to do. First, you say this man and I could be soul mates. Now you want me to destroy that. Well, I won't do it. The answer is no."

"You selfish child," Bethel said from the back of the room, her voice low and harsh. "She knows exactly what she's asking you."

Tadgh turned to yell at her, but before he could speak, Tamara put a gentle hand on his chest. "What I'm asking,

Tadgh, is for you to do something unbelievably hard so I can save my son's life. You've never met him, but he's only eight years old. We're all exhausted and need a few hours rest. After that, the Sage will teleport all of us to DunDegore. The island is overrun with the living dead, and we are walking in blind. We need you to use your ability to take control of Samar's mind. Force him to tell us what he knows."

"Which might be nothing."

Bethel growled. "Or it could be the difference between her child living and dying!"

Tamara glanced over at Menphis who sat quietly on the couch.

Menphis cleared his throat and said one word. "Please."

Tadgh wanted to punch something, but the only thing in front of him was glass. If he gave into his anger, the window would shatter. So instead of lashing out, he closed his eyes and let tears fall down his face. After a moment, he turned to Menphis.

"Fine," he said. "I'll do it. Now get out. All of you."

Tamara motioned for Bethel to leave. The bodyguard went to Menphis and helped him to his feet. When they left the room, Tamara walked over to Samar and touched his forehead. The blond man stirred and his breathing deepened. Afterward, she followed Bethel and Menphis out of the room and closed the door.

Alone in the room with Samar, Tadgh pulled up a chair and sat directly in front of him. As if stirred by Tadgh's proximity, Samar's eyes opened. At first, his expression was bright with recognition and affection. Then he looked around the room and down at the restraints tying him to the chair and his expression changed.

"It's over," Tadgh said. "We know you're working with the Quadumvirate. Tamara read your mind. Because of you, her son ran away and is now in grave danger."

"I...."

Tadgh interrupted. "She also told me how you feel about me."

"Oh." Samar stared at the ground.

Tadgh pulled his chair closer to Samar and put a hand on Samar's leg. The man jolted at the contact.

"You know about me," he said. "Know what I can do. If you truly have feelings for me, don't make me do this. We need to know what's happening on DunDegore. Tell me what you know."

Samar shook his head. "I can't. I just can't."

"Damn it! I can't believe I liked you."

Samar's face brightened. "You do?"

"Past tense! There can't ever be anything between us now. You shot my friend."

"Can't we get past that? Look, you're just like me, Tadgh. You don't have to play their game anymore. You and me, we could just run away and…"

"I can't just get past it! You shot my friend."

"Only a little."

"Stop it!" Tadgh jumped out of the chair so quickly it fell over. "Stop treating this like it's some big joke. Their son's life is in danger and…"

"No, it's not," Samar interrupted. "The kid is bait. They won't let the graunskyegs anywhere near him. They need him alive to trap you. Don't you see? All of this is to get you to the island, to get you to…." Samar clamped his mouth, realizing he'd said too much. After a moment, he spoke again in a quiet voice. If you go there, you're doing exactly what they want you to do. I know what the plan is, Tadgh. If you go to DunDegore, you will lose."

"So help me." Tadgh picked up the overturned chair and placed it back in front of Samar. He sat and reached out to touch Samar's face. "Tell me everything."

Samar looked back at Tadgh with hope in his eyes. And hunger. For just a moment, Tadgh allowed himself to feel that hunger in return.

Samar closed his eyes and shook his head. Tadgh realized he needed to be logical. Still touching his face, Tadgh leaned forward and spoke softly.

"Look at you. I've only known you a few days. I won't deny I have feelings for you. But Menphis? He's my best friend and his son is in danger. Bethel was right. I can't be selfish. I need to think of the greater good. You are a beautiful man, Samar. And I hate you for making me do this."

Tadgh extended his will through his fingertips and took control of Samar's mind. Samar gasped and squeezed his eyes shut. Slowly, his facial muscles relaxed and his lips turned up in a smile. "Master," Samar said. "How can I serve you?"

Tadgh bit his lip and fought back tears. Standing slowly, he went to the door. Opening it, he looked down the hallway. There was no sign of Menphis or Bethel, but Tamara stood nearby speaking with the Sage. Both turned to look at him, their faces blanketed with pity.

"It's done," Tadgh said.

Tamara bowed her head and touched her chest in prayer. "Thank you." She walked past Tadgh back into the room.

The Sage folded his arms and sighed. "It was the right thing to do."

Tadgh grunted. "It still sucks."

"Doing the right thing often does." The Sage walked toward Tadgh and briefly squeezed Tadgh's shoulder in an act of consolation. "After everything that happened between you and Shonn, this must be especially very difficult for you. Maybe I'm supposed to tell you that you'll find love again, that everything happens for a reason. But that's all nonsense. This might have been it for you. He could have been the love of your life. But I've learned the hard way, not everyone gets what they want."

Tadgh nodded. Surprisingly, the Sage's words comforted him. He preferred it to empty platitudes. He wiped his eyes with the back of his hand. He glanced into the room and watched as Tamara removed Samar's bindings.

"You said before you had something to tell me," Tadgh

said.

"Right." The Sage cleared his voice. "It's important you know before we head to DunDegore. You and I need to have a conversation but let's finish with Samar first."

Tadgh followed the Sage back into the room and shut the door.

Samar refused to answer questions from anyone but Tadgh. So, for the next hour, Tamara and the Sage took turns asking questions through Tadgh. Samar told them his only role was to keep track of Tamara's party and make sure Tadgh made it to the island. They learned there were five greater graunskyegs on the island, including Teric who had previously worked with Lord Vyken. Each greater graunskyeg had raised a force of one thousand lesser graunskyegs. Samar told them the plan was to feed the inhabitants and tourists on the island to weaker graunskyegs to build an undead army.

"So basically we're walking into *World War Z*," Tadgh said. "The book, not that horrid movie."

The Sage smiled. "Yeah. That movie did suck. But remember, these creatures may look like zombies, but there are fundamental differences. Their bites are not infections. The only way to create a graunskyeg is by dark magic. Unfortunately, it will also take more than a shot to the head to end them. You need to completely destroy the body. Fire is the best option. The lesser ones are only dangerous in groups. But if they feed enough, they become a real danger, something close to the vampires of earth."

"Do they sparkle?" Tadgh asked.

The Sage groaned. "Don't make me hit you. You remember the Umbral Knight we faced months ago? Think of that as a cybernetic graunskyeg. Imagine facing five of them during the zombie apocalypse and you have yourself a situation."

Tadgh grinned. "On the plus side, no dragons."

Tamara put a hand to her forehead and sighed deeply. "Only a man could joke at a time like this. What I don't understand is why the Norshire government has allied themselves with the Quadumvirate."

Tadgh absorbed the question and repeated it to Samar.

"I only follow orders," Samar responded. "I have no idea why the government is working for her."

"Her who?" the Sage asked.

"Myan." Samar shivered as he said the word.

The Sage inhaled sharply. Seeing the questioning look on Tadgh's face, he spoke. "Myan is one of the Quadumvirate, the four beings who rule in the absence of Dispayre. Amir Durgen is the head of the dem straki, although, according to rumor, he hasn't been seen in months. Myan is the Oracle. The other two, twins, rule the senate. She says Dispayre speaks to her from beyond the Void. I'm honestly not sure if she actually speaks to him or she's simply schizophrenic. I'm also not sure which option is more terrifying. So, your government is in league with the Quadumvirate? Hmm. Something will need to be done about that. But not today."

"Is there anything else I can do for you, master?" Samar asked. "Anything for you."

Something inside Tadgh roiled, and he felt nauseous. "Have we learned enough?" Tadgh asked.

"I believe so." Tamara reached down and touched Samar's forehead again. "Thank you again, Tadgh. I will never forget what you've done for me and Grandwyn. You should get some rest. We'll leave in the morning."

Tadgh nodded weakly and left without another word. The further he went from the room, the more somber his mood became. His mind whirled with so many thoughts he couldn't process them. He stopped in front of the hotel room he shared with Menphis. He stood at the door and heard voices inside. Bethel and Menphis spoke in hushed tones. He knew he couldn't be around either of them yet. He needed to be alone.

Walking further down the hall, he found a set of glass doors leading to a patio garden. Lush green plants sprouted from clay pots next to wicker couches. A stone wall created a safety barrier around the edges of the patio boxing it in. Tadgh walked to the edge and watched the lights of the city flicker and dim.

He took a deep breath. The cool night air helped to clear his head and dull the ache inside. For the first time in months, he wanted to be back home in Cleveland. A few months ago, his biggest concern was passing high school, getting into a good college. Everything changed when three bigots murdered his first boyfriend, Colin. Beaten and left for dead, Tadgh had wished for revenge. And his wish came true. Bes came to him and grafted the cat spirit to Tadgh, giving him the power to avenge Colin's murder. Driven by rage, Tadgh had killed the young men who had murdered Colin. He felt justified at the time, but now…? Whenever he thought back to the murders, which was often, he felt like a monster. If he returned to Earth, he would have to deal with the consequences of his actions. Would his life be any better if he stayed?

He heard the patio door open behind him and glanced over his shoulder to see who it was. Seeing it was the Sage, he put his forearms on the stone ledge and leaned forward. For several minutes neither said anything.

"How are you?" the Sage asked.

"Seriously?" Tadgh felt nauseous as bile built up inside. "I want to throw up. What's going to happen to Samar now?"

"The city guard took him into custody. He'll be tried for treason and probably spend the rest of his life in prison. Tamara is convinced she may be able to break through his conditioning with time. But I'm less hopeful. Some things, once damaged, cannot be replaced."

Tadgh mimicked the Sage's pose and leaned over the stone wall. "So what's the plan for tomorrow?"

"Oh, the usual. Race in. Blow stuff up."

Tadgh laughed quietly. "Sounds fun. But wouldn't it make more sense to send in the army or something?"

"First off, there is no army. Not like they have back on Earth. Each country has its own militia, but their weapons are limited to siege weapons. Think *Lord of the Rings*. The only ones with any real technology are the nizarians, and I've never trusted them."

"Why?" Tadgh thought for a second. "You know, their flying ships look an awful lot like flying saucers."

The Sage raised an eyebrow and smirked. "Really? I never noticed that. There is a man who lives among the nizarians I do trust. His name is Elmontrazar, a very old and powerful fieldbender. I tried to send him a message earlier today but was told he'd already been called away on a mission. He was the only hope I had of a quick response. Politicians move at their own speed. The nearest militia to DunDegore is in Karaj Robat. You may remember that is the same government that sent a hit squad after you. The head of the city guard here will make Karaj Robat aware of the situation while we make our initial assault. The militia will arrive as soon as possible. Which, knowing them, will be in a few days. At best. And that's assuming they agree to help. My relationship with them is…complicated. I'm betting they will look past that to see the greater threat. But Grandwyn may not have that long." The Sage hesitated for a moment and cast a side glance at Tadgh. "And, don't tell Menphis I said this, but the fate of his child is not even my biggest concern."

Tadgh nodded. "We can't let those graunskyegs off the island."

The Sage waved the statement away. "That goes without saying. But there is something else. You remember how shocked I was to see you earlier today. There was a reason for that. You already know I saw Bes and overheard him speaking with a demon. They were speaking about you. Specifically, about how you got your powers."

Tadgh frowned. "What do you mean? I thought you said I was fod sel-ondc. That I was born this way. You're saying I wasn't?"

The Sage closed his eyes. "No. Not even close. You are something much more dangerous. This is a long story. I will tell it as quickly as I can. I was born thousands of years ago in Atlantis, long before it fell into the ocean. As a child, I was stolen from my parents. Captured, if you will, by a djinn. You're from America, so the only exposure you've had to the djinn was *I Dream of Jeannie* and *Aladdin*. But the djinn are nothing to be laughed at. They are creatures of immense power who live in a parallel dimension known as the Kaz. I lived among them for thousands of years raised by a monster who insisted I call him father. When I escaped, my father was not pleased. He spent centuries trying to drag me back to the Kaz. Not long before I came to this world, he and I had a final battle. I won. I killed my father, and I thought that was the end of it."

Tadgh shook his head. "Even if I believed half of what you just said, what does that have to do with me?"

The Sage rubbed his hands over his scalp and took a deep breath. "Unfortunately, everything. When I killed my father, his essence should have returned to the Kaz to be reincarnated. But a portion remained on Earth."

"You've completely lost me."

The Sage turned to face Tadgh. "I've been playing the dates in my mind and it all adds up. The day you were attacked, the day Colin was murdered, was the same day I killed my father. His essence sought out a host, a being filled with rage and loss. In the whole world, for some reason, it found you."

Tadgh walked over to one of the wicker couches. His head felt light, and he was no longer sure he could stay on his feet. His skin tingled with tension.

"So you're saying my wish power came from an actually genie? Does that mean I only get three wishes or something?"

The Sage sat on the couch beside him. "Djinn have unlimited ability to alter reality. There's no way of knowing how much of his power lives in you now. Maybe your wish power is limited. Or maybe, with time you will develop more of the djinn's abilities. It's too soon to tell."

"And that's why Bes wants me." Tadgh laughed and leaned forward, his elbows on his thighs.

"Yes. He wants to study you, to find out why the djinn's energy went into you. I know how I got my abilities. I lived in the Kaz. I ate, drank, and breathed fire elemental energy for millennia. But you are something different. I've never had anything close to your wish power. That's why the demons want to drag you to hell."

"What if..." Tadgh gave the Sage a sidelong look. "Look, I'm not eager to die or anything, but if I'm really so dangerous, maybe I should...you know..."

The Sage nodded. "I thought of that."

"Really? You were seriously going to kill me?"

"No offense, but if that solved everything it would be an easy call. One life to save the entire world. I like you Tadgh, but I wouldn't hesitate." The Sage folded his hands on his lap. "Here's the dilemma. The djinn's energy is inside you. If you die, I fear it would simply find another host. I'd rather keep it exactly where it is."

"Really? Why?"

"Because you don't want it," the Sage answered. "Or at least you're hesitant to use it. Imagine that power in the wrong hands. So, no pressure here, but don't die."

Tadgh grunted. "Thanks. I'll see what I can do."

For a moment, the Sage grinned. Then his expression grew very serious. "If they find out how to put a djinn's power inside a human body, they'll invade the Kaz. They want to make an army of soldiers with your abilities. We can't let that happen. If things go badly on DunDegore, if it looks like Bes is about to capture you, I need you to wish for my ability to teleport."

Tadgh's jaw dropped. "But you said..."

"I know what I said. If you use your wish ability, you risk weakening the bonds of the Void and releasing Dispayre. Right now that is the lesser of two evils. No matter what the cost, you cannot let the demons use you. Do you understand?"

Tadgh stared at the ground. "And here I thought my day couldn't get any worse. Thanks for proving me wrong."

The Sage patted Tadgh briefly on the back before leaving the patio. Tadgh sat alone for a long time before heading to his room for a few hours sleep.

Chapter Fifteen

It was morning on the isle of DunDegore. Grandwyn woke to find himself alone. He heard Mikhel's voice filter in from elsewhere in the house, chanting something softly. He followed the sound to the top of the stairs. Below, Mikhel kneeled by the front door, his fingers slowly tracing the wood.

"Whatcha doin'?" Grandwyn asked. "Removing the wards?"

Mikhel glanced back, nodded, and continued with the work. Minutes later, he stood and turned to face Grandwyn.

"How did you sleep?" he asked.

"Poorly." Grandwyn rubbed the sleep from his eyes.

"Nightmares?"

Grandwyn nodded. "Is it safe out there?"

"No. Don't give me that look. You're the one who said I shouldn't lie to you. What we aim to do this morning is downright foolish. But, honestly, I don't know what the safe thing to do is. Are you sure you're up for this? I could always…."

"No," Grandwyn interrupted. "I want to do this. Are we going now?"

Mikhel flinched, avoiding Grandwyn's eyes. "The sun's been up for about twenty minutes now. From what I've read, the stronger the graunskyeg, the more the sun affects them. Only the weaker ones will be out during the day."

"You mean the ones that haven't eaten enough. The ones that are still hungry."

Mikhel laughed, a sound without humor. "Doesn't sound so safe when you say it like that. Listen, kid, this is your last chance. Once we leave this house there will be no turning back."

Grandwyn thought for a moment. "I don't want to do this. But we have to. If my mother was here she'd try to save all those people."

"Who is your mother anyway?"

"Tamara Billyan, head of the Temple of Fricka in FleshPrayer."

Mikhel's eyes went wide. "Seriously? Damn. I met your mother once. It was at a fundraiser in Karaj Robat. Don't you go dying on me, kid. Your mother has some powerful friends. Anything happens to you I might as well die too."

Grandwyn smiled. "Well, I guess you shouldn't let anything happen to me."

Mikhel laughed for a moment then inhaled deeply. He put a finger to his lips, motioning for Grandwyn to be quiet. He opened the front door. Soft rain still fell, bouncing off the streets and rooftops with a gentle staccato. Mikhel stepped outside and looked around. After a moment, he motioned for Grandwyn to follow him.

The docks were only a block away. Seagulls flew in the air above, their harsh cries echoing through the empty streets. Grandwyn's head spun in all directions. He was hyper alert as he watched for signs of movement.

As they reached the dock, Mikhel put a hand on Grandwyn's shoulder to stop him. He knelt down and pointed at the horizon. Grandwyn squinted and shielded his eyes from the sun. Then he saw it. A tiny white speck in the distance.

"That's the ship," he whispered. "We got here in time."

"Yeah. Which means we need to find a place to hide and wait. They won't reach dock for at least half an hour. As soon as the crew starts to tie off, we'll rush over and tell them to get away."

"But not before we get on board, right?"

Mikhel tousled Grandwyn's hair. "Right. Now where's a good spot to wait?"

Grandwyn looked around. The area by the docks was in ruins. It was hard to believe it was the same place he'd landed two days ago. Back then, the streets had been packed with people. Now, only shadows moved in the empty shops.

"Wait." Grandwyn stared in the window of one of the

shops. "Shadows don't move."

"Did you see something?" Mikhel asked.

Grandwyn pointed at the window. "In there."

They stared at the window for several long moments but saw no other sign of movement.

"I believe you, kid," Mikhel said. "Maybe it was nothing, but we can't take a chance. We should get off the street. Let's head for that building over there. See it? It's a bank. They have bars over the windows and thick doors. It's the safest place around here I can see."

Grandwyn nodded and turned away from the window. As they walked toward the bank, an eerie feeling built up inside Grandwyn. He scanned the streets but saw nothing to justify how he felt. He listened. His mouth dropped open and he stopped.

"What is it?" Mikhel asked.

"The birds," Grandwyn answered. "Where did all the birds go?"

Mikhel looked up. There was not a single seagull in sight. Moments before the sky had been filled with them. Even the rain had stopped. The entire dock area was deathly quiet.

Mikhel gripped Grandwyn's hand tightly and looked down at him. "Run."

Both raced quickly toward the bank. Then Grandwyn heard the moans. Glancing over his shoulder, he saw doors open from all the shops. From each door, a steady stream of undead creatures poured out, filling the previously empty streets. A thought entered Grandwyn's mind.

"They're in the stores," he screamed. "The bank isn't safe!"

As he spoke, the door to the bank opened and a dark-skinned graunskyeg appeared. Half of his face was missing skin. He was horrifying to look at.

Without slowing, Mikhel pointed and shot a blast of Akashic energy at the graunskyeg. It knocked the undead creature back into the building…right into the twenty other graunskyegs behind it.

"There are too many of them!" Undead creatures poured out of buildings everywhere Grandwyn looked. In less than a minute, hundreds of graunskyegs stood on the docks.

"There!"Mikhel pointed at the docks. "Do you see it?"

Grandwyn shook his head. "No I…Wait! Yes. I do." Sitting at the edge of the docks was a small row boat, the type larger ships used as life boats. Somehow, this one boat had escaped sinking.

They raced toward it. Behind them, the moaning of the dead grew louder. Grandwyn knew they had to slow the graunskyegs down or he and Mikhel would never reach the boat. Glancing to his left, he saw a merchant cart filled with clay replicas of the Ruins of DunDegore. Reaching out with his power, he threw the cart backwards, right into the approaching graunskyegs. The cart slammed into three of the undead, knocking them down. Dozens tripped over the fallen creatures, slowing down others.

Mikhel looked over his shoulder. "Nice one, kid. Hang on. We're almost there.

They reached the docks, their feet pounding on the wooden planks as they ran quickly toward the boat. Mikhel stopped, throwing a hand in front of Grandwyn's chest to prevent him from going further.

Behind them, the graunskyegs stopped as well.

Grandwyn watched as a small furred creature jumped out of the boat and onto the dock. He'd never seen anything like it: a four legged animal the size of a small dog that looked like the great cats he'd seen in zoos. It was covered in orange fur, and its eyes glowed with bright green light.

"What is it?" he asked.

"My name is Bes," the creature answered. "And I'm afraid you aren't going anywhere, Grandwyn Billyan."

As soon as the creature began to talk, Grandwyn realized what it was. This was the demon Mikhel had spoken about, the one who attacked the monastery and stole the object. And, somehow, it knew his name.

"What do you want?" Mikhel asked.

The creature grew in size, now the size of a lion. "You're not too bright, are you? Isn't it obvious?" Bes turned to stare at Grandwyn.

"You can't have the boy." Mikhel pulled Grandwyn closer to him, shielding the boy from Bes with his body.

"Who's going to stop me?" Bes grew yet again until he was the size of a horse. "You? You're not even a real fieldbender yet. I ate your comrades for breakfast. Literally. They were quite tasty. Since you seem intent on dying a hero, give it your best shot."

Mikhel looked down at Grandwyn, a sad look in his eyes. "I'm sorry, kid. I wish I was stronger. You need to be really strong now. Remember the roses."

Then, as hard as he could, Mikhel pushed Grandwyn. The boy went over the side of the dock and into the water. As Grandwyn sank beneath the waves, he heard a monstrous roar followed by the sound of Mikhel's scream.

Chapter Sixteen

Tadgh collapsed to his knees and elbows, gasping. It took him ten minutes to get control of the nausea and the sensation of being strangled. When he got to his feet, he found the others were as pale-faced and sickly as he felt. Tamara, once again wearing her crimson jacket and the weighted chain as a belt, leaned on Bethel for support. Gnocko looked especially affected. He repeatedly waved away Eiodeesh's attempts to help him to his feet.

The Sage looked particularly troubled. "Well, that was…different."

Menphis wiped spittle from his lips. "You have a gift for understatement. That was nothing like the time you teleported us away before."

"Exactly." The Sage wiped his forehead and studied the sky. "Ah. I see it now. They've erected some sort of energetic barrier over the city. Probably to prevent the fieldbender guild here from leaving or calling for help. I should have expected something like this. We should be grateful we got in at all."

Tadgh used his quarterstaff as a walking stick and looked around. They had arrived in the alley behind the fieldbender guild. The Sage had chosen the location because it was hidden and near the center of town.

"I don't like this." Bethel turned in a slow circle. "It's too quiet."

The Sage motioned to Eiodeesh. With a nod, the trofast drew her axe and ran to the end of the alley. Crouching , she peered both ways around the corner. After a moment, she looked back and signaled that the road was clear.

Gnocko walked over to the Sage and kicked him in the shin.

"Hey!" The Sage said. "What was that for?"

"For making me feel like my insides were on the outside. I must be out of my mind for working with you."

Gnocko picked up his weapons, which had fallen to the ground. They were two small sickles joined by a length of chain. Tadgh had heard the Sage call them kusari-gama. Gnocko, annoyed, had corrected the Sage and called them climbing gear. Tamara leaned against a brick wall. Appearing still shaken, she looked at the Sage. "Remember the last time we were here?"

The Sage nodded. "The conference on inter-denomination cooperation last year. We had lunch at that restaurant at the end of the pier, Magdalene's. They have the best fish and yogurt on the island."

Tamara smiled briefly before looking down. "Had. It's all gone now, isn't it?"

Bethel squeezed Tamara's shoulder and the two women shared a moment of silence.

"Alright," the Sage said. "You all remember the plan. Gnocko and I are heading to the ruins. According to Samar, that is where the demon Bes is keeping the Sword of Kassandra. The rest of you will follow Tadgh's lead. He's our best chance of finding Grandwyn."

"Because apparently now I'm a bloodhound." Tadgh looked down at his hands. He held Grandwyn's stuffed animal, the one Tamara had kept with her in the carriage on the trip here. For the last hour, he'd studied the scent. The Sage was fairly certain Tadgh would be able to track Grandwyn.

The Sage flicked his wrist and opened another portal.

Gnocko kicked him in the shin again. "Are you trying to kill us? Barrier, remember? You can teleport if you want. I'm going to walk. Stop being so lazy. The blasted ruins are just at the edge of town."

"Good point." The Sage closed the portal and put his hands on his hips. "Everyone, a few last words. Be careful out there. Remember, all your skills and abilities mean nothing if you're rushed by a horde of graunskyegs. You serve no one by dying needlessly. Run if you need to."

Tamara touched her forehead and chest in pray. "The

same to you, old friend."

The Sage put one hand around Gnocko's waist, lifting him off the ground. Then he jumped. He flew to the nearest rooftop and ran off toward the ruins.

Tadgh lifted the stuffed animal to his nose. He walked to the end of the alley as he inhaled Grandwyn's scent one more time. As he approached, Eiodeesh rose from her sentry position and entered the street. Menphis followed Tadgh, his quarterstaff held at the ready. Bethel walked in the rear, protecting Tamara. When Tadgh hit the main street, the scent of death and old blood overpowered him. Gagging, he dropped to his knees.

Eiodeesh crouched beside him. "Can you do this?"

Tadgh nodded and rose back to his feet. "I think so. Give me a minute."

He closed his eyes and practiced the deep breathing he'd learned at the monastery. At first it was difficult because of the stench. But, slowly, he gained control of his senses. That's when it hit him. His eyes flashed open.

"I have it! Grandwyn's scent." He ran to the front door of the fieldbender guild. Lowering himself to the ground, he sniffed the air.

"Is he inside?" Tamara asked.

Tadgh stepped through the open door and shook his head. "No. He never made it inside. The scent isn't fresh. Sorry, I can't tell how old it is. This is all new to me, but I don't think he's been here in awhile." Coming back outside, he opened his mouth slightly to improve the acuity of his olfactory sense. "The scent leads in two directions." He walked up and down the street repeatedly sniffing the air. "But this way seems most recent."

Bethel stood beside Tadgh and looked up the street. "This leads to the docks. Everyone keep your eyes on the buildings. We'll hear the graunskyegs if they come by street, but we have no way of knowing how many are hiding inside."

Menphis walked backwards for a bit, checking what was

behind them. "Eiodeesh. Can you do your trofast thing? Check for thoughts?"

Eiodeesh put her hand on the side of her head and closed her eyes. "Nothing."

"I've heard trofast can sense thoughts for miles," Bethel said. "If there are no active thoughts nearby, perhaps we should…"

"No," Eiodeesh interrupted. "I was raised by a sirian. I've never had any real training. I can only sense thoughts within a hundred feet or so. It's enough to tell if there's anyone alive in the buildings around us. Nothing more. That's why the Sage put Tadgh in charge of tracking."

The sound of the group's footsteps echoed through the empty streets. On the left-hand side of the street was a string of tourist shops advertising trinkets and memorabilia with the name DunDegore emblazoned on them. Along the right-hand side was a string of hotels.

Bethel stepped forward. "Did you see that?" She pointed at the open door of one of the hotels.

Tadgh looked at the hotel's name: Voltryp Hotel. He had seen the name several times before, once in GardenKeep, once on the way through Gateway. Apparently, Maghe Sihre was advanced enough to have hotel chains.

"What did you see?" Tamara asked.

Bethel withdrew her sword. "Movement. We should check it out."

"No!" Tadgh squealed. "That is the absolute last thing you should do in a zombie movie. Bar the door if you need to but stay out in the open."

"I don't know what a zombie movie is, but we are not in one." Bethel went to the glass doors and pushed them further open. "We're in a city crawling with potential enemies. Best to know where they are. Agreed?"

"Agreed." Eiodeesh put her hand to her forehead again. "There's someone alive in there." Eiodeesh went through the door. Bethel followed leaving the others behind.

Tadgh flung his head back in frustration. "In a world of bad ideas this one is looking to win awards. Please tell me you guys know this is just asking for trouble."

Tamara looked up as she unwrapped the weighted chain from around her waist. "This hotel has multiple stories. Perhaps we can take to higher ground and get an overview of the city. For all we know, the next street over is crawling with graunskyegs." Holding the chain like a weapon, she turned to Menphis for support.

Menphis nodded. "Sounds like a good idea."

"You are all insane." Tadgh shook his head and watched as Tamara and Menphis entered the hotel. For a moment, he was alone on the streets of DunDegore. "I still say this is a stupid idea. Watching all those scary movies taught me something. Don't tempt disaster."

Minutes passed. No one came back out of the hotel. Tadgh grew increasingly uneasy being alone. The only sound was the wind blowing through the empty streets.

"Screw it," he said. "But if I get eaten by a zombie, I am so going to haunt someone."

Holding his quarterstaff in front of him, Tadgh walked into the hotel.

He stood in a lobby with gold-colored walls. Directly opposite the main entrance was a black reception desk that stood chest-high and ran twenty-feet long. Past the reception area was a small restaurant with round wooden tables, and chairs upholstered with white and gold fabric. Ten-foot-tall oil paintings hung on several of the walls.

There was no sign of the others.

"Splendid," he said. "They wandered off."

Walking past the reception desk, he saw something out of the corner of his eye.

A severed hand lay in a pool of blood on the floor.

With a grunt of disgust, Tadgh turned away. He walked into the dining room. There was still no sign of the others. At the back of the dining room, a simple white door swung gently back and forth on its hinges. His heightened hearing picked up sounds of movement on the other side. He went to it and pushed it open. The door led to a kitchen. Pots of cold soup were spilled over the floors. Chunks of meat lay on the counter, mid-butchering. A human ear was caked to the wall in a splatter of blood.

An unexpected scent hit his nose. Tadgh followed it to a wooden pantry door. When he opened the door, the woman inside screamed.

"It's okay." Tadgh crouched and extended a hand as if trying to calm a nervous animal. The brown haired woman wore a torn white uniform heavily stained with blood. Her wild eyes moved past Tadgh, looking at something over his shoulder. She screamed again.

On instinct, Tadgh slammed the pantry door closed. Jumping to the left, he shot a bolt of Akashic energy behind him. The purple bolt struck the torso of a graunskyeg knocking the creature back. It wore a white servant's uniform, its flesh in the early stages of rot. Tadgh recognized this as a sign it was only recently a graunskyeg and had not fed often. It snarled at Tadgh, black mucousy rot dripping from its mouth. Tadgh swung his quarterstaff, striking the creature in the knees and driving it to the ground before it could rise to its feet. Tadgh jammed the butt of his staff into the creatures head over and over again.

The creature stopped moving.

"Huzzah!" Tadgh said. "Head shots do work. Looks like the Sage doesn't know everything after all."

Tadgh opened the pantry door. Reaching in, he pulled the terrified woman to her feet. As they ran out of the kitchen and into the dining room, two more graunskyegs walked slowly toward them. One was a bald woman wearing the same type of white uniform as the woman from the pantry. The second was a naked man missing his right hand.

Eiodeesh appeared from somewhere and chopped off the female's head. Right behind her was Bethel. With three swift movements, Bethel sliced the main tendons in the graunskyeg's arms making it impossible for the creature to raise them in attack. She kicked it in the chest, pushing it backwards. It fell against one of the tables, several of its bones snapping with a wet sound.

Bethel turned to Tadgh. "Get outside! Menphis and Tamara are already there." She turned to the male graunskyeg and swung her sword at its head. Her blade could not go all the way through the flesh. She had to swing several times before the head fell to the floor.

Tadgh dragged the survivor toward the lobby.

Another graunskyeg appeared on the stairs, walking down from the upper floors. Tadgh shot a blast of Akashic energy at the approaching graunskyeg. Its flesh was so weak and decayed the mystic bolt sliced right through its chest. The creature did not slow. Tadgh heard the sound of a door opening and looked back toward the kitchen. The white door had opened. Several graunskyeg appeared, including the headless one he thought he'd dispatched. It appeared the Sage was right after all.

Tadgh yelped. "Watch out! They're coming to get you, Bethel." Tadgh did a double take. "I can't believe I honestly just said that."

Before the headless graunskyeg could get far, Eiodeesh swung her mighty axe, cutting off its arms at the shoulder. Another swing took out its knees.

"Are you going to kill it or keep it as a pet?" Bethel asked.

Eiodeesh grinned at Bethel. "I think I like you." Holding the axe above her head, she slammed it down where the creature's head had once been, neatly slicing the creature in two. She turned to face the other graunskyegs.

The woman from the pantry screamed again. She pulled away from Tadgh and ran outside. Only then did Tadgh realize he'd stopped moving. Shaking his head, he looked away from Bethel and Eiodeesh back to the graunskyeg with the hole in its chest.

'The Sage said fire worked best,' he thought. 'But I don't see any fire around. Both my quarterstaff and purple energy thingies don't seem to do anything. I think this might be the time to amscray.'

Sprinting out of the building, he saw Menphis comforting the woman who was sobbing uncontrollably. Tamara stood nearby, swinging one end of the weighted chain. Bethel ran out of the building right after Tadgh. Eiodeesh, the last out, slammed the door shut behind them.

"What did I tell you?" Tadgh screamed. "Did I not say this was a bad idea?"

Menphis glowered at him. "If we hadn't gone in there you wouldn't have saved this young woman. I think her life that was worth the risk. Don't you?"

Tadgh glared back at Menphis. "Just because you make a valid point doesn't mean I have to agree with you."

"Shh." Eiodeesh held up her hand. "Do you hear that?"

Tadgh held his breath and focused on his hearing. What he heard scared him more than anything in his life ever had. Although he'd never experienced it in real life before, he'd heard it all too often in movies.

"What is that?" Menphis asked.

"That," Tadgh responded, "is the moans of the dead. We need to be anywhere but here. Like yesterday. Everybody, run!"

Chapter Seventeen

Grandwyn released his hold on the wooden pier post, allowing his body to float to the surface.

"Remember the roses," Mikhel had said. It took a moment for Grandwyn to realize what the fieldbender meant. The idea terrified him, but he also knew it was his only hope. As he was thrown off the pier, Grandwyn called upon his power and created a thick sphere of ice over his head, trapping in breathable air. The only problem with the plan is that the air made him float. He swam beneath the pier and held on tightly to one of the wooden posts. When his head grew dizzy, he rose to the surface but quickly realized it wasn't yet safe.

"Find the brat," came the cat demon's voice. "If he gets away the whole plan could fall apart."

Grandwyn didn't know what that meant and didn't want to find out. He heard footsteps above him as dozens of bodies walked over the pier.

'I have to go down again,' he thought. 'They'll find me if I try to swim ashore.' He used his ability again, this time creating a much larger ice sphere filled with more breathable air. He dove beneath the water's surface again and waited until the ice began to melt. Still unsure if it was safe, he let go of the beam and floated to the surface.

It was quiet now.

He swam toward a ladder attached to the pier and climbed out of the water. Dripping wet and getting steadily colder, he looked around. The small row boat he'd seen earlier was gone now. A large splash of blood marred the wooden pier. It was where Mikhel had been standing. He didn't want to think about what that meant.

Turning around, he saw a ship tied to a pier at the other end of the dock. He assumed it was the ship Mikhel and he had seen in the distance. Dozens of tourists had already left the ship, looking at the destruction around them. Grandwyn wanted to cry out to them, to warn them, but he was too frightened. He knew the graunskyegs would be close by. If he cried out, they would find him and whatever had happened to Mikhel might happen to him. So instead, he ran.

Not long after he left the docks, the screams began. Tears flowed freely down his face, blurring his vision. He was in an open-air market filled with covered stands. Beside one of the stands stood a graunskyeg. Once it had been a teenage girl. Now, its bruised skin showed beneath its tattered and bloody green dress. It sniffed the air.

Grandwyn dropped down behind an overturned cart and held his breath. The graunskyeg moved in his direction, moaning. Then its head cocked to the side as if it was listening to something. It growled and looked directly at Grandwyn. Then it moved away.

'Must be my lucky day,' he thought. Then he realized what a silly statement that was and laughed quietly.

He wiped his eyes and moved away from the cart. He paid close attention to his surroundings now, staying low and using the stands for cover. He passed a fruit standing selling blast berries and yellow nuts. Behind that stand was another graunskyeg, an old man with gray hair and wrinkles. It chewed on something that appeared to be a thigh bone. Grandwyn crept forward, careful not to make a sound. The next few stands were thankfully empty: nothing but souvenirs and baubles.

He reached the end of the open-air market and realized where he was.

'That's the mall,' he thought. He'd seen it in the brochure. It was the largest indoor shopping area outside the Great Castles. Three hundred stores all lit by nizarian lights. There were two large buildings, one of which featured a massive grocery store. The brochure claimed it sold food imported from around the world, something Grandwyn found hard to believe. The world, after all, was very big. And why would people want to eat food from around the world when there was so much local food?

Outside the mall were dozens of statues, each forty feet tall. Beherskers, he realized. He let his eyes fall over them, momentarily stunned by the spectacle. The statues were almost two hundred years old, created in the renaissance after StarFall. Some statues were male, others female. All had straight, shoulder-length hair. In place of their eyes were large gems: fist-sized rubies in some, luminescent jet in others. The women wore flowing garments like sheets wrapped around their bodies. Some men wore skin-tight jumpsuits while others wore scaled jerkins and trousers. Most statues had some form of jewelry. From here it looked like the gold necklaces, the earrings, and the arm bands were constructed of real gold and real gems. Most surprising to Grandwyn was the smiles on their faces. Back home, most statues were stolid representations of quiet dignity. These seemed more like snapshots of family life.

The front door of the mall was open.

'I'm scared,' Grandwyn thought. 'The mall could be crawling with graunskyegs. Still…' He looked down at his soaked clothes. 'I'd really like to get out of these things. Maybe I could borrow some dry clothes. I'm sure my mom will pay them back.' He stopped, suddenly realizing how silly his thoughts were. The island had been overrun with graunskyegs, and he was still worried people might thing he was stealing clothes. 'No one's going to care if I steal clothes because they're all dead.'

Grandwyn started to shake. He wanted to cry, to hide. He regretted every decision he'd ever made. Why had he come here, anyway? If he'd only done what his mother told him to, he'd be safe at home. He wished his mother was here. She would know what to do.

'But she's not here,' he thought. 'I have to figure this out myself. So, first I'll get dry clothes. After that, I need to find a way off this island.'

With one last look around, Grandwyn ran toward the front door and entered the mall.

Chapter Eighteen

The Sage set Gnocko down beside him and studied the ruins of DunDegore: fifteen jagged spirals, each over a hundred stories tall, spread out over forty acres. They jutted out of the ground like the shattered teeth of some monstrous animal. Dozens of smaller buildings filled the space between the larger towers. The doorways and windows were designed for much larger beings than sirians. The Beherskers, legend said, were giants with an average height of twenty-five feet. The oversized scale made the Sage feel small and vulnerable.

They walked along a chain fence erected to keep tourists at a distance from the buildings. Random acts of vandalism were not uncommon. The Ruins of DunDegore were one of the most revered places on the planet, similar to Stonehenge back on Earth. Normally, the area was under guard. Now the streets were empty.

He stopped in what must once have been a public square. At the center of the square was a recently-constructed fountain featuring statues of Beherskers. The gurgle of water splashing in the fountain was the only sound in the city.

"Remarkable, isn't it." The Sage put his hands on his hips and looked up at the nearest spire. "Best estimate is these buildings are over three thousand years old. Still structurally sound, for the most part. We had many cities like this on Earth. The one this reminds me of the most was called Tokyo. Well, what Tokyo would look like after a few centuries of neglect."

"You know what's remarkable?" Gnocko straightened his clothes and readjusted his glasses. "You carry me like a sack of potatoes as you jump around rooftops like a charging rheiballough without so much as a warning or an apology. That is remarkable."

The Sage patted Gnocko on the head. "Did I ever tell

you how cute you are when you're grumpy?"

Gnocko tried to kick the Sage in the shin again, but this time the Sage laughed and nimbly avoided the attack.

Dejected, Gnocko glared up at the Sage. "If you're done making jokes at my expense, we're here to look for the Sword of Kassandra. Any idea where to start, smart guy? It'll take days to search the whole ruins."

A flash of blue fabric drew the Sage's attention to one of the smaller buildings. "Something tells me it won't take that long. Follow me and stay low."

"I'm 3' tall. I always stay low." Gnocko grumbled something else, but the Sage could not understand what he said.

'Why is she doing this?' The Sage knew instinctively that the flash of blue he'd seen was Echo. It was the same dress she'd worn when he had last seen her. 'She's leading me somewhere, but why? I know we have a troubled past, but if she wants to show me something why not come to me directly? The way she pops up so sporadically she might as well be a ghost.'

As they turned a corner, the Sage saw her more clearly. There she was: Echo, the only woman he'd ever truly loved. She stood beneath a tarp supported by wooden scaffolding, her long brown hair curling slightly in the damp air.

Echo stood at the entrance, arms to her side. She did not motion to him, but he could feel the weight of her stare. She looked back at him. Her face a mixture of melancholy and fear, she turned and went inside.

"Wait." Gnocko held his hand out to stop the Sage in place. "Is that her? The woman Tadgh keeps seeing?"

The Sage looked down at Gnocko and nodded. "When I first met Echo, her name was Andromeda but she changed it. She said the name Andromeda reminded her too much of what she'd lost. She called herself Echo to hurt me."

"How so?"

The Sage winced. "Back on Earth, Echo is a character in several myths. In one, she is chased by a lust-filled god named Pan. She denied his advances, so Pan used his power to enrage a group of shepherds. They killed her."

"You…killed this woman?"

The Sage sighed deeply. "Quite the opposite. I gave her immortality. I also gave her power and wealth. At the time, I thought that's all anyone could want. But I also killed her family. Destroyed her entire village and kidnapped her. I was a different man back then. Consumed by anger. I abused my power, took advantage of everyone weaker than me. For many years, I looked at Echo as a toy, a pretty bauble to be exploited. Over time, she became much more to me. She knew that. In her own way, I believe she loved me back. But she never forgave me."

"Huh." Gnocko looked up at him nodding extremely slowly. "And this is the woman we're following right now? How do you know she's not leading us into a trap?"

The Sage crossed his arms. "I've known Echo for thousands of years. I think she's moved past what I did to her. Well, as much as anyone can move past it. A few days ago, she helped me learn what was happening on DunDegore. Months ago, it was Echo that helped Tadgh learn the extent of Lord Vyken's invasion plans. When I was captured, she helped Tadgh rescue me."

"And maybe she got you captured in the first place. Did you ever think of that?"

"I have. Often." The Sage looked away. "Before I lost consciousness, Echo looked at me with terror in her eyes. Whatever game she is playing, she didn't want me captured. I know that in my bones. I don't expect you to trust her, Gnocko. I'm asking you to trust me. I believe she's leading us somewhere. I need to know why."

Gnocko shook his head and stared at the ground. Then, he flicked his arm forward motioning for the Sage to lead the way.

When they entered the excavation site, Gnocko once again took his weapons in hand. The path, wide enough for several people to walk shoulder to shoulder, led steadily downwards. It was lit by well-spaced nizarian lights, so Gnocko kept his sunglasses on.

Gnocko glanced over his shoulder. "You realize heading underground is the worst possible thing on an island of graunskyegs. The lesser ones have a weak connection to the Void which allows them to move about in the sun. But the sun will burn the greater graunskyegs. If there really are five of them on the island, underground is where they'll be strongest."

"We're both capable of throwing fire, Gnocko. We don't need the sun's protection."

Gnocko shivered. "Flames didn't save me last time. I told you what happened the last time I met Teric. I was stupid. Tried to break into his fort and got myself captured. The things he did to me…And now there are five of those things."

"Don't forget the hermadur." The Sage smirked. "Don't worry. Believe it or not, I've faced worse odds."

They traveled in silence for some time through the carved-out tunnels. The main path branched off occasionally leading to separate chambers. Most were small empty rooms discovered long ago. The best discoveries were further on. The Sage knew that's where Echo would be. Sometimes, to get to the good stuff, you have to go really deep.

The stopped at an elevator shaft. Dozens of lesser graunskyegs stood guard.

Gnocko glared up at the Sage with a look that clearly said 'Told you so.'

The Sage simply shrugged and sent a mental message. *'Don't worry. We're not going to fight them. Too loud. I'll take care of them.'* He opened a teleportation disk beneath the graunskyegs. In a flash of light, they fell through the portal and silently disappeared.

"Where did you send them?" Gnocko asked.

"Mogul tower."

Gnocko did a double take. "Wait. Isn't that were you sent Ein and his soldiers?"

The Sage's eyes widened. "Oh yeah. I forgot about that. He's really not going to like me anymore. Remind me to teleport him out of there later so he doesn't starve to death. Come on."

The elevator was a simple device of weights and pulleys. They rode it to the bottom where it stopped with a loud clunk. They stepped out into a vast natural cavern. Large beams of black crystal jutted from the ceiling. Dozens of floodlights filled the chamber with light. Near the center of the cavern was the only artificial structure in the area: a complex metal and crystal device.

Gnocko's thoughts spoke in the Sage's head. *What is that?'*

'A generator.' The Sage wandered closer to the structure, his eyes searching the cavern for a sign of Echo. *'Each of the Great Castles has one similar to this. If we had all the parts, this could create enough energy to power nizarian lights throughout the entire southern continent.'*

'What's it missing?'

The Sage shrugged. *We don't know. Not exactly. That's why the archeologists keep digging, hoping to discover the technology of the ancients.'*

A pool of shadow formed at the base of the generator. The Sage tensed, hoping it would be Echo. Instead, he saw a pale-skinned man with snow-white hair that hung to his shoulders. The man's robes were black as the Void. Around his waist was a leather belt and simple sheath.

"It's not here," the man said. "Bes and the hermadur left with the Sword a few moments ago."

"Who are you?" Gnocko lowered himself into an attack pose.

"Can't you tell?" The man put his hands behind his back and cocked his head to the side.

The Sage studied the man's features. They were not familiar. He looked above him at the black crystal in the ceiling. It dawned on him where he'd seen this crystal before. The same material formed the hilt of the Sword of

Kassandra. He looked back at the man and inhaled sharply, realizing who he was.

"How did you get out of the Void, Tempertin?" he asked. "Did you slip out with the sword?"

"Tempertin?" Gnocko put his weapons away, his mouth open in awe. "You mean THAT Tempertin? The hero of StarFall? The one who used the Sword of Kassandra to imprison Dispayre?"

The white-haired man bowed deeply at the waist. "One and the same. And I've been out long before our friend Tadgh Dooley cracked the Void and released the Sword of Kassandra. Years, actually."

"But why didn't you come forward?" Gnocko lifted the glasses from his head. He looked to be on the verge of kneeling prostate before Tempertin. "You saved the world! Now that you've come back there should be celebrations and…"

"Do you honestly believe everyone would be happy I returned?" Tempertin interrupted. "If Castle Dispayre realized I had returned, they would burn the world looking for me. Only my brothers-in-arms knew of my return. We fell to this world together. They were the only ones I could trust."

The Sage narrowed his eyes. A train of thought was becoming distressingly clear to him.

Tempertin studied the Sage's expression. "Ah. It appears you are as smart as they say. Please continue to use that brain of yours so we can avoid any…unpleasantness."

The Sage clenched his fists and a blast of fire flew from him toward Tempertin. The other man stepped backwards into the shadows, reappearing a few feet away.

"What are you doing?" Gnocko shouted. "Don't you know who that is?"

"I know exactly who he is," the Sage growled. "And what he's done. He destroyed my planet."

Gnocko gripped the Sage's arm. "You're not making any sense. That was Defksquar not…"

"Think, Gnocko. You seem to know the legends. Who are Tempertin's brothers?"

Gnocko's eyes dimmed, and he glanced back at Tempertin. "Four aliens fell to the world from a place they only refer to as The Rock. The first was Trusselman who helped my people, the frie stav, reclaim our subterranean land from the marauding Shee Empire. The second, Peter, is currently king of the Isle of Enkh. Tempertin is the third, hero of StarFall, who spent years with the nomadic moduners fighting monsters. The fourth was Defksquar, freer of the oppressed." Gnocko, realizing what he'd said, glanced quickly up at the Sage. "Well, that's what the legends say of him anyway."

The Sage waved the comment away. "I've found a consistent gap between legend and reality. Tell me, Tempertin, whose idea was it?"

Tempertin shrugged. "I can't take all the credit, but I was the first to recognize the situation. I spent over two hundred years trapped in a dark dimension with a powerful, insane god. I've seen firsthand what evil people can do with unlimited power. Remember, Dispayre was a normal man once. But you never met him, did you? You came to Maghe Sihre after he was imprisoned. We could have used your help during StarFall. Why didn't you go back further."

"I couldn't." The Sage shifted uncomfortably. "The disruption to the time fields were too severe."

"Oh really?" Tempertin grinned widely. "Is that what you're telling yourself?"

A long moment passed as the Sage reevaluated his experiences. When he arrived on Maghe Sihre, he had a brief encounter with Defksquar that convinced him he could go back in time and change events. Tweak them in the hopes of saving Earth. He'd opened a portal and traveled not across space but across time. But something had prevented him from going back past a certain point. Repeatedly, he had tried to arrive before the period known as StarFall. Each time he had failed.

"It was you." The Sage turned away from Tempertin, shaking his head. "You stopped me from going further back in time. You disrupted my teleportation. How?"

"Now that would be telling." Tempertin's grin grew even wider.

"But why?"

Tempertin yawned. "You're the Sage. Work it out."

The Sage found he was chewing on his fingernails and threw his hand away from his mouth. "Something must have happened during StarFall that you don't want me to change. Some key event that, if I was there, I could have altered."

"You're getting warm."

Gnocko tugged at the Sage's pant leg. "We don't have time for this. Tadgh and the others are expecting us to get the sword, not sit down for a chat."

The Sage brushed Gnocko away. "I've recently found out this bastard has been manipulating my life for years. I'm not leaving here until I find out why." The Sage raced through every detail he could recall of StarFall. "The next sun over in the constellation of Boah went supernova. The energies disrupted the dimensional barriers of every planet it touched. It took three years to reach Maghe Sihre. Powerful beings from other realms appeared. Gods and demons walked among mortals. That was the beginning of StarFall."

"Cooler. Almost ice cold."

Annoyed, the Sage tried again. "If that's cold, perhaps it was near the end of the war when Dispayre conquered the realms of the Ventori."

"Ah. Very warm." Tempertin looked over his shoulder, appearing to listen to someone. "Why not? It's not like he can…" Tempertin sighed and turned back to the Sage. "My brother Peter tells me I'm being foolish. Perhaps he's right."

The Sage jumped forward too quickly for Tempertin to dodge. He grabbed the white-haired man by the throat and hurled him against the nearest stone wall. The cavern shook. Tempertin, momentarily stunned, tried to get to his feet. The Sage opened a small portal that, for an instant, connected with the surface of the sun. A thin stream of plasma shot through the air. Tempertin raised his hands and a dome of shadow covered him, absorbing the superheated flame. The Sage opened another portal. And another. The air in the cavern grew faint as the plasma ate more and more oxygen.

Gnocko fell to his knees. "Stop! You're killing me too."

The Sage looked back at Gnocko and decided to change his tactics. He opened a portal to an elemental plane of air, replacing the lost oxygen. Then he opened a large teleportation disk right in front of Tempertin. From out of the yellow light charged a five-ton quadruped with grey leathery skin covered in dozens of spikes. It charged the first thing it could see, bashing its horns repeatedly against Tempertin's shield.

"Seriously?" Gnocko yelled from behind him. "You summoned a rheiballough?"

The Sage grinned. "Well, you're the one who gave me the idea."

Tempertin pressed his hands against the side of his shield, his face straining with exertion to keep it up. With a grunt, he pushed his hands outward forcibly. The shield expanded, pushing the rheiballough back toward the Sage. It landed on its back. Before it could rise to its feet, Tempertin hurled a bolt of solid shadow at the creature. The rheiballough exploded, throwing meat and gore in all directions.

"Enough!" Tempertin, his white hair soaked in blood, turned toward the Sage and flicked his fingers. Nearby, a pool of shadows opened and a single figure walked out. Echo. She stood, head bowed, unwilling to look at the Sage. "Stop this immediately or this is the last time you will ever see Echo."

Chapter Nineteen

Tadgh looked out the front window of the dress shop in which they were all hiding. It had been several minutes since they'd seen a graunskyeg. Now the streets were clear. Eiodeesh stood nearby, her hands on her axe. Tadgh wondered if she ever tired. She'd held the weapon since they arrived on the island but showed no signs of needing to put it down.

"Are they gone?" The woman from the pantry stared at Tadgh with wide, frightened eyes. He realized that with all the running he'd forgotten to ask her name. He glanced at her uniform. The name Beqa was embroidered on the left-hand side.

"Looks like." Tadgh nodded and watched the woman's face relax.

Menphis came to stand beside Tadgh. "Do you think you can find Grandwyn's trail again?"

"No problem. May have to backtrack a bit but I've got his scent now." Tadgh clapped his friend on the shoulder. "Don't worry. We'll find him. How is Tamara holding up?"

Menphis looked toward the back of the store. Tamara and Bethel sat together, speaking in quiet tones. Tamara had wrapped the weighted chain around her waist again. The bodyguard's sword lay on the floor beside her.

"She is one of the strongest women I've ever known."

"I saw the way she holds that chain thing. Can she fight?"

"Yes." Menphis smiled. "But that is not what makes her strong." He turned to the others and raised his voice to be heard. "The way is clear. We should go before the graunskyegs come back."

Bethel stood and resheathed her sword. She helped Tamara to her feet. Meanwhile, Eiodeesh opened the door, standing watch as, one by one, everyone left the dress shop.

They retraced their steps back to the hotel and Tadgh

quickly found Grandwyn's scent again. He followed it until the trail stopped at a house near the docks.

"The scent is strong here. I think that means he was here for awhile." Tadgh sniffed the door. "It smells like there was someone else with him. A man, I think." Tadgh backed away from the door. "The trail is fresh. Grandwyn and the man were here not that long ago. They went this way."

With Tadgh in the lead, the group retraced Grandwyn's steps and arrived at the docks. A single ship was docked at the pier. The air was filled with dozens of recent scents, but there was no sign of any people. Grandwyn's scent led him to the end of a pier. The trail stopped at a splotch of blood by the water. Tamara cried out when she saw it.

Bethel walked forward and placed her hand over the blood. "Still warm. This is recent."

Kneeling beside Bethel, Tadgh sniffed the blood and felt the tension in his chest relax. "It's not Grandwyn's. This belonged to the man that was with him." He lifted his head, taking several short sniffs of the air. "Weird. Grandwyn's trail stops here."

Eiodeesh looked over the side of the pier. "He may have gone into the water. That could explain why you've lost his scent."

"Or he could be dead." Tamara touched her forehead and chest and closed her eyes.

"Stay strong Tamara." Tadgh went to her. "Remember what Samar said. They need Grandwyn alive. Besides, I think I'd smell something if they killed him. A change in his scent or something. The trail just stops. I believe Eiodeesh is right."

Tamara looked only slightly consoled. Menphis pulled her close to him and the two shared a brief embrace. When Tamara pulled away, Menphis kissed her lightly on the cheek.

"What now?" Bethel asked. "If the trail has gone cold, how do we find Grandwyn?"

Tamara stroked her chin as she said. "We could head to the Aerie." Seeing the confused look on Tadgh's face, she explained. "It's the local temple for the Pheonides, a monotheistic religion that shuns the true gods. Sorry. Old habits. The old gods. Their faith has many followers in Celtica. I know the woman who heads the temple, Torch Karehn. We've met repeatedly at interdenominational seminars."

Tadgh scratched his head. "Unless the temple is actually a fort, I'm not sure why it's the safest place on the island."

Tamara explained. "Graunskyegs have only two weaknesses. Fire and positive spiritual energy. Aside from the monastery outside of town, the Aerie may be the holiest place on the island. Thousands flock to it each year in pilgrimage. Whatever happened here, if Grandwyn…" She faltered for a moment then squared her shoulders. "If Grandwyn escaped, he will look for shelter. There's no place safer than the Aerie."

***

"This isn't right," Bethel said. She, like the others, huddled behind a large fountain in a town square. Less than a block away was a massive red-stone building with a raised dome at its center. It reminded Tadgh of St. Paul's Cathedral in London, England. Along the roof, dozens of white flags flapped gently in the breeze. On each of the flags was a red bird, wings flared behind as it flew up from flames beneath it.

Between them and the Aerie was a throng of silent graunskyegs. None of them moved. All faced the front doors of the Aerie. It appeared they were sentries, quietly waiting for a cue to make their attack.

"That doesn't mean it's not happening," Menphis said. "How many do you think there are?"

"Two hundred." Tadgh said. "Maybe three. Thankfully, it's not a full-on zombie horde because that would be scary. Not that this isn't scary, but honestly if you'd seen the last Resident Evil movie this would look a lot more manageable."

Tamara bit her thumbnail. "I've never seen a graunskyeg before, but if the legends are accurate, they shouldn't be able to get this close to a faith-based building."

"Maybe they sense people inside," Tadgh said. "In the movies, these things are always drawn to the living."

Tamara shook her head. "My gut says that's not it. Something is controlling them, pushing them to act outside of their instincts. There is powerful fieldbending here, and that scares me more than the graunskyegs we can see."

Eiodeesh exhaled, her breath a whistle. "Look at them all. If those things get off this island and continue to feed…."

"One disaster at a time," Tamara whispered. "We need to get inside."

"I'm open to suggestions." Menphis placed his quarterstaff on the ground and ran a hand through his hair. "There's too many to fight our way through. If the Sage or Gnocko were here we'd have a chance. Both of them can fieldbend fire."

Tamara bit her lower lip. "I have an idea. It's a bit risky, but it might work."

"What do you need?" Bethel asked.

"Keep them off me as long as you can." Tamara stepped out from behind the fountain and walked toward the graunskyegs.

Tadgh's eyes went wide. "Is she crazy?" No one answered him.

Everyone left the cover of the fountain, weapons in hand. Tadgh watched as Tamara unwrapped the chain around her waist and let it fall to ground. Then she did something completely unexpected.

She started to sing.

It began with a low ululation. With each step her voice grew louder, more confident. With each step she removed another layer of clothing. When she was within one hundred feet of the graunskyegs she stood completely bare. In a slow wave, the throng of graunskyegs turned toward her. Their mouths opened in hungry snarls. A few of them moaned, the eerie sound rumbling through the crowd. Ten graunskyeg stepped forward. Then twenty. Then twenty more.

Tamara raised her hands above her head and the ululation became haunting lyrics. The wind swirled around her body, creating a vortex with her at the center.

"What is she doing?" Tadgh asked.

Menphis bowed his head. "She's praying. I've heard of this but never seen it. She's calling on the goddess, Fricka, asking for an audience."

"Really?" Tadgh searched the sky above. "Do you think it will work?"

Bethel knocked on Tadgh's shoulder. "Eyes on the ground. The graunskyegs are making their move."

Tadgh looked forward and saw Tamara's song was having an effect on the graunskyegs. Most put hands over their ears, trying to block out the sound. But not all of them. Other graunskyegs seemed enraged by her actions. These ones broke from the pack, stalking toward Tamara.

"Protect her," Eiodeesh said. She ran to stand between Tamara and the approaching graunskyegs. When one came too close she sliced her axe across its neck, beheading it. Bethel unsheathed her sword and stood far enough away from Eiodeesh that the trofast could safely swing her axe. Tadgh shot bolts of Akashic energy at other graunskyegs. Since he couldn't hope to kill them with the blasts, he focused on applying their concussive force. He aimed at kneecaps, shattering their joints. Unable to walk properly, the graunskyegs fell, tumbling over each other.

Tamara's voice rose again, now unnaturally loud. To Tadgh it sounded as if stadium-sized speakers projected her voice. The wind grew stronger. Tadgh watched in amazement as an invisible force lifted Tamara off the ground. She hovered in midair, arms raised, head back. Her hair lashed about wildly in the vortex.

"It's working," Menphis shouted. He ran over to collect her discarded clothes and her weighted chain. Hands full, he couldn't fight but stood next to Tadgh.

Tadgh took his eyes of the graunskyegs in front of him and looked around. Nearly all the graunskyegs had their hands over their ears now. They were also moving, slowly, away from Tamara. She floated through the air heading toward the front door of the Aerie. Now, no graunskyeg would come close to her. It was clear to Tadgh what they needed to do.

"Gather around her," he shouted to the others. The others ran inside the vortex. Backs to Tamara, they followed her as she moved through the square. The graunskyegs crowded, always just outside the area of effect. It only took a minute, but each second was laced with tension.

Bethel pulled on the door and, finding it locked, banged loudly with the ball of her fist.

"Open up!" Menphis shouted.

A second later, the door flung open. A man with brown hair and green eyes ushered them in. In his hands was a crossbow. He held it with trembling fingers as he looked up at Tamara, still floating in the air. Behind him was a group of at least twenty people, all of them armed.

"Hurry," the man with the crossbow said. "Before whatever she's doing stops working."

Tadgh was the first inside. Tamara lowered her hands and stopped singing. The vortex dissipated, and she lowered gently to the ground. Menphis passed Tamara her clothing and helped her inside. Bethel, the last inside, backed into the Aerie.

A sigh of relief went through the crowd. The man with the crossbow lowered his weapon and motioned toward two muscular men who pressed thick metal levers on either side of the door. Tadgh heard a loud clunking sound which he assumed was the mechanism that locked the door. He felt his shoulders go slack, the tension fading from his body. He did a quick survey of the area and turned toward the man with the crossbow.

"Are you in charge?" he asked.

"No sir," the man answered. "Just a clerk. Name's

Henri." He bowed toward Tamara. "And you are Mistress Tamara Bethel. I remember you from your last visit. Come. Torch Karehn will want to see you immediately."

"She's alive?" Tamara slipped back into her dress, seemingly unperturbed by her nudity. "That is the best news I've heard so far today."

"We're looking for her son." Menphis wet his lips and tensed. "I mean, our son. Have you seen him?"

Henri's eyes narrowed. "Little redhead boy? I remember him. Sorry, Miss. There are a few children inside, but he's not here."

"I guess it was too much to hope for." Menphis sighed and helped Tamara put on her crimson jacket, lacing it to her waist.

Strangely, Tamara looked at Menphis with an expression of glee. "We have much to hope for, Menphis. Have faith. Lead on, Henri. Take us to Torch Karehn."

Tadgh and the others followed Henri through the foyer and into the cathedral. He wasn't sure if that was term they used on Maghe Sihre, but it was the closest description for what he saw. The air was thick with a strange incense that enticed Tadgh to breathe more deeply. Looking up, he saw the ceiling was painted to show numerous scenes. In one section, fire rained down from the heavens and healed the sick. In another, a giant flaming bird was superimposed over a bearded man in a white robe.

"That's the Phoenix Lord," Menphis whispered to him. "Look to the front of the Aerie. See the large fire burning in that copper cauldron? That is called the eternal flame. Both are things everyone here should know. Understand?"

Tadgh nodded. "Got it. No weird questions."

The walkway to the front of the Aerie was lined with ornate columns. Beyond the columns were rows and rows of wooden benches, most of them empty now. Small pockets of people huddled together around the church. Kneeling in front of the eternal flame was a woman with gray hair. She looked to be in her early fifties, with deep wrinkles along her face and hands. As they approached, the woman stood and faced them. Her eyes were bluish gray. Tadgh thought they might have been the kindest eyes he'd ever seen. When she saw Tamara, she raced forward and embraced her.

"What are you doing here?" the woman asked. "I'm glad to see you but…"

"I'm glad to see you too, Karehn," Tamara said. They embraced for a moment before Tamara pulled away. "May your light be a torch in the dark times. As for why I'm here, that is a long story best told in private. But first, some introductions."

Tamara introduced each of them. When Torch Karehn turned to face Tadgh, she blinked rapidly as if startled by something she saw in Tadgh. Whatever she saw, she said nothing. When the introductions were completed, she bowed to each of them.

"May the fire of the Phoenix Lord warm your heart," Torch Karehn motioned to empty benches around the eternal flame. Tadgh saw they were far out of earshot of anyone else. Once everyone was seated, Torch Karehn spoke, her words focused on Tamara. "We feared there was no one left alive in the city. When the graunskyegs first appeared, we gathered as many as we could and bolted the doors. Did you come by boat?"

"No," Tamara said. "It was the Sage. He used his light disks."

"The Sage?" Torch Karehn looked back toward the front door. "Thank the light. Where is he? Is he safe? Silly me. Of course he's safe. Do you think he can get the pilgrims off the island?"

"I know what he means to you." Tamara placed a comforting hand on Torch Karehn's knee. "The Sage was safe the last we saw him. But he has his own mission. He won't be joining us. At least for now, we are on our own."

"Mission?" Torch Karehn touched the nape of her neck. "So you know what's happened here. Did he tell you about…?"

Tamara glanced around nervously before answering in a whisper. "Yes. We know about the Sword of Kassandra. He said you were one of the few that knew it was on the island. Here's what we know so far."

Tamara spent several minutes detailing the events that led them to the island: Grandwyn's flight, the soldiers in Gateway, the Sage's capture, and everything they learned from Samar. When she finished, Torch Karehn leaned back against the pew, her eyes dim with worry.

"Sad oak," she cursed. "There are things I should tell you, as well. We kept the Sword outside of town at a monastery. It disappeared days ago, and we feared the worst. Still, we never imagined this. When we lost the Sword, I ran to the fieldbender guild to tell them. After that, I came here and tried to call the Elmontrazar. I had hoped the nizarians could help us but..."

"What happened?" Eiodeesh asked.

"We had a device." Torch Karehn looked toward the back of the Aerie at an open door. "Some sort of sender/receiver that allowed instant communication between here and Castle Nizaria. But when I got back to the Aerie it was gone. That's when I knew."

Bethel grunted. "Spies."

Torch Karehn nodded. "We'd been infiltrated. I honestly have no idea who it was. The Aerie employs dozens. We have almost two thousand in our flock. Any one of them could have been the spy. But that doesn't matter now. The damage is done. When I realized I couldn't call for help, I went back to the fieldbenders. They told me they would travel en masse to the monastery. I wanted to join the search for the Sword, but duty forced me to stay behind for my flock."

"Just as well," Tamara said. "We've seen the fieldbender guild. There was no one left. You're here. You're alive. Obviously your god has a use for you."

Torch Karehn touched the medallion around her throat, a silver phoenix. "It would appear so. I felt what you did out there. Did she come to you?"

Tamara nodded. "Yes. Fricka spoke to me."

Tadgh did a double take. "She did? I didn't hear anything?"

Menphis glanced at him, slightly annoyed. "And why would you? Do you expect the voice of a goddess to be heard by everyone?" Menphis sighed. "Never mind. Of course you do. Sometimes I wonder why I even ask."

Torch Karehn turned to Tadgh. "In my faith, we believe the Phoenix Lord speaks to all when they need to hear him. Be not concerned that you didn't hear the voice of Fricka. If ever your need is great, have faith. You will hear what you need to." She turned back to Tamara and grasped her hand. "What did she say to you?"

Tamara smiled, her eyes filling with tears. "She told me my son was alive. He's holed up in a shop in the mall, the one that sells the replicas of Behersker artifacts. There are graunskyegs everywhere. And there's something else, something dark and dangerous beneath the mall. He's safe for the moment, but we have to go to him."

Tadgh groaned. "Seriously? You want us to go to a mall in the middle of a zombie invasion? This is not going to end well."

Menphis stomped on his foot. "Stop speaking nonsense. Of course, we are going to get my son. But you, Tamara, you're staying here." Tamara opened her mouth to protest, but Menphis stopped her before she could speak. "We both know I can't force you to stay, but I'm asking you to be reasonable. What you did out there was amazing. But it also tired you. I can see it in your eyes. Tell me I'm wrong."

Tamara turned away, her lips pursed.

Menphis knelt beside her. "I will bring our son back to you. I promise."

Tamara touched his cheek and, leaning forward, kissed him gently on the lips.

Standing, Menphis turned to Tadgh. "You'll come with me?"

"Duh." Tadgh stood and leaned against his quarterstaff. "But only if you promise to listen to me when I say something is a bad idea."

Menphis grinned. "I promise nothing."

"I'll come with," Eiodeesh said. "If you'll have me. I can accomplish more out there than I can in here. Bethel, are you coming?"

Bethel stood but glanced down at Tamara. "I should stay with Mistress. We're safe in here for now, but if those graunskyegs rush the front doors, everyone in here will be in trouble."

"We could use your sword," Torch Karehn said. "But we're not defenseless. I have several Pheonides in the Aerie. Ten of them have the Voice of Fire."

Tadgh had no idea what the Voice of Fire was, but based on the knowing nods around him, everyone else seemed to understand what she meant.

"Is there another way out of here?" Menphis asked. "We estimate over two hundred graunskyegs by the front door. I'd rather not tempt fate by trying to get through them again."

"Of course." Torch Karehn stood, her old bones creaking noticeably. "There's an old tunnel that links the catacombs beneath the Aerie to city hall. I sometimes use it during the winter. Saves me from trudging through the snow. Follow me."

Chapter Twenty

The Sage focused on Echo, looking for a signal that the woman he loved was truly there. She still refused to look at him.

"Are you sure that's really her?" Gnocko asked.

The Sage snorted. "Honestly? I'm not sure of anything anymore. Echo died. I watched her die in my arms. I buried her. But I would know her anywhere. Every ounce of me tells me that's her." He turned toward Tempertin, taking several deep breaths to avoid lashing out again. "How did you bring her back? And more importantly, why?"

Tempertin crossed the room to stand between the Sage and Echo. "See, Echo? I told you he could be reasonable." With a smile, he turned back to the Sage. "She tried to tell me there was no way you would talk to me, that your rage would overrule you. But here we are talking like adults. We both know the soul is more resilient than the body. There is always a way to bring someone back if you are willing to pay the price. Tell me, are you willing to pay the price?"

"I don't like this," Gnocko said.

Tempertin glared at the frie stav. "No one asked you. Be silent or go away."

Gnocko looked like he was going to say something else, but the Sage motioned for him to be still.

"Better," Tempertin said. "I brought Echo back for one reason and one reason only. You, the mighty Wisdom, or the Sage, whatever you're calling yourself these days. You were the one variable I couldn't control. That had to change. Twenty years ago, I escaped the Void, but not before I met an old friend of yours, a man from Earth who also spent time in the Void."

The Sage glanced at Echo. From the mix of terror and sorrow on her face, he knew the man Tempertin spoke of. He covered his eyes with his hand suddenly feeling very tired.

"Propates," the Sage said. "I should have known. He had power over the shadows too."

"Yes. Propates." Tempertin held up his hand. Waves of darkness wormed their way across his fingers. "Of course, he didn't spend as much time in the Void as I did. My abilities are, shall we say, more refined. In your long life on Earth, you only gifted two mortals with the essence of your power. Echo, the woman you loved, and Propates, who viewed you as a father. Propates hated you, wanted Echo for his own. And when she chose you over him, he killed her."

"He only claimed to love me," Echo said. "You don't kill people you love."

Tempertin backhanded her. "Speak again. I dare you."

Echo glared back at Tempertin but said nothing. The act of violence enraged the Sage, more so because he knew how strong Echo was, emotionally and physically. For her to suffer the injury silently suggested this was not the first abuse.

"Now where were we?" Tempertin lowered his shoulder, as if trying to stretch away the tension. "Ah, yes. Dearly departed Propates. We first met after the djinn attacked you in Africa. We rescued him, bringing him into the Void."

"Who is we?"

Tempertin ignored the question. "Propates spoke of you often. Sometimes we would watch you. There's little else one can do in the Void except watch. He helped me realize you were the one variable I could not control." With a smug smile upon his lips, he motioned toward Echo. "But now I can. Up until now, you've been very helpful, whether you knew it or not. But your time in this play has ended. Events on DunDegore have to proceed without you. So, here is the price you pay to have Echo back. Walk way."

The Sage frowned. "That's it?"

"Not quite." Tempertin waved his hand and three chairs made of solid shadow appeared. "Have a seat. Let me tell you a little story. It involves my brother, Defksquar."

"I hate it already." The Sage sighed and looked over at Echo. She motioned her head toward one of the chairs so, unwillingly, the Sage sat. Gnocko took a seat beside him.

"Oh, but you'll love the ending." Tempertin sat across from him and leaned forward. "As I said, I left the Void twenty years ago. How I broke free is a story for another day. Why I broke free is the important issue. I watched over Maghe Sihre as well as Earth, and I saw something terrifying. The Verdenstab."

"What exactly is a Verdenstab?" Gnocko asked.

The Sage turned to Gnocko. "Part of a terraforming device, a machine capable of transforming a lifeless planet into one that can support life. The Beherskers used one on Maghe Sihre. Evidence suggestions they used one on Earth, as well. You've seen Tadgh. Humans and sirians look almost identical. I don't believe that's a coincidence."

"Neither do I," Tempertin said. "I believe I was shown the Verdenstab for a reason. Before I came to this planet, I did many things I'm not proud of. This was my opportunity for redemption. I knew the Verdenstab was somewhere on Maghe Sihre, but it took me years to pinpoint its location. While I searched, Defksquar found the perfect hiding spot. Earth. We sent it there and activated it to ensure it could not be brought back to Maghe Sihre. Now, it's beyond the reach of the Quadumvirate. My actions saved the lives of millions."

The Sage clenched his fists. "You murdered millions of people. People on Earth."

Tempertin shrugged. "Sacrifices had to be made."

"Why are you telling me this?" The Sage leaned forward, mimicking Tempertin's posture.

"Because I need your help." Tempertin leaned back. He was no longer smiling. "My brother didn't stick to the plan. After the Verdenstab was activated, he was supposed to head to the Isle of Enkh and wait for me. Instead, he gave into his guilt and did something heroically stupid. He tried to infiltrate Castle Dispayre. He's been captured."

"And I care why? He should feel guilty. Do you have

any idea how many children died when that device was activated?"

Tempertin scratched his forehead. "If you keep harping on small details...."

The Sage stood. "Children are never small details!"

Tempertin cocked his head to one side and simply stared back at the Sage until he returned to his seat.

"As I was saying," Tempertin continued. "Defksquar was captured three weeks ago. Since I left the Void, I can't see as much as I used to. Castle Dispayre is heavily shielded against prying eyes. I know he's there but little else. For various reasons, I can't get to him. Which is where you come in. You need to head to Castle Dispayre and rescue my brother. Once you have him, bring him to the Isle of Enkh. I'll be waiting there with my other brothers. Do this and I release Echo." Tempertin snapped his fingers. A wind appeared out of nowhere and pushed Echo back into the shadows. In an instant, she was gone. "Or stay and you'll never see Echo again."

The speed of her withdrawal hit the Sage like a slap to the face. He wanted to scream, to punch something, but he fought past his rage. He knew that acting in anger would only make the situation worse. Still, something didn't add up.

The Sage stopped and chewed the inside of his cheek. "Why are you here?" He looked up at the ceiling. "Here in DunDegore, I mean. You could have come to me in GardenKeep with this offer. Why drag me all the way out to DunDegore?"

"I never wanted you here." Tempertin's cool demeanor slipped, showing a hint of anger. "That was Echo. She's constantly sneaking away, meddling in plans. She's lucky I need her for leverage. Enough talking. What's your answer? Stay or go?"

The Sage scratched his head. "I'm not making any decision until I know all the facts. Defksquar's been imprisoned for three weeks. I get why you want me out of the picture. But you've been meddling with Tadgh for months. If you want me to rescue your brother from a different mother, tell me the truth. What are you trying to stop me from doing?"

Gnocko gasped. "Oh lord. The sheath. Remember the legend."

The Sage looked at the empty sheath at Tempertin's waist. For a moment, Gnocko's words did not make any sense. Then it clicked.

"Damn it. He's just a boy. You can't do that to him."

"Of course I can," Tempertin said. "Do you know why, out of all the possible worlds, Defksquar chose Earth? It's the DNA. Humans have very malleable genetics, even more so than sirians. When the djinn's energy entered Tadgh, well, everything became clear to me." He looked down at the sheath. "As long as I wear this, Void energy has no effect on me. Among other things, I don't age, I don't get sick, and graunskyegs are unable to feed from me."

"But it also binds you," Gnocko said. "According to legends, as soon as you used the Sword of Kassandra in battle both it and the sheath were bound to you. You were the only one able to use the blade."

"And now you want Tadgh to use it." The Sage closed his eyes, exhausted. "What happens if he uses the Sword of Kassandra? Be exact."

Tempertin touched his chin as if weighing his options before finally speaking. "Fine. I can't go back to the Void. I won't. The indecencies I suffered in that place are unspeakable. The Void was never meant as a permanent prison for Dispayre. The barriers have been disintegrating for decades. And now that Tadgh's power has torn a hole in the Void, it is only a matter of time before Dispayre returns. Let someone else fight him. I'm done. All I want to do is leave this miserable planet and find a new home." All traces of anger and bitterness left his voice. "But I won't leave the world unprotected. It needs a new hero. I choose Tadgh as my replacement. I won't let you stop that from happening."

"You don't have to do this," Gnocko said. "Go to the Great Castles. I'm sure hundreds of people would willingly take up the sword."

"Ah, but do they have the power to wield it?" Tempertin shifted his belt as if suddenly aware it was a heavy burden. "I've searched long and hard for a new host. Tadgh is the only one who stands a chance against Dispayre. As soon as he uses the sword, the sheath will leave my waist and materialize around his."

"What about Bes?" the Sage said. "I heard the conversation between the hermadur and Bes. As soon as Tadgh uses the Sword, he's to be handed over to the demon."

Tempertin spat. "I'm not working with either of those demons. As far as they know, I don't exist. I'm playing a separate game. Remember, the sheath gives its owner control over void energy. Bes can try, but he won't be able to drag Tadgh to whatever hell that demon is from. As far as I'm concerned, this is a win win. Both Tadgh and I will have our freedom."

"I see." The Sage was quiet for a long moment, running the details over and over in his mind. He turned to face Gnocko and crossed his arms. "I'm sorry, old friend. Looks like my part in this battle is over."

"What?" Gnocko's jaw dropped. "You can't be serious! You're the Sage. You don't give up."

"I'm also a man in love. Tadgh will have to take care of himself." As he spoke, he sent Gnocko a mental message. *'Run. Get to Tadgh. Whatever happens, you have to stop him from using the Sword of Kassandra.'* He cleared his throat and put a hand on Gnocko's shoulder. "I hope you can understand."

Gnocko, taking the cue, kicked the Sage in the shin. "I understand completely. You can rot, you bastard."

As he ran away, Gnocko sent back a mental message. *'Godspeed, my friend. Godspeed.'*

Only when Gnocko was free of the cavern did the Sage stand and face Tempertin. "Alright. I'll leave for Dispayre immediately. I expect you to hand Echo over to me as soon as I return with Defksquar. Cross me and it won't be the armies of Dispayre burning the world to search you out."

With a curt nod, the Sage opened a portal and stepped through. He arrived in his office back in GardenKeep, went to the door, and opened it a crack. He heard Pwella and Barnes speaking downstairs in the kitchen, their voices low and affectionate. He realized it was nearly supper. He thought of calling out to them, but there was something he needed to do first.

He changed out of his clothes, putting on a black shirt and black pants. Over this he wore a dark red jacket similar to the type he'd worn on Earth. Going to his desk, he retrieved the nizarian memory chip that Eschandel had given him days ago. With so many things happening, he'd not yet had a chance to review it.

In a few minutes, he would head to Castle Dispayre, perhaps the most dangerous place on the planet. They had an army in the hundreds of thousands, many of them dem straki capable of fieldbending. They also had legions of wypera, the fire-breathing dragons of Maghe Sihre, and Umbral Knights, cybernetic undead warriors. The Sage had not faced such a formidable enemy in years.

A white leather couch sat beneath a large window. He lay down on it, placed the memory crystal on his forehead, and allowed the images of recent events to filter down through his third eye.

***

The Verdenstab was activated, destroying the old world to create something new. Radiant energy spread over the entire planet disrupting electronics. Planes fell from the sky, cars crashed, and life support systems failed. The energy ate through the bodies of everyone exposed to it, forcing their bodies to evolve. The process killed many who were too weak to survive the change. Hundreds of millions died within seconds.

He saw the good things as well. Lands of legend – Lemuria, Atlantis, and Mount Penglai – rose up from the oceans. But all of this had happened before he left Earth. The images changed to reveal what he had not yet seen: the aftermath. He witnessed a planet in chaos: frightened people in a world without electricity, surrounded by death and riots. He watched armies attempt, ineffectually, to restore order. Then he saw something that gave him hope: a young blond man stood on a train surrounded by familiar faces.

'It's Josh,' he thought. 'He's with Garnet and Todd. That means they escaped the Axeinus. And there's Ms. Ryerson. Why is she in a wheelchair?' The image pulled back giving the Sage a better view of the train. It was far beneath the ground, part of the underground railway constructed to allow hyper-fast travel around the world. 'But where are they headed?'

The image flashed forward, showing him the answer to his question. 'They're heading to the Black Pyramid! Good. The people there will know what to do.'

The image flashed again to Windsor, Ontario. He saw a group of young people running away from an army. 'And there's Jessica! She's alive too. Oh and I see the others, David, Elaine, Josh's cousin Travis. Not sure who that other guy is. Looks like they all survived. But who is that chasing them?'

The memory crystal refocused showing the Sage an unexpected person leading the charging army.

'That's Amir Durgen, one of the Quadumvirate. What is he doing on Earth?'

***

The Sage removed the memory crystal from his forehead and sat up. Most of what he'd seen gave him hope. But seeing Amir Durgen filled him with a very different feeling.

There was a knock on the door. A moment later, Barnes walked in. "I thought I heard you, sir. We weren't expecting you, but Pwella has dinner almost made. How are things going in Gateway?"

"I won't be staying." The Sage placed the memory crystal back in his desk. "I have to leave on a mission, Barnes. A big one. I'm honestly not sure when I'll be back. I'm counting on you to hold down operations until I return. How are things going with Eschandel and the fieldbenders?"

Barnes, his face distorted by concern, took a moment to respond. "Very well, sir. The engineers checked the fort outside of town. Thankfully, it's structurally sound. Now that the city council has bequeathed it to you, people are calling it Fort Apostate."

"By people I assume you mean Eschandel. Does anyone else call it that?" The Sage went to a cupboard beside his desk and removed a fist-sized crystal. He held it up to the light, studying it carefully before placing it in his coat pocket.

"Not yet, sir. But Eschandel is trying very hard to convince them. The clearing crews say they will be finished by the end of next week. We should be able to start moving fieldbenders into the new guild by the end of the month."

The Sage flicked his wrist and another portal of light appeared. "Excellent. I'll check in on them as soon as I get back."

"Sir…" Barnes' eyebrows furrowed. "You are coming back, aren't you?"

"Of course I am. Have a little faith." The Sage opened another teleportation disk. 'Just one more stop before I'm off to have fun storming the Castle.'

Chapter Twenty-One

Tadgh stared at the building before him. It looked more like a museum than a shopping mall. He had never been the type of person to visit museums. More to the point, his family had never been the type to visit museums. He had, however, seen many of them from the outside. The mall was actually two buildings, side by side, each nearly as wide as the Aerie and three stories tall. A series of gentle steps rose along the entire façade. The steps were lined with statues of beings similar in appearance to trofasts with subtle differences. The foreheads seemed a little too short, the eyes a little too close together. He noticed as well that the torsos seemed overly long and the hands eerily small.

"What are those?" he asked.

"Did you hit your head?" Menphis pointed at the dozens of graunskyegs that crowded around the front doors of the mall. Like those at the Aerie, these ones were silent and unmoving. However, these ones all faced outwards. "They are graunskyegs. Living dead things that feed on flesh. We've been running from them all day."

Tadgh rolled his eyes. "Not those things, bozo. The other things. Statues."

"Oh," Menphis said. "Those are Beherskers. At least we think they are. No one's really sure what Beherskers look like."

"If we're finished with the art history lesson can we focus on the situation?" Eiodeesh shifted her battle-axe. It appeared to Tadgh that she was finally starting to tire. "If I didn't know better, I'd swear they're trying to keep us out."

"Fantastic." Menphis shook his head. "That means whoever is controlling the graunskyegs knows my son is inside."

Torch Karehn had led them to the tunnel, passing them a few candles to light the way. As soon as the three of them were alone, Tadgh had switched to feline form to better navigate the darkness. The other end of the tunnel ended in a supply closet. After that, it was a short walk to where they stood now. Tadgh, still in feline form, was surprised to see how high above them the sun was. The day was passing faster than expected.

"So what's the plan?" Tadgh asked.

"We'll have to try to sneak in." Menphis pointed at the front door. "Or rather, you sneak in. Eiodeesh and I will lead the graunskyegs away. Something may be controlling them, but you saw the way they acted at the Aerie. One look at flesh and they forget their orders. We're faster than them. When you get in there, track Grandwyn and bring him out. Eiodeesh and I will circle the block and be back in a few minutes. We'll meet up with both of you and race back to the Aerie."

"Remember that thing I said about bad ideas?" Tadgh thought back to one of his favorite zombie movies, *Shaun of the Dead*. He seemed to remember a similar tactic in that film that ended badly.

"I vaguely recall you speaking and me promising nothing," Menphis answered before turning to Eiodeesh. "Are you up for this, my friend?"

Eiodeesh smiled. "Why not? That last time you and I worked together, I almost died, and you were captured and tortured by a monster. I'm sure things will work out better this time."

Tadgh coughed and shook his head. "You realize I have zero confidence in you guys now, right?"

"Think of it this way," Eiodeesh said. "At least people can tell interesting stories about you at your funeral."

Tadgh glared back at her, blinking slowly. He tightened his grip on his quarterstaff. "Oh, what the heck. Ready when you are."

Eiodeesh and Menphis rose from their hiding position and charged toward the graunskyegs. The creatures responded quickly to their appearance. No longer motionless, they snarled and moaned, leaving their sentry position to attack the others. Menphis and Eiodeesh turned, running away from the mall. The graunskyegs followed.

Tadgh waited until the last of them disappeared, then walked toward the front doors. They were massive, at least twenty feet tall and equally as wide. Splotches of blood covered the steps. A child's toy lay abandoned beneath one of the columns. The sun slipped behind the building creating long patches of shadow. Everything was quiet, still. As he searched the shadows, he realized graunskyegs could be lying in wait anywhere. Watching him. Waiting.

"Nothing at all like a Romero movie." He pushed on the door and it swung open easily. Inside, the marble floors were covered with broken glass and overturned furniture. Looking up, he saw ornate stained glass skylights. Balconies from levels two and three looked down on the main entrance. Tadgh walked past discarded shopping bags and a small booth selling flavored yogurts. The cart, no longer refrigerated, reeked of spoiled dairy. To the right he saw open-aired pods selling soft, flowing gowns and well-tailored suits. To the left was a shop selling exotic children's toys.

He sniffed the air. Grandwyn was definitely here somewhere. He wasn't close enough to pin down a location, but the boy had definitely walked through the front doors. The scent of death and decay was stronger inside than outside. He looked deeper into the mall. The only sound was the dim hum of electricity. Nizarian lights created dim pockets of shadows between toppled-over mannequins and bare countertops. At the far end was a set of stairs.

'So not doing that,' he thought. 'Torch Karehn said Grandwyn is in a store on the third floor. I think I'll take the express route.'

Tadgh ran toward the balconies and jumped. He grabbed the railing on the second level and vaulted over. He ducked down, back against the railing and looked around. The shadows were equally dim here. The open-aired pods were replaced by a food court: a semi-circle of open-faced, closed-in areas offering a variety of dining options.

Hundreds of chairs were arranged around pristine white tables.

Every single chair was filled by a graunskyeg. Each of them was perfectly still, staring off into nothingness. They looked almost like normal corpses except several of them swayed slightly. Others, he noticed, occasionally blinked.

For a moment, Tadgh was paralyzed. He could not will his muscles to move.

'I have to get out of here before they notice me.' He kept his eyes on the food court instead of the railing behind him. It took him a little longer to get into position, but he could not take his eyes off the graunskyegs. Thankfully, his balance in feline form was even better than his jumping. He crouched down slightly and jumped thirty-five feet in the air again. He reached for the railing on the third floor.

A graunskyeg stood there, a shirtless man covered in blood who was missing an arm.

Tadgh screamed when he saw it and forgot to reach for the railing. At the last second, he fumbled and tried to reach out for a handhold. He missed. The graunskyeg, up until then, had been staring off into space. Tadgh's flurry of movement woke it up. It howled.

As Tadgh fell backwards, he heard the graunskyegs on the second floor come to life. Chairs pushed back, tables toppled. Fear gripped him as he fell graceless to the main floor. Time seemed to slow. At the last minute, his body took over for his conscious mind, flipping his feet beneath him. Dropping his quarterstaff, he put his hands to the side to steady himself. That was a mistake. He smacked into the marble floor on all fours. His legs completely absorbed the shock of the fall. His hands, however, were not so lucky. Pain shot through him, and he roared. The sound of his voice echoed throughout the first floor.

He looked down at his hands to assess the damage. Shards of glass cut into his flesh. Blood flowed steadily from his palms. One of his fingers bent sideways at the knuckle.

Tadgh held his breath and listened. The moans from

the food court grew louder. Worse, he heard shuffling of feet and additional moans coming from stores all around the first floor.

Panic pushed him to his feet. 'I'll heal,' he thought. 'As long as I'm not torn to pieces first.'

He looked above. Graunskyegs lined the balcony, staring down at him. Some showed surprising coordination and were attempting to climb over the railing. Most were simply throwing themselves forward. Three bodies landed around him with sick wet splashes.

Tadgh screamed and picked up his quarterstaff. If these were zombies from the movies back home, a fall like that might damage its head re-killing it. But he'd already established that headshots didn't work. The first of the graunskyegs who had thrown themselves over the edge rose to its feet. Despite shattered bones and loosely-held-together flesh, the creature walked toward Tadgh.

He shot it with an Akashic bolts hoping the inertia from the blast would throw it back slightly.

'I have to get to Grandwyn,' he thought. 'Only way out of this is up.' Looking above, he saw his exit: a ledge of flowering vegetation above the front doors. He jumped for it. Not thinking, he reached for the ledge with both hands. Pain from his broken finger shot through him. He nearly lost his grip and fell again but, pushing through the pain, managed to pull himself up. He dropped behind the plants, hiding.

Five more graunskyegs fell over the second story balcony. Looking down, Tadgh saw other graunskyegs crawling toward the spot he'd been in moments before. They weren't looking at him anymore. He noticed two fighting for a spot of ground. He felt nauseous as he realized why.

'Gross. They're licking up my blood from the fall.' As the adrenaline started to fade, he looked down at his hands. Aside from the broken finger, two other fingers were out of place. 'Not my first broken bone. Just have to get them back in place. Should heal within the hour.'

Biting into his forearm, he twisted the fingers back into place.

For several long minutes he waited, hoping the graunskyegs would settle down with no prey in sight. If anything, the small amount of blood seemed to have agitated them even more.

'Looks like they're not going back to sleep, and I can't wait much longer,' he thought. 'Menphis and Eiodeesh will be back soon. It's getting darker, and the Sage said that's when the greater graunskyegs come out to play. We have to get Grandwyn and get back to the Aerie.'

He looked back up at the third floor. He could clearly see the graunskyegs who had startled him. Unlike the others, its eyes were still on Tadgh, watching him. As far as Tadgh could tell, it was the only one there.

'I can make that jump,' he thought. He looked down at the thrashing graunskyeg beneath him. 'Not so sure I'll survive a second fall. Not with those things down there. Here's hoping this works.'

He crossed his fingers and nearly yelped in pain. Though, technically back in place, his fingers still throbbed.

'Someday I will be smart,' he cursed. 'God help the world when that happens.'

He jumped to the third floor balcony. The graunskyeg ran at him, reaching out with his one arm. Tadgh swung his quarterstaff at the creature's knee, throwing it off balance. He focused his life energy on his fist, a practice Menphis referred to as iron fist. Tadgh punched at the graunskyeg's shoulder, dislocating it. Unable to move its arm, the creature snarled at Tadgh and tried to get to its feet. Tadgh used his claws to grab the creature and, picking it up over his head, hurled it over the balcony. He watched as it fell to the main floor landing on several blood-drinking graunskyegs. He glanced at his hand, shocked to discover the punch had not caused him pain.

'What do you know?' Tadgh thought. 'Looks like my training might be coming in handy after all.'

A quick glance around showed there were no visible graunskyegs. Both sides of this level were lined with art galleries selling paintings and sculptures.

He couldn't hear anything over the moans and howls of the graunskyegs on the main floor, so he sniffed the air. Grandwyn's scent was stronger now. That meant he was close.

He walked down the middle of the aisle, his eyes sweeping the stores to the left and right as he went. He passed a store selling $5,000 handbags, one selling life-sized statues of children dressed as Beherskers, and a rare-book store. The air was putrid with rotting flesh, but he could not see the dead bodies. Then he found the replica store.

'Finally.' He slid open the glass door and looked around. The lights in the store were out as they were in nearly all the stores. Still, his feline sight allowed for excellent night vision. Something move by the cash register. Someone screamed.

Tadgh turned around just as a rather ornate mace slammed into his head.

Chapter Twenty-Two

Unprepared for the blow, Tadgh's body twisted with the impact, and he fell to his knees.

"Jeebus!" he cursed, bracing himself for another blow. Nothing came.

A moment later he heard a young boy's voice. "Yikes. He's alive!"

"Stop yelling at me. I didn't know!" The second voice was also young, female. "I thought one of them had gotten into the store. Do you think I killed him?"

Tadgh turned slowly in the direction of the voice. His head was dizzy from the blow, so it took him a moment to focus. He saw a teenage girl in a short black dress. She had deep black hair. Her face was damp and slimy with several-day-old makeup. Then he saw the boy beside her.

"Wow," he said. "You really do look like him. Your name's Grandwyn, right?"

The boy looked startled. "How do you know my name? What kind of monster are you?"

"I'm not a…" Tadgh stopped and realized he was still in feline form. Flicking the switch in his mind, he became, once again, human. Suddenly, it was darker and the pain in his fingers was more intense. He found it difficult to hold his quarterstaff. "What did you hit me with?"

The girl pointed to a decorative mace at her feet. It was two feet long with a large spike at the top. The handle was covered in shiny black leather strips. Just his luck, the mace was pure silver.

"Figures," he said. "My name is Tadgh Dooley. I'm here to rescue you. I'm here with your mother and father."

Once again, Grandwyn looked shocked. "I think you injured your brain. I don't have a father."

"Of course you do. He'll be here in a few minutes. Is it just the two of you in here?"

"I just got here," Grandwyn said. He spent a few

minutes describing his past few days. To Tadgh, it appeared Grandwyn was speaking very carefully, hiding certain aspects of the story. He wanted to ask about it, but when he noticed the sidelong glances Grandwyn gave the girl, he decided not to push him. "When I got out of the water, I was soaking wet. I ended up at the mall and wanted to find some dry clothes. I found the first store that sold clothes I could wear and put these on." He pointed down to his clothing: a bright orange tunic and matching pants. "I'll pay for them later, I promise."

"I told you, nobody cares if you pay for them," the girl said.

"I do." Grandwyn looked up at her, sullen. "Anyway, after I changed, these graunskyegs appeared out of nowhere. They chased me but..." Grandwyn stopped and frowned. "It was weird. I kind of got the feeling they weren't trying to get me. Not really, I mean. They pushed me up the stairs. Every time I tried to leave they pushed me further into the building. Does that make sense to you?"

Tadgh grimaced. "Unfortunately, yes. That's a long story. I'll tell you as soon as we get out of here. Grandwyn, have you seen that orange cat since you got to the mall?

Grandwyn shook his head.

"Good." Tadgh looked at the girl. "What's your name?"

The girl leaned back against the counter. "Re-dha. I've been here since this whole thing started. I work here. I was ringing up some rich snob from Norshire. She was getting this gaudy dagger for her daughter. I was trying to tune her out, just smiling as she prattled on about how quaint the whole town was. I think she was a politician's wife or something. Anyway, just as I passed her the receipt, I heard the first screams. Everyone in the store just kind of turned toward the entrance and froze.

"When nothing else happened, the snob took her bags and left. Everyone else in the store went to see what all the screaming was about. I was kind of freaked out, so I stayed. A few seconds later, there was another scream. Then another. Soon all you could hear was screaming. I ran back to the store and closed the door. Everyone else ran for the exits."

Tadgh glanced over his shoulder. "Based on what I've seen out there you made the right call. The entire island is crawling with those things. The only survivors we've seen are at the Aerie. Grandwyn, that's where your mother is."

"How are you going to get us out of here?" Re-dha asked. "Are you a fieldbender? Is that how you were able to turn into that...thing."

Tadgh shook his head. "No. Not really. I'm a ...." He almost said a fod sel-onde but remembered his conversation with the Sage. Perhaps there was no name for what he was. "I'm with the Brotherhood of Tyche. I'm here with another member of the elmire ahk, Menphis. He's Grandwyn's father. We also have a trofast with us. She's really good with an axe. But none of that is going to stop the graunskyegs if they swarm us. It's crucial we leave quietly. Menphis and Eiodeesh should be here in a few minutes. I'd like to be out by the front doors when they arrive. But the main stairs are out. Too many graunskyegs. Re-dha, how well do you know this mall?"

Re-dha's eyes brightened. "Pretty well. I've worked here for two years. Past the candy stand there's a metal door that leads to the maintenance area. Mostly storage and janitorial stuff but there's also a separate stairwell. It goes down to a side entrance used for deliveries." She stopped, suddenly looking scared. "I saw a whole bunch of people run that way when this started. I don't know if they got out. If not, there could be anything in there."

"I'll go check it out." Tadgh went back to the glass door. "You stay here. Close this door behind me and stay out of sight. I'm going to shift into my other form, so don't freak out. I know it's big and scary, but it helps me not get killed."

Tadgh left the relic store and walked toward the metal door Re-dha had described. The lights flickered above him, and he had the distinct impression that someone was watching him. He searched the shadows but nothing moved. Still, there seemed to be a new sound, a whisper beneath the constant drone of hungry graunskyegs.

When he reached the metal door, the stench of blood was so strong he nearly gagged. Before he opened the door, he knew what he would find. The door swung open easily, and he stepped into a long hallway lined with metal doors on either side. At the far end, a door was propped open by a dead body. He could tell it was dead because it was headless. Along the hallway were several other corpses torn into long, shredded sections.

'Well isn't this just precious,' he thought suppressing his urge to vomit. 'Grandwyn will never be able to make it through this. Neither will the girl, especially if she knew any of these people. Still, if it's the only way to safety…'

Tadgh realized he had to check out the exit. 'I could always move the shredded bodies if I need to. And wow, there is a phrase I never thought I'd use.'

He walked to the end of the hallway and looked past the headless body. The stairwell beyond looked clear. Surprisingly so. It took him a moment to discern what the problem was.

'There's no blood,' he thought. He looked back at the hallway to confirm it was bloody mess. Yet the metal stairs beyond were absolutely clean. 'Almost like they've been licked clean.'

Voices whispered from the bottom of the stairs. The voices were too low for him to make out most of the words, but one word kept repeating.

"Soon."

Tadgh pushed the headless body out into the stairwell and closed the door. Remembering what he'd done back at the warehouse, he gripped the doorknob, pushing inwards and twisting it. No sooner had he done that when something tried to open the door from the other side. The whispers were louder now.

"….not ours…." one said.

"…stronger than him. Take what we…."

"Shh. He's listening."

Tadgh bolted, quickly running back toward the relic store. He slammed the metal door behind him and found a surprise waiting for him on the other side. Eiodeesh and Menphis stood nearby, looking into the stores, their faces wrinkled with confusion. Menphis, hearing the door slam shut, spun toward Tadgh, quarterstaff raised.

"Tadgh," Menphis said. "What is it?"

Tadgh pressed his back to the metal door. "Not sure. Not sticking around to find out. Something horrible is on the other side of that door. Something worse than zombies." Tadgh stopped. "Wait. It's quiet. What happened to all the graunskyegs?"

"We don't know," Eiodeesh said. "We got back here and you weren't outside. We waited for a bit and decided to check inside. We haven't seen a single graunskyeg since we came in here."

Tadgh stared at the ground, thinking. "That can't be good. There were hundreds of them in here. Hundreds."

"Let's not look our fortune in the face," Menphis said. "We should find Grandwyn and get out of here before they come back."

"He's over here," Tadgh said. "Follow me." Tadgh led them to the relic store. He knocked on the glass door before sliding it open to let them know he was coming in. "I'm back. Please don't hit me again."

Re-dha stood up first, once again holding the ornate mace. Grandwyn came out of hiding second. When he did, Tadgh heard Menphis cry out. Tadgh turned to look at his friend and saw tears falling freely down his face.

Grandwyn stared at Menphis and scratched his ear. "Um, are you my dad?"

"Yes." Menphis cried out again, a sound that was half joy and half something else. "Yes, I am your father."

Grandwyn walked forward and held out his hand,

waiting for Menphis to shake it. "I'm pleased to meet you. My name is Grandwyn."

Menphis grabbed the boy with both arms, pulling Grandwyn close to him as he sobbed uncontrollably.

Eiodeesh put a hand on Menphis' shoulder. "We should move. It might not be safe for long."

A strange laughter danced between the shadows seeming to come from all directions and no direction at once. Menphis got to his feet, standing protectively in front of Grandwyn.

A voice spoke from the shadows. "I told you boy. You can't run from me. The game is almost over now. Just one last piece of the puzzle to put in place."

"Who was that?" Re-dha asked.

Tadgh shook his head, but he knew who it was. The voice was impossible to forget. "Menphis. You need to get your boy out of here now."

Menphis hesitated. "You can't fight them alone."

"And the boy can't lose his father. You've just found each other. Go."

Eiodeesh pushed Menphis and Grandwyn out into the mall. "I'll stay with Tadgh. Go quickly. The sun will set soon." She looked over at Re-dha. "Girl, if you want to live I suggest you leave with Menphis now."

Re-dha did not need to be told twice. Still carrying her ridiculous weapon she ran out of the store.

Menphis knelt. "Grandwyn, do you know what a piggy-back rid is? I want you to get on my shoulders. I can run very quickly, but I'll need you to hold on tight and be very brave. Do you think you can do that?"

Grandwyn nodded and climbed upon Menphis' shoulders.

With his son settled in place, Menphis looked Tadgh in the eyes. "I can't carry him and my weapon. Can you put my quarterstaff somewhere safe? I'll come back for it later."

"Of course." Tadgh took Menphis' weapon. "Good luck out there."

Menphis smiled and looked up at his son. Without another word, he ran out the door after Re-dha.

Tadgh placed Menphis' staff at the back of the store away from easy view. Eiodeesh, hands on her axe, kept guard by the door.

"Are you sure about this?" Tadgh asked.

Eiodeesh nodded. "My father was an honorable man. He taught me well. I would never leave a comrade to face an evil alone."

"I appreciate that but..." Tadgh hesitated remembering his conversation with the Sage last night. "That voice we heard belongs to a demon. His name is Bes. He's the one that turned me into what I am. He's orchestrated all of this simply to get me here, but I can't let him catch me. I won't go into details, but I spoke with the Sage last night. He told me if worst came to worst I should use my wish power and teleport off the island."

"Is that wise?" Eiodeesh lowered her axe, letting it rest on the floor. "Won't it tear another hole in the Void? And what about the fieldbenders from Karaj Robat? They will feel you use your power and send more assassins after you."

"Yep. The Sage knows that and still thinks it's better than me falling into the demon's hands. The only reason I'm staying right now is I hope to be a bit of a distraction. I'm the only thing Bes truly cares about. Grandwyn was bait. If I stay..."

"Menphis and Grandwyn will have time to get back to the Aerie." Eiodeesh smiled and picked up her axe again. "Well this might not be the death sentence I thought it was."

Bes, the size of a horse, jumped out of the shadows and chomped his teeth down on Eiodeesh's neck. The trofast tried to raise her weapon but the angle was wrong. She could not get a solid swing at the demon. Bes slightly shifted his teeth and Eiodeesh's neck snapped with a loud pop. A moment later, the axe fell from her hands.

"You bastard!" Tadgh swung his quarterstaff smashing Bes repeatedly in the head. "Let her go! Let her go goddamn you!"

Bes backhanded Tadgh with an enormous paw sending him flying into a rack of replica weapons. Rising quickly to his feet, Tadgh shot a blast of Akashic energy at Bes. The demon bounced away, shrinking down to the size of a house cat. He landed on a glass counter top.

"You realize this is your fault," Bes said. "All of this. Every person that died on this island is dead because of you."

"Liar!"

"Demons don't lie." Bes licked his paw and wiped a splotch of blood from his mouth. "We just tell selective truths. Back on Earth, if you had come with me when you were supposed to, I would never have come to this world. So, like I said, all of this is your fault."

Tadgh's eyes filled with angry tears. He looked over at Eiodeesh's still body and wanted to destroy everything. But he remembered the Sage's words. No matter what Bes had done, Tadgh could not surrender. He could not allow himself to be captured. He had to run.

"I will make you pay for this." Tadgh took one last deep breath and said "I wish…"

"Not this time."

Before Tadgh could finish wishing himself away, Bes opened his mouth. A hot stream of sickly green goo shot into Tadgh's face. He closed his mouth to avoid swallowing it. Bes pounced, sinking his claws into Tadgh's head. The pain lasted only an instant before Tadgh fell unconscious.

Chapter Twenty-Three

The first thing the Sage noticed when he stepped out of the teleportation disk was the heat. Even though the tower was completely sheltered from the sun, most would find the heat oppressive. Having spent most of his life in a fire dimension, he found it rather comforting.

The second thing he noticed was the screaming.

"Oh goodie," he said. "They're not dead yet."

The Sage ran toward the screams.

The center of Mogul tower was hollow, allowing people capable of flight fast travel between floors. The Sage was on the top level. Ein and the others were two floors down. The Sage assessed the situation, quickly understanding what they had attempted to do. There were no doors in Mogul Tower, which made it hard to defend if anyone got inside. Ein and his soldiers had piled tables in front of the archway, trying to barricade it. It hadn't worked. The graunskyegs had smashed through the furniture. One soldier was on the ground, a graunskyeg gnawing at his leg.

"Stop that," the Sage said. He shot a blast of fire past the soldier, hitting the graunskyeg in the chest. Remembering that normal people need air, he called the fire from an elemental plane, not the sun. It wasn't as hot as solar fire, but it was still intense enough to set the decayed body aflame.

The Sage looked to his left. Ein was there, hands glowing purple, watching the Sage with a look of pure unadulterated rage.

The Sage waved back at him and shouted down to him. "Hate me later. Pull your man free, so I can save your butts."

Ein grumbled something and his soldiers pulled their comrade away from the burning graunskyeg. Once the soldier was clear, the Sage teleported down. He held his hands out in front of the barricaded archway and set the furniture on fire. The graunskyegs on the other side ran away from the flame, no longer eager to get through.

The Sage smiled at Ein. "Hey there. Long time no see."

Ein threw a blast of Akashic energy at the Sage. The Sage deflected the magical attack with a lazy wave of his hand.

"We've been here for two days!" Ein shot at the Sage again. This time, the Sage opened a teleportation disk in front of him sending the attack away harmless.

"Sorry," the Sage said. "Trying to save the world and everything I got a little distracted. I kind of forgot you were here."

Ein's face grew a deep purple. "You…forgot?"

"Woah." The Sage held up his hands. "We can fight if you want but admit it. You know you're going to lose. Besides, I'm your only way out of this place. You know about Mogul Tower, right? This place is five stories tall with no external openings larger than an arrow slit. Back before the Badlands was a desert, this used to be an academy for fieldbenders. Only way in or out was teleportation. And you can't teleport. And that's why it was later used to house undesirables."

Ein bit his lip, his color darkening even more.

"This is the perfect prison," the Sage said. "Well, at least it was until the fieldbenders bowed to political pressure. Some people thought it inhuman to imprison people in conditions like these, if you can imagine that."

"I'm going to kill you." Ein punched a hole in the wall. "I don't know how, but I will find a way."

The Sage frowned. "This isn't going as well as I expected. Let me try again. I need you to do me a favor."

Ein blinked. Then he started to laugh. "You're insane. You are literally insane if you think I'll do anything to help you after what you've done to me."

"Hey," one of the soldiers said. "Gregor's leg is pretty torn up. We need to do something to stop the bleeding."

"Oh shut up," Ein said. "Nobody cares about Gregor."

The Sage went to the injured man and examined the leg. "Yeah, this is pretty bad. Healing others isn't one of my specialties. Let me send him to the hospital in Gateway. They can take care of him."

He opened a teleportation disk beneath the injured man and then stood to face the others. "I'll be happy to get the rest of you out of here but I'm going to need something in return." He pointed at the still-burning doors. "I need your decision quickly. That door is only going to burn for so long. The graunskyegs will be back. We all know what that means."

"You're a monster," Ein said.

The Sage shrugged. "Maybe. I have done a lot of questionable things in my life. What I'm going to do next maybe one of the worst. Gaysun Defksquar has been captured by Castle Dispayre, and I need to rescue him. And I need you to help me."

Ein did a double take. "You want me...to help you...invade my homeland?" He shook his head slowly and snorted. "I was right. Total madman. Why in the world would I help you?"

The Sage stepped close to Ein and spoke in a whisper. "Because if you don't, I'm going to break your hands so you can't fieldbend properly. Then I'll leave you here. Oh, and I'll also leave your soldiers who'll know you are the reason they've been condemned to death. Look at your men, Ein. Take a good, hard look at their eyes. Between you and me, I don't think you'll be alive for more than a few minutes after I leave." The Sage sighed deeply. "I'm not usually one for blackmail, but someone has a knife to my throat. I don't have time to be nice."

Ein snorted. "When have you ever been nice?"

The Sage thought for a moment. "You may have a point there. So, Ein, what's it going to be?"

Ein looked around the room at the stony gazes of his soldiers. He took a step away from the Sage, mumbling beneath his breath. Then, without looking at the Sage, he nodded.

"I'm going to need a stronger commitment that that," the Sage said. "You and I are going deep into the heart of the enemy empire. Well, my enemy not yours. I need to make sure you won't turn on me. Which is why you're going to let me bind you."

"No!" Ein smashed his fist into the wall again. "I won't do it. Go on. Leave me here. We'll find another way out."

The Sage stepped forward, his voice so low only Ein could hear it. "I'm not a healer. But I happen to know you are. You will let me bind you, or I'll tell your soldiers you were prepared to let one of them bleed to death without lifting a finger. You won't last minutes. You'll last for hours. They'll play with you, turn you into a toy until eventually the graunskyegs devour all of you. So please, stop wasting my time. Let me bind you. Once the mission is over, I'll remove the binding. You have my word."

Ein glanced over the Sage's shoulder. His face was nearly ashen now.

The Sage knew the request for a binding was risky, but it was the best leverage he had. Most of his abilities came from his time in the fire dimension, but he'd picked up a few tricks from the fieldbenders on Maghe Sihre. One of them was soul binding. He would rip a small portion of Ein's soul and imprison it in a vessel. The experience was said to be painful. Victims of the bind suffered terrible nightmares. If the piece of soul remained apart for too long, victims often succumbed to insanities and, occasionally, death.

Ein's shoulders sank. "Fine. Do what you need to do and get us out of here. But my men don't come with me, you here? I won't have them see me like that." Ein hesitated for a moment. "And I suppose they've more than earned their freedom. Send them home."

With a nod, the Sage flicked his wrist. A teleportation portal opened beside the soldiers. As they stepped through it, the Sage could see Ein eyeing the portal covetously. He assumed that Ein was calculating his chances of running toward the portal and making his escape. Before he could carry through on the wish, the last soldier made his escape. The Sage closed the portal.

"Are you ready?" the Sage asked.

"No." Ein began to take off his shirt. "We both know what fieldbending of this level does to a body. No sense getting blood all over my clothes. I assume you won't bring the container with us."

"Of course not." The Sage reached into his jacket pocket and brought out the fist-sized crystal he'd brought. "I'll keep it in a safe location."

Clothless, Ein lay down on the floor. "Please tell me you've done this before."

The Sage placed the crystal on Ein's chest. "Don't worry. I know the ceremony well, but I abhor the soul bind. I hate what it stands for, what it does to the victim and the caster."

"And yet here you are about to do it." Ein closed his eyes. "Get on with."

The Sage looked away for a moment. A little while ago, Tempertin had asked him if he was willing to pay the price to get Echo back. He wondered if there was any price too high, anything he would be unwilling to do to get her back.

The Sage began to chant. Ein began to bleed.

Chapter Twenty-Four

A splash of water on his cheek startled Tadgh awake. When his eyes fluttered open, the first thing he saw was drops of rain falling on his hands, hands currently bound by thick metal chains. He rode on the back of a white horse with a bright orange mane. The mount glanced back at Tadgh with eyes that burned with the same orange color, and he realized this was no ordinary creature. Looking down he saw the horse walked on a stone paved path. Tiny weeds sprung up between small cracks.

Lifting his head, he became aware of a weight around his neck. Though impossible to see without a mirror, he knew he wore a power dampener around his throat, just like the one he'd removed from the Sage in Gateway. He tried to shift into feline form and found himself unable to do so.

Five strangers walked in front of his horse. He could not see their faces. Each wore identical black cloaks that hung to their ankles. A large blood-red moon was embroidered on the left side above a word in a language Tadgh could not read. Bes, once again the size of a lion, walked several paces ahead of the five. Tadgh glanced over his shoulder and cried out in shock. Trailing behind him was an army of graunskyegs, thousands of them, all silently walking along the stone path.

Tadgh spun his head around to the front again, for the first time noticing how dark it was. Thick clouds covered the sky hiding both moons. Night had fallen on DunDegore, which suggested the five strangers ahead of him could be the greater graunskyegs. One of them, a male with long black hair, turned to face Tadgh. It grinned, showing monstrously sharp teeth that gleamed even in the moonless night. It whispered to the figure beside him, a female with long red hair, who also looked back briefly at Tadgh.

'I have to get out of here,' he thought. The rain intensified, making it difficult for him to see very far. It seemed with the power dampener on he lost his improved night vision as well. 'They must be leading me to the Sword of Kassandra. They want me to use my wish power, which means they'll have to remove the collar. That will be my only chance for escape.'

The stone path led up a slight incline and buildings came into view. He'd only seen them from the distance before, but he clearly recognized the Ruins of DunDegore. The white stone gleamed despite the darkness. He opened his mouth to ask a question, but another of the five figures, this one a female with short white hair, turned to face him, a finger at her lips motioning for silence.

Tadgh became more and more unnerved by the ruins. To him, the structures looked far too modern to be ruins. The spires appeared to be nothing less than large skyscrapers made of concrete and steel. Glancing up, he noticed several winged beings flying around the top of one of the buildings. Instantly, he knew what they were.

'Just when I thought the day couldn't get any better,' he thought. 'Wypera. At least ten of them.'

It soon became clear the procession was aiming for the tower around which the wypera circled. When they reached the base of the tower, one of the graunskyegs, the male with the long black hair, lifted a hand. Tadgh's horse stopped as did all the graunskyegs behind him.

Bes continued inside, as did two of the cloaked figures. The one with the long black hair walked over to Tadgh and held out a hand. Tadgh realized the man wanted to help Tadgh down off the horse. He took the man's hand to steady himself, swung his leg over the horse, and jumped to the ground. The man's hand was cool and wet, like melting ice.

"I have heard so much about you." The man put his arm around Tadgh's shoulder, gently guiding him closer to the building. "We've yet to be introduced, but I have met several of your colleagues. You may call me Teric."

Tadgh jolted and tried to break free of Teric's grasp.

The arm around his shoulder held him firmly in place.

"Ah." Teric smiled. "I see that they have spoken of me. Good. So you know how foolish it would be to run. Tell me, how is Menphis doing? He and I shared several special moments together when last I saw him."

Tadgh simply shook his head, not trusting himself to speak.

Teric grasped Tadgh's chin with his free hand. "Does the wind have your tongue? I asked you a question, boy?"

Bes walked out of the building, his green eyes glowing brightly. "Step back, Teric. He's not yours. Find another toy."

Teric release Tadgh's chin and stepped away. "Of course. I have my heart set on Menphis anyway. As soon as we finish here, I will pay him a visit. I can still remember the taste of his blood on my lips."

Teric smiled and Tadgh turned away, disgusted. His eyes widened when he saw something unexpected. A grey mist swirled along the ground like a tangle of giant serpents. The mist faded and two figures appeared, walking arm in arm. One was a tall bald man with bronzed skin wearing a white sleeveless tunic. He carried a quarterstaff that he used as a walking stick. The other was a wide-hipped woman with soft brown hair that hung down over her bared breasts.

Tadgh glanced back to Teric and Bes, but neither reacted to the appearance of the two newcomers.

"They can't see us," the woman said.

The man nodded. "But we can't stay long, or they will feel us. You know who we are."

Tadgh realized the statement was not a question, but he had no idea who the two people were. He shook his head uncertainly.

Teric glanced at Tadgh, his deep black eyes scrutinizing him. Tadgh found himself unable to meet that gaze and looked back at the strangers. He was startled to discover the rain did not seem to touch either of them.

"No need to speak," the man said. "We came to show

you something. You cannot use the Sword of Kassandra to open the Void."

"I won't," Tadgh said. Realizing he'd spoken aloud, he glanced back at Teric. Seeing Teric and Bes engaged in a quiet conversation, Tadgh turned back to the others and shook his head.

The woman stepped closer. "You will be tempted. Both Tyche and I believe you will overcome temptation, but the others are not so certain."

Tadgh blinked rapidly. Did the woman actually mean to imply the man beside here was Tyche? Tadgh studied both of the figures again.

"No way!" Unable to control himself, Tadgh fell to his knees, his head bowed. "Lord Tyche. Lady Fricka, I'm unworthy…"

Teric smacked Tadgh upside the head. "Get to your feet boy and stop praying. I'll have none of that holy nonsense around me."

Head ringing, Tadgh got to his feet. "Yes, sir. Of course." When Teric returned to his conversation with Bes, Tadgh turned back to the figures.

The man, Tyche, was smiling. "You're not overly bright, are you lad? Stop talking. Listen. Watch."

The goddess Fricka lifted her hands above her head, an exact replica of the motion he'd seen Tamara do earlier that day. The rain stopped, and an unseen hand pushed aside the clouds creating a wide circular opening through which he could see the stars above. As Tadgh watched the sky, a tear appeared in the fabric of reality. Three-dimensional space folded like paper, creating the impression that the solid world around him was nothing more than an illusion. At first the wound was small, little more than a thin line between him and the moons beyond. Then it widened.

"Witness the opening of the Void," Tyche said. "Witness the return of Dispayre."

Purple and green lightning flashed from within it, lighting up the night sky. Horrified, Tadgh watched as colossal hands appeared on either side of the tear, ripping the opening wider. Dark shapes, visible only against the flashes of lightning, poured out like swarming locusts. Hundreds of thousands of creatures fell from the Void and all of them headed downwards, swarming over the lands of Maghe Sihre. But that was not the worst part. The tear in reality was not large enough for the colossal creature inside to reach out. One of its hands stretched forward, a giant arm the color of glistening blood extending down to the planet. Along its skin marched other monsters, those incapable of flight. They ran down the arm, their howling voices raised in celebration.

Tadgh turned away. "Make it stop!"

Teric grabbed Tadgh by the throat. "I told you to…" Teric stopped, his head turning as he searched the night. Although Tyche and Fricka were still there, it appeared he could still not see them. Teric turned back to Tadgh, his nails digging in slightly to Tadgh's flesh. "Tell me, boy, who are you talking to?"

Tadgh shook his head. "No one."

Bes walked forward, his nose lifting as he sniffed the air.

"That is our cue to leave," Tyche said. He backed away from Tadgh, Fricka matching his movement. "For hundreds of years, Dispayre has been trapped in the Void. In that time he has grown, in size and power. You cannot allow him to come back to the world, Tadgh. No matter what the cost. Understand?"

Tadgh, unable to respond, simply closed his eyes. When he reopened them, the gods were gone.

Bes growled. "Gone. I thought I smelled something for a moment, but it's gone now." He came closer to Tadgh and his green eyes narrowed. "Tell me who it was."

Tadgh attempted a moment of bravado. "Or what? We both know you won't kill me."

"Not yet," Teric said. He pressed his sharp teeth close to Tadgh's throat. The heat of his breath and the stench of blood made Tadgh want to gag. He held his breath.

Teric threw Tadgh to the ground. "Bah! Let's get this over with. The sooner he does his thing the sooner we can…"

Bes stepped between Tadgh and Teric. "The sooner you do nothing. The boy is mine, remember? We do this and he leaves with me. Cross me at your peril."

Teric threw his head back and laughed. "The peril would not be mine, kitty cat." He pushed aside his black cloak to reveal the nizarian battle armor beneath it. A menacing mace made from black metal hung at his waist.

Bes glared at Teric, unmoving.

The black-cloaked woman with red hair came out of the building. Arms crossed, she watched the standoff for a moment before speaking. "The hermadur is ready for Tadgh. Bring him."

Teric bowed his head and walked past the woman into the building.

"Get up," Bes said to Tadgh. "Or do you prefer I carried you in my teeth?"

Tadgh got to his feet and followed Bes into the ruins.

Chapter Twenty-Five

Grandwyn huddled in his mother's arms. She held him so tightly he found it hard to breathe, but he didn't want to let her go. She spoke to him, but he couldn't focus on her words. He only understood the message. He was safe.

After a long time, his mother pulled back from him. She brushed his damp hair away from his forehead and kissed him.

"I'm sorry," he said. "I should never have run away."

"Oh my poor baby." His mother kissed him again. "You are not to blame. None of this is your fault."

"Glad you're okay, Wynnie." Bethel, his mother's bodyguard, looked down at Grandwyn looking less than amused. She was wearing her fancy black leather armor again. He often wondered if she ever wore anything else. "But we're going to upgrade security when we get home."

Grandwyn narrowed his eyes. "Don't call me Wynnie."

Bethel laughed.

Grandwyn's mother motioned toward someone Grandwyn could not see. A moment later, Menphis approached them and knelt down so he was eye to eye with Grandwyn.

"Grandwyn, have you met your father?" his mother asked.

Grandwyn shrugged, saying nothing.

Menphis cupped Grandwyn's neck with his calloused hands and smiled. "We made it kid. I know I've been a horrible father. That changes today. I promise you. I may have to make some changes in my life…"

"Menphis…" Grandwyn's mother interrupted his father. "Don't make promises you can't…"

"I've made up my mind." Menphis looked at Grandwyn with wide, wet eyes. Grandwyn thought he looked very happy, and also very sad. "If I've learned anything these last few days it's that my priorities were backwards." Standing, he lowered his voice. "Listen, Tamara, I'm not sure what this means for you and me, but…"

"Hush." Grandwyn's mother touched Menphis' chest. "We'll talk about that later."

Grandwyn had a million questions. If this man was his father, why had they never met before? How had Menphis met his mother? And why had his mother never mentioned him. All these things ran through his head, but he knew instinctively that this was not the time. Grownups became very awkward when you asked difficult questions.

"How did you get past the graunskyegs?" his mother asked.

Menphis frowned. "That's the weird thing. There were no graunskyegs. Anywhere. The streets are completely empty."

"We thought it was just here," Bethel said. "The guards noticed it a few moments ago. The graunskyegs gathered in front of the Aerie all wandered away. Where do you think they went?"

There was a pounding on the front doors of the Aerie. A moment later, a little man with orange-skin and thick black glasses walked toward them.

"Gnocko!" Menphis ran to the orange man. "It's been so long I was starting to get worried. Where's the Sage?"

Gnocko glanced at Grandwyn and then looked back up at Menphis. "Perhaps we should have this conversation in private."

"Nonsense," Grandwyn's mother said. "My son's been wrapped up in this since the beginning. He can stay for the end. Tell us what happened?"

Gnocko readjusted his glasses. "Let's hope this is not the end. I need to get to Tadgh before he does something foolish."

"Have you met Tadgh?" Menphis asked. "When is he not doing something foolish?"

"This is no time for games!" Gnocko removed his glasses revealing his strange white eyes with small red dots.

"We found out why Tadgh was brought to this place. The reason. The hermadur is going to force him to use the Sword of Kassandra to reopen the Void."

"Mother of flesh," Grandwyn's mother said. She touched her forehead and chest like she did whenever she prayed. "Surely he won't do it."

Gnocko sighed. "From what I heard he might feel like he has no choice. The Sage is away on his own mission. I have to warn Tadgh. Where is he?"

Menphis looked toward the front door. "Damn. He stayed at the mall. That's where Grandwyn was. He hoped to draw off the graunskyegs until and give me time to get my son back here. Don't worry. Eiodeesh stayed with Tadgh. She can talk some sense in to him."

A spinning circle of shadow appeared near the front of the Aerie. Several people shrieked and ran away from it. One woman with short gray hair actually ran toward the shadows. For a moment Grandwyn thought she looked familiar, but he couldn't place her.

"Reveal yourself," the gray-haired woman said.

A beautiful woman in a blue dress stepped out of the shadows. Her, Grandwyn recognized.

"It's you!" he shouted. "She's the woman from the boat."

His mother looked down at him with that strange look that always indicated she had no idea what he was talking about.

Grandwyn hit his forehead. "Sorry. I didn't have a chance to tell you about that yet. I talked with her on the boat, and she told me I didn't have to go to DunDegore, that I could just take the ship back to the mainland and head home. Don't you see? She tried to warn me. She's a friend."

Grandwyn's mother waved at the gray-haired woman. "It's okay, Torch Karehn. Grandwyn knows her. Let her through."

The woman from the boat bowed respectfully to Torch Karehn and walked toward Grandwyn. Torch Karehn walked close behind her.

The woman in the blue dress touched her forehead and chest, mimicking the actions of Grandwyn's mother. "If only I'd been able to convince you to go home. Perhaps none of this would have happened. Or perhaps they would have tried to unleash the graunskyegs in Karaj Robat. Or FleshPrayer. The loss of life here is a tragedy. It would have been tenfold worse elsewhere."

"Who are you?" Grandwyn's mother asked.

"Her name is Echo," Gnocko said.

Menphis scratched his head. "You told me and Tadgh your name was Andy."

The woman in the blue dress threw her hands over her head in frustration. "Whatever. Can't a woman have two names? We have more important things to discuss, and I don't have much time." She looked over her shoulder at the swirling circle of shadows. "I can never get away for long. Tempertin's momentarily distracted which is why I was able to sneak away. And it's why you have to hurry."

Torch Karehn inhaled sharply. "Did you say Tempertin? As in…"

"Yeah yeah yeah," Gnocko said. "Hero of StarFall, companion to Defksquar. Blah blah blah. Have to tell you not so nice in person. Echo, I came here looking for Tadgh. Menphis left him at the mall. Do you know if he's still there?"

Echo shook her head. "He's been taken to the ruins. Do you know the names of each tower?"

"I do!" Grandwyn said proudly. "I memorized the travel pamphlet."

Grandwyn's mother ruffled his hair. "Of course you did. But you are out of your mind if you think I'm letting you back out there. You're not leaving my side until morning. Understood?"

Grandwyn crossed his arms. "I'm not a child."

Menphis laughed. "I see what you mean about his stubborn streak."

Grandwyn pouted. "I'm not stubborn." Suddenly, he wasn't sure he liked this Menphis guy.

"I know the numbering," Bethel said. "I'll head over with you."

"Are you sure?" Grandwyn's mother put one of her hands on Bethel's waist.

Bethel looked around the Aerie. "I'm not doing much good around here, am I? The graunskyegs are gone for the moment. From the sounds of things, it's important we stop Tadgh from doing whatever they want him to do. I'll go if you'll allow me, mistress."

Grandwyn's mother touched her lips and, closing her eyes, nodded.

'She could have just said yes you can go, Bethel' Grandwyn thought. 'Why do adults have to be so dramatic?'

"Fine," Echo said to Bethel. "The ritual site is at the top of the Tower Four. You don't have much time."

Menphis looked at his hands. "Damn. I just realized my quarterstaff is back at the weapon store. I don't suppose we have time to retrieve it."

Echo shook her head.

"Bare-fist fighting it is then. Gnocko, are you coming with us?"

The orange man put his glasses back over his eyes. "I must have a death wish. Lead the way." Gnocko chewed his lower lip. Then his eyes bulged, and he looked up at Echo. "Where's Eiodeesh?"

"I...I don't know." Echo turned away, as if she didn't want to look at Gnocko. Grandwyn thought she was being very rude.

Gnocko didn't seem impressed either. His face drained of color, and he stared at the floor. "Oh. I see." He covered his mouth with his hand and sobbed loudly. A moment later, he recovered his composure. Menphis put a hand on Gnocko's shoulder, but the orange man knocked the hand away, angrily.

Grandwyn scratched his head. 'I think I missed

something.' He looked up at his mother and found she, too, was crying.

Gnocko looked as if he was about to scream. Instead, he took a deep breath and wiped tears from his eyes. "Okay. Let's do this. For Eiodeesh."

Everyone nodded and said Eiodeesh's name. Grandwyn watched them altogether convinced he'd missed something important but unable to figure out what it was.

Chapter Twenty-Six

Inside Tower Four, Tadgh followed Bes up flight after flight of stairs. They looked to be made of concrete, but his steps made no sound. It seemed to him the material somehow absorbed sound vibrations. The silence made the ascent even more eerie.

'My legs are killing me,' Tadgh thought. 'Not that I'm in a hurry to get to the roof or whatever, but seriously? Who builds a hundred-storey building and doesn't put in an elevator? Guess these Behersker people weren't so civilized after all.'

"Keep moving," Bes growled at him.

"Couldn't you have just flown me to the roof on one of those wypera?" As soon as he said it, Tadgh told himself to shut up. He wasn't supposed to be helping the bad guys finish their plans more efficiently.

"They wypera are part of the ritual," Bes said. "At least according to the hermadur. Me? I think everyone is making this more difficult than it needs to be."

Tadgh looked over the side of the stairs. It was a long way down. He thought about jumping over the side, but even if he had access to his powers he wasn't sure he'd survive the jump. He also noticed they were quickly approaching the top of the stairs. That meant he would have to make his move soon, and he still didn't know what waited for him on the roof.

"What's going to happen to me up there?" he asked.

"Simple. You touch the sword, you make the wish, and the Void opens. Dispayre slips back into the world, and we leave."

Tadgh grunted in annoyance. The skin beneath the chains around his hands itched. He tried unsuccessfully to scratch it. "Guess there's no chance of you taking these chains off, huh?"

Bes chuckled. "Not going to happen."

As they reached the final flight, Tadgh stopped. It took Bes a moment to notice. The demon turned and growled at Tadgh.

"Just a minute," Tadgh said. "Obviously I'm not going anywhere. Can you answer one question before this all goes down?"

Bes shifted in size, shrinking to the size of a housecat. "Why of course dear master. I live only to serve."

"Jeesh," Tadgh said. "You don't have to be so snarky about it. It's just, I don't understand why we need the Sword of Kassandra. Not that I want to help you – although annoyingly I keep thinking of ways to improve your plans – but why don't you have me just wish the Void was open? Is my wish power not strong enough?"

Bes sat on his hind legs and cocked his head to one side. He studied Tadgh for awhile before answering. "I told you demons can't lie, but we are very selective with the truth. Give me one reason why I should tell you anything and the truth is yours."

Tadgh, realizing his next few words were very important, did something he rarely did. He thought before he spoke.

'Menphis would be so proud of me right now,' he thought. "What if I told you there was another player in this game, someone you know nothing about who's been manipulating events all along."

"Nonsense."

"Really?" Tadgh smiled. "So that means Andy is working with you, too?"

Bes blinked. "Who is this Andy you speak of? Was that who you were speaking to earlier? Who is he?"

Tadgh couldn't help himself. He laughed. "Ha! I was right. You don't know about her, do you? She's been helping me for months. When I was being beaten to death on Earth, she's the one who chased off the attackers. If it wasn't for her, I'd be dead. And she's done so much more than that. And you, apparently, are completely clueless. So, to quote from one of the creepiest movies of all times, quid pro quo, Clarice. Quid pro quo."

Bes stalked down the stairs toward Tadgh, sniffing him. Bearing his teeth, he walked back up the stairs until he was eye level with Tadgh. "Fine. I'll even go first. Do not feed me nonsense, boy. When we leave here, you and I will be spending much time together. I can't kill you now but, there is always time for that after. The Sword of Kassandra will give you control over Void energy."

"What's that?"

"Every dimension has a level of background radiation. On this plane, it comes from the stars. I believe you call it electromagnetic radiation on your planet. Other dimensions are called elemental planes. They radiate pure fire or water or…Well, you get the picture. The Void, is a series of interlocking pocket dimensions soaked through with a dark energy. The people of this planet call it Void energy. There is no name for it on Earth because you idiots have not discovered it yet. People on Maghe Sihre have learned to harness it. They crafted a prison for Dispayre within the Void, trapping him in only a small corner of the dimension. They also use the energy to create graunskyegs."

"How?"

"I said one question. That was your third. Don't push your luck."

Tadgh tried his best to look innocent. "How about I guess? Just tell me if I'm right."

"Why should I?" Bes sounded annoyed. "I've already told you more than enough."

Tadgh ignored him and continued speaking. "I've heard people say the graunskyegs get stronger as they feed on flesh. So somehow eating people – which is gross by the way – strengthens the bond between the graunskyegs and the Void. The Sword of Kassandra somehow gives the wielder control over Void energy which means you could probably use it to create graunskyegs or make them stronger."

Bes growled but nodded hesitantly.

"But the Sword must have limited power. That makes sense. Otherwise you would have just zapped all the graunskyegs and turned them into an army of unstoppable vampires, right?" Tadgh rubbed his forehead. "I'm not used to playing Sherlock Holmes. All this deduction is hurting my head."

Bes' eyes flashed green. "Feel free to stop. I've answered your questions. Now tell me about this Andy."

Annoyed, Tadgh continued. "Give me a minute. Graunskyegs are kind of like killing machines. They run on Void energy. If you feed them, they grow stronger, like over-clocking the video card on your computer or over juicing a battery. If you had enough energy you could..."

Tadgh stopped. Suddenly it was very clear what the demon intended to do.

"Enough games." Bes grew back to the size of a lion. "You have no idea the trouble you've caused me. If I wasn't under orders, you wouldn't be breathing. The next words out of your mouth had better be about Andy or I will take off an arm. Understand?"

Tadgh realized two things. First was that he had to give Bes something big. Giving a small detail could infuriate the demon. He'd been on the receiving end of Bes' rage before and had no desire to witness it again. The second thing, more important than the first, was that Tadgh was not a demon. And that meant he could lie.

"Andy is a powerful wizard from earth. You've seen the way the Sage teleports? Well, she does pretty much the same thing, but her disks are shadows instead of yellow light. And the best part? She doesn't work alone. Andy has an army of wizards."

Bes hissed. "Lies. The only army of wizards on Earth is the Council of Peacocks. And the Sage decimated them."

Tadgh frowned. "I've heard the Sage mention this Council of Peacocks before. He thought my parents might belong to it. But Andy doesn't work for the Council of Peacocks. If anything, she's an ally of the Sage. She helped me rescue him after you imprisoned him at the warehouse in Gateway. That's how we got to the island so quickly. The Sage teleported us."

"The Sage is here?" For the first time, Bes seemed genuinely uneasy. He sniffed the air several times before turning back to Tadgh. "Funny. I don't sense him on the island any more. Perhaps he has gone off somewhere with your invisible friend, Andy?" Bes growled. "We've delayed long enough. Get to the roof."

Tadgh followed Bes up the final flight of stairs. He understood now what they wanted him to do, but he still could not figure out why they thought he would actually do it.

The roof was surprisingly intact without visible sign of erosion. At the center of the roof, a circle of thirteen mauve-skinned trofast in purple robes chanted. Seeing them was an unwelcome reminder of Eiodeesh. Although her complexion was similar to the trofast before him, none of them looked anything remotely like her. In one corner stood Teric and the other black cloaked figures. Tadgh felt a breeze blowing down on him and looked up. Circles of blue-scaled dragons – or wypera as they were called on Maghe Sihre – flew in a careful formation. With each rotation, the wind grew stronger, the chants grew louder.

"You're late," boomed a voice like pebbles in a blender. "I was beginning to think you lost the boy again."

The circle of trofast parted, giving Tadgh his first glance at the speaker. The hermadur. Although he knew Bes was a demon, the creature before him actually looked like he imagined demons should. Wings made of pure fire spread out from its back making its blood-red armor glisten. In its hands was a weapon that Tadgh assumed was the Sword of Kassandra. It looked massive: five feet long and as wide across as Tadgh's open hand. The blade was clear and translucent, like quartz. The hilt was black and opaque but also gleamed like crystal.

But it was what sat at the hermadur's feet that truly terrified Tadgh: three people, bound and gagged. All of them were familiar. Now he understood how they would make him use the Sword of Kassandra.

Tadgh fell to his knees, numb. The first figure was a woman with brown hair and very frightened brown eyes. His mother. Beside her was a black-haired man with hazel eyes. His father. The third figure was a pale-skinned man with blond hair and blue eyes. Shonn, Menphis' cousin. The man who still owned his heart, the one he chose over Samar.

Teric walked over and pulled Tadgh to his feet. "Let me make this clear to you. We can kill these fine people and turn them into graunskyegs or you can make a wish."

Tadgh looked into his mother's eyes. Saw her trying to scream his name. He started to shake, his eyes blinking uncontrollably fast.

Teric slapped him across the face. "Focus. Pass out on me, and I'll slice into your family."

The hermadur walked toward Tadgh and passed him the Sword. "I have waited a long time for this, Tadgh Dooley. You know what will happen to your loved ones if you don't cooperate. Nod if you understand."

Tadgh looked over at his father, the man whose features were so similar to his own. The last time they'd spoken was at the hospital after Tadgh's attack. He knew his father was disappointed in him, wanted him to be something, someone other than who he was. But in that moment his father looked at him not with anger or disappointment, but with absolute terror. His father shook his head, trying to tell Tadgh not to do whatever the demon wanted him to do.

Tadgh nodded. "I understand." He gripped the Sword of Kassandra. Despite its size, it was nearly weightless. Tadgh lifted it up and looked at the blade. It seemed there was writing on it, but he could not read it.

"Good." The hermadur produced a key from somewhere and held it in front of Tadgh's face. "In a moment I will remove your power dampener. You will lift the sword above your head and say the following words. 'I wish to drain the energy of the Void currently imprisoning Lord Dispayre and transfer it into the bodies of the graunskyeg army below.' Repeat it."

Tadgh hesitated.

Teric jabbed him in the back. "Go on boy. Your power won't work right now. You've got the collar on."

The hermadur cast Teric an annoyed glance. "As the undead thing said, think of this as a trial run. I want to ensure you have the wording correct. We only get one chance at this."

Tadgh glanced over at Shonn. Unlike Tadgh's parents, Shonn did not look frightened. He looked back at Tadgh with nothing but love. Tadgh's mouth felt dry, but he forced himself to say the words.

"I wish to drain the energy of the Void currently imprisoning Lord Dispayre and transfer it into the bodies of graunskyeg army below."

When nothing happened, he sighed with relief.

"Excellent." The hermadur snapped his fingers and several of the chanting trofast led Tadgh's mother, father, and Shonn out of the circle. Teric stood watch over them as the hermadur led Tadgh to the center of the circle.

Tadgh quickly considered his options. If he did what the hermadur wanted him to, the energies of the Void would rupture forth, entering the thousands of graunskyegs. They would no longer be mindless zombies. They would be powerful creatures like Teric.

If he decided to do anything different, he would only have time for one wish. He could repeat the wish he'd made months earlier, but that carried its own risks. When he had wished all of Lord Vyken's army were dust, he'd caused a massive earthquake and flooding in GardenKeep. The disruption to the reality field on Maghe Sihre was so strong he ripped a hole in the Void. That might stop the hermadur from creating an army of powerful undead creatures, but it could still free Dispayre.

He could simply wish he and his family were far away from here. He could save their lives. But there would still be the army of graunskyeg. And there was no way to guarantee that the hermadur would not simply track down his family again. Once someone knows they have leverage over you, the blackmail never stops.

With that in mind, Tadgh knew there was really only one choice.

"Ready?" The hermadur unlocked the power dampener around Tadgh's neck. Immediately, Tadgh felt his abilities rush back to him. His vision changed and his sense of smell improved. He smelled his mother's perfume, the cigar smoke imbedded in his father's clothing. He turned to them, looking each in the eye. Teric stood nearby wearing a smug expression.

Tadgh closed his eyes and whispered "Forgive me."

He swung the Sword of Kassandra high above his head slicing down one of the chanting trofast. A bright light appeared within the blade and the sword cut completely through the trofast's body. The other trofasts quickly dodged to either side creating a wide gap in the circle.

He couldn't look in the direction of his family. He didn't want to see Teric cut their throats. Instead, Tadgh tightened his grip on the Sword of Kassandra and started to run.

Chapter Twenty-Seven

Tadgh jumped down the first flight of stairs, already knowing he wasn't fast enough in human form. Only in feline form did he have a chance at survival. He also knew that he'd never mastered transforming mid-run. If he fell now, it was very likely the demons would capture him again. Escaping a second time was unlikely.

'Does it even matter?' he thought. 'They're dead. My mom, dad. Shonn. All of them dead because of me.' But he knew it was unlikely they were all dead. The demon would probably kill one of them to punish Tadgh, keeping the others alive for leverage. It would keep killing people he loved until he did what they wanted. The only way he knew this would end is if he was dead. However, thanks to the Sage, he knew that wasn't an option. The djinn's energy inside him would simply find a new host and the process would begin again.

'I need to do what the Sage suggested,' he thought. 'I have to use my wish ability to learn how to teleport like him. But I can't do it while being chased by graunskyegs and the hermadur and God knows what else. I need to get somewhere quiet for a second. Carefully word the wish. It's not enough to be able to teleport. I have to be able to teleport as well as the Sage. No use leaving the island only to end up someplace worse."

Bes charged down the stairs toward him. Tadgh ducked at the last minute and Bes landed gracefully on all fours at the bottom of the flight.

'Although, at this point I'm not sure a worse place exists.' Tadgh vaulted over the side of the stairs angling himself to land on the steps several flights down. He relaxed, allowing his body's natural sense of equilibrium to help him land on his feet. He took a second to kick off his shoes and started running again.

'Now or never,' he thought. 'I need to get into feline

form or Bes will be on me again in a second. He slowed his running ever so slightly and called on the feline demon inside. He was vaguely aware of the fur sprouting over his body but kept all his attention on his feet. That was always the hard part. He always ended up tripping over his big feet. His tail pushed free of his pants and…

He kept on running.

"Woohoo! The movies are right. The threat of imminent death is exactly the motivation you need to do what you've never been able to do before."

Teric landed on the steps directly in front of him. Tadgh tried to dodge the graunskyeg, but Teric was too fast. He grabbed Tadgh's tunic with claw-like fingers.

"Not happening," Tadgh said. "Today, I'm on fire." He vaulted over the side of the stairs. Teric's claws tore the tunic, ripping it to shreds. Tadgh lifted his hands over his head and, twisting free of the ruined tunic, fell through the air. Once again, he landed several flights below only this time he immediately jumped again. He repeated this action several times, always slightly ahead of Teric. In no time at all he was on the main floor.

He raced out the front door quickly seeing one small hole in his plan. Before him stood thousands of graunskyeg.

"Oh, crap." Tadgh made a hard right turn and sprinted past the graunskyeg.

The hermadur hovered in the air nearby, its fiery wings flapping furiously. "Don't just stand there, you idiots. Get him!"

The graunskyegs began to moan, snarling and gnashing their teeth as they began to chase after Tadgh.

"Can this get any better?" Tadgh shouted.

A blast of acid hit the ground to the right of him erupting into bright flame. He glanced up at the sky to see several wypera flying directly toward him.

'Yay. It got worse. At least they're not trying to kill me. They just want to slow me down so the graunskyegs can catch me, but that's not going to happen. I just sacrificed the lives of three people I love. Their deaths will not be in vain.'

A torrent of dark energy shot up from the ground. From out of it stepped the red-headed female graunskyeg. She threw her hands to her side and the darkness swallowed Tadgh completely. The Sword of Kassandra still shone, the light inside the crystal pushing back at the darkness. But the illumination did not reach far. Tadgh couldn't even see his hand holding the sword's hilt.

Claws raked at his fur, drawing blood.

"Think you're so clever, don't you clever boy?" The female graunskyeg's voice cackled with laughter. He couldn't pinpoint her location. The voice seemed to come from every direction at once. "Well, your cleverness got your parents and lover killed. Teric slit their throats and drained them. we have other ways to make you cooperate. We'll see how clever you are without your legs. You don't need to be able to stand to make a wish."

Tadgh fought past his fear and reached out with his awareness like he'd learned at the monastery. For a moment it didn't seem to be working. Then, he felt it. One section of the darkness felt more wrong than the others. Tadgh dropped to one knee and swung the sword back and to the right.

There was an unearthly howl and the torrent of darkness disappeared. The Sword of Kassandra had sliced into the female graunskyeg. He watched as she flaked apart like burnt paper, parts of her floating away on the night breeze.

But there wasn't time to celebrate. The army of graunskyeg was getting closer and closer.

Tadgh glanced down at the sword in his left hand. Then it hit him.

"I am a complete and utter idiot. Why didn't I think of this sooner?"

Lowering himself into an attack stance he turned to face the approaching army.

And Tadgh Dooley made a wish.

"I wish I knew how to properly use this blasted sword."

The earth rumbled softly and a rush of energy passed through Tadgh. The light inside the sword grew brighter spreading out in all directions. He also noticed for the first time that there was a leather belt and matching sheath at his waist.

'When did that get here?' he thought. 'Did they put it on me before the ceremony? It can't be meant for this sword. It's barely three feet long and only a few inches wide.'

But Tadgh's wish had worked. He knew the sheath was tied to the Sword of Kassandra and that as long as he wore it the graunskyegs could not feed on him. As the nearest graunskyegs approached him, Tadgh raised the sword over his head sending all of his willpower into the blade. The light grew stronger and stronger until he was forced to close his eyes or risk going blind. When the sword would not take any more of his willpower, he swung it down like an axe cutting wood.

The moaning of the graunskyegs stopped.

Relaxing his control over the sword, he dimmed the sword's light. Tadgh opened his eyes and looked at the graunskyegs. The entire army had been cut in two. The light from the Sword of Kassandra had chopped off each of their bodies at the waist. There was no sign of the tops of their bodies.

Tadgh grinned and looked at the sword in his hand. "Well alright! Not that's what I'm talking about."

A voice called out to him from somewhere nearby.

"Tadgh, over here!"

The light of the blade was too bright. With a mental command, Tadgh dimmed the sword and put it inside the sheath. Miraculously, the blade shrank to fit the much smaller sheath. With the blade away, he clearly saw who spoke to him. And his heart broke.

Menphis ran to Tadgh. "We came to stop you from using the Sword but..." He glanced down at the sheath around Tadgh's waist. "It looks like we're too late."

Tadgh shook his head. "It's okay. I didn't do what they wanted me to do, but there was a price. Listen, Menphis, I have to tell you…"

"No time." Menphis put his hands on Tadgh's shoulders and spun him around. "Or did you forget about them?"

Tadgh saw the hermadur and a dozen wypera flying toward them. Teric and the remaining greater graunskyegs kept their distance. Apparently, seeing the Sword of Kassandra in action was enough to give them pause.

Tadgh sighed. "It will have to wait. Let me guess. We're going to run."

Menphis smiled and patted him on the back. "Good guess. Follow me."

They ran toward wooden scaffolding that supported a tarped off area. Immediately inside the entrance, Gnocko and Bethel stood with their weapons drawn.

"What's the plan?" Tadgh asked.

Gnocko glared up at him. "Don't make a sound."

Tadgh winced. "That's it? Don't make a sound? That's a horrible plan."

"Just do what I say." Gnocko sighed. "Please, Tadgh. I can't handle…Not after…" His voice trailed away, and he closed his eyes. "Eiodeesh."

Tadgh crossed his arms not sure what to say. Maybe Bes was right. Maybe all of this really was his fault. Eiodeesh had died because she wanted to stand beside him. And now his parents and Shonn were dead. All because of him.

Gnocko sheathed his weapon and stretched his hands out before him.

"What's he doing?" Tadgh whispered.

Bethel leaned close to his ear. "Casting an illusion. His people have the natural ability to create visual illusions. It won't register as fieldbending, so if you are capable of shutting your mouth we should be able to hide here until morning."

Tadgh nodded. He'd heard of Gnocko's illusions before

but never actually witnessed them. As he wondered how effective they were, the hermadur walked in front of the entrance. Although he stood no more than ten feet from Tadgh, the demon did not react to their presence.

When it left, Tadgh sighed with relief. Menphis pinched his earlobe and motioned for him to be quiet. Tadgh pulled Menphis further into the tunnel. He didn't risk making another sound until they reached an elevator shaft far from the main entrance.

"What is it that can't wait until morning?" Menphis asked.

Tadgh couldn't look at him. "I don't even know how to say this."

"Just spit it out. I don't want to leave Gnocko and Bethel by themselves for long. We've lost enough people today.

Tadgh made a sound that started as a laugh but quickly became something very different. Menphis watched him nervously for a moment then covered Tadgh's mouth, muffling the sound. It took Tadgh a long time to regain composure. Only when he could ensure he would speak in a whisper, did he pull away from Menphis. He told his best friend about being captured by Bes and the walk to the tower. He spoke of the gods appearing before him and the warning they gave. Then, his voice barely audible, he told Menphis about the hostages on the roof and the impossible choice he'd been forced to make.

"I didn't see any other way out," Tadgh said. "Maybe if I'd been thinking clearly I would have wished I knew how to use the sword earlier. But I had no way of knowing what it could do. Every decision seemed to lead to one of two outcomes. Choose the world or choose the people I love." Tadgh flicked the switch in his mind again, changing back into human form. As he became human, the claw marks from the graunskyeg's attack faded. The blood still stained his skin. "And I couldn't do it. I couldn't allow their lives to be more important than the entire world. I'm sorry,

Menphis. I'm so, so sorry. I couldn't save Shonn."

Menphis walked away, his face ashen, his eyes unfocused. "I…I don't understand. How…?" He ran his hands over his face. "How did the demons get to Shonn?"

Tadgh shook his head. "Don't know. Same way they got to my parents, I guess. Same way they got to me. They seem to be able to teleport. Not like the Sage, but…"

"That's not what I mean!" Menphis immediately realized how loud his voice was and punched the air in frustration. When he spoke again it was with a quiet voice. "That's not what I meant. Shonn is supposed to be in Castle Nizaria training to be a neurotech. The nizarians have technology so advanced it might as well be fieldbending. They may have the highest level of security on the planet. So how did they get to Shonn?"

Bethel came down the tunnel, sword drawn. When she saw there was no danger, only the two men talking, she put her sword away. "Have you both lost your minds? Whatever tiff you're having can wait until morning. Gnocko's illusion won't do us any good if you keep yelling like that."

An idea flashed through Tadgh's mind. He glanced at Menphis and could tell from his friend's expression they were both thinking the same thing.

"Is it possible?" Tadgh asked. "They looked solid. I could smell them."

Menphis turned to Bethel. "Go get Gnocko."

"But the illusion…"Bethel began.

Menphis interrupted, his voice a harsh whisper. "He can cast it from here!"

"Please, Bethel," Tadgh said. "It's important."

Bethel glared at them, rolled her eyes and headed back to the entrance. Tadgh was trying very hard not to get his hopes up, but the more he thought about the possibility, the more sense it made. Several minutes later, Gnocko and Bethel arrived at the elevator shaft.

"This had better be important." The frie stav took his glasses and blinked at the light. "We don't know how long we have before one of those things comes by here again."

Once again, Tadgh recounted everything that had happened to him since he left the mall. When he finished, he explained his theory to Gnocko and waited for a response.

Gnocko stroked his chin. "Yes. I suppose it's possible. Very difficult to recreate all of the senses, though. Tell me, did you hear them speak?"

Tadgh gasped and shook his head. "Not. Not a peep. I saw them trying to speak, but I didn't hear a sound."

"Oh, thank Tyche," Menphis said. "It had to have been an illusion."

Bethel exhaled slowly. "Look, I understand why you both want it to be an illusion, but there's only one way to be sure. In the morning, we'll find a way off the island, and you can contact your cousin in Castle Nizaria. If you're right, he'll be there. If not…"

"He'll be there," Menphis said. "I'm sure of it."

Tadgh clued in to something Bethel said. "Wait. What do you mean find a way off the island? Where's the Sage? Why isn't he here?"

Bethel's eyes went wide, and she cocked her head in Gnocko's direction.

Gnocko shook his head. "Nope. That's a story that can definitely wait until morning." Placing his glasses back over his eyes, he turned to face the entrance. "Now, everybody shut up and let me do my damn job."

Chapter Twenty-Eight

Tadgh jolted awake, unaware of when he'd fallen asleep or what had woken him. He was seated on the floor, his bare back leaning against the dirt wall. Bethel crouched before him, touching his leg as she smiled at him.

"The sun's up?" he asked.

"Finally." Bethel extended a hand and helped Tadgh to his feet. "We're leaving now. Menphis is eager to get back to the Aerie."

"I'm eager to get a new shirt." Tadgh brushed dirt off his bare arms. "And bathe. But is it safe?"

"Should be. The hermadur and greater graunskyeg can't survive in the sunlight. We think whatever you did with the Sword of Kassandra last night destroyed all the lesser graunskyegs. That leaves your cat demon, Bes, and the wypera."

"And the chanting trofast," Tadgh added. "Don't forget about them."

Bethel shrugged. "I kept watch for most of the night. There was so sign of any trofasts. The only way we're going to know if it's safe out there is to try."

Tadgh checked his waist to make sure the Sword of Kassandra was still at his side. He pulled it free of the hilt and watched as it grew to full size. Although it no longer shone, he stared at the translucent crystal blade in wonder for a moment before slipping it back into the sheath.

"Pretty handy," Bethel said. "Maybe I should get a fieldbender to make me a sheath just like that."

"Something tells me this is a one of a kind."

Menphis and Gnocko stood at the mouth of the cave speaking quietly to each other. The rain from the night before had stopped, leaving the ground damp. Tadgh stepped outside and noticed the sky was cloudless and bright.

"I know it looks safe but don't let your guard down," Menphis said. "Tadgh, you wouldn't happen to know where your quarterstaff is, would you? I'd feel much better with a weapon in my hand."

"I haven't seen it since the mall," Tadgh responded. "If you want, we could swing by the relic store and pick up your old one."

Gnocko grumbled. "Or you could get yourself another long twig when we are safely off this gods-forsaken island. Let's get back to the Aerie and avoid any unnecessary detours. Speaking personally, I'm done with adventures. The sooner we leave, the sooner I can head home."

Although Tadgh had heard Gnocko make similar statements before, something in the frie stav's tone of voice indicated he meant it this time. Tadgh suspected the loss of Eiodeesh had robbed him of the last of his desire for adventure. It might also be the reason he didn't want to go to the mall. That, after all, was were Eiodeesh's body was.

They encountered no graunskyegs of any sort on the way back to the Aerie. There was also no sign of Bes or the trofasts from the evening before. As they passed Tower Four, Tadgh searched the skies for signs of wypera. He saw something very different instead.

"Ak ak ak." Tadgh was vaguely aware he was making incoherent sounds as he pointed at the objects in the sky, but he was too startled to form real words.

"What?" Gnocko looked where Tadgh pointed and sighed with relief. "Thank the holy fire. We're saved. Looks like you won't have to wish for the Sage's teleportation power, Tadgh. We have our way off the island."

Three silver disks hovered above the center of DunDegore. As they spun, alternating lights of red, yellow and blue pulsated in a thin line alone their edges. Though it was hard to judge their size from this distance, Tadgh estimated each was the size of a baseball stadium.

"What's the problem?" Bethel looked at Tadgh with a puzzled expression on her face. "You look like you've never seen a Pharocai before."

"That's not a freaking Pharocai!" Tadgh felt like jumping up and down. "That's a freaking UFO! A real freaking UFO. Oh my god. I'd kill to have my camera. No one back home would believe this."

Menphis snorted. "But they would believe you singlehandedly defeated a thousand graunskyeg with a magic sword? Use your brain, Tadgh. In the grand scheme of things, is a flying ship really that big a deal?"

"Big deal?" Tadgh pointed at the Pharocai again. "Big deal? I've heard about those things my entire life. I always thought only crazy people saw them, and now there's not one but three freaking UFOs just hovering there." Tadgh went pale. "Oh my god. Does that mean there are going to be aliens?"

Bethel slapped him on the back. "You're babbling. Far as I'm concerned, you're the alien here, Tadgh. Nizarians have been on this world for hundreds of years."

"And it looks like you're about to meet them." Gnocko's voice was riddled with derision. "I know I'm asking a lot here, Tadgh, but please don't make a fool of yourself."

Tadgh walked slowly after the others, his eyes glued to the sky. He wasn't sure why the appearance of the Pharocai affected him so much. Menphis was right. He'd seen hundreds of improbable things in the last few months. Was it really so hard to believe in UFOs?

The square in front of the Aerie was filled with people. Many of them were survivors who had spent the night in the Aerie, but there were at least a hundred others who were definitely not sirians. They were small creatures, roughly the same height as Gnocko. They even wore the same strange black outfit that Gnocko wore, a nizarian battlesuit. From a distance, Tadgh couldn't make out their faces. Each wore a deep cowl attached to the battlesuit.

"Are those nizarians?" Tadgh asked.

"I think so," Menphis answered. "This is one time it's

okay for you to act surprised. Many people go their whole lives without seeing a nizarian. That's why they hide their faces. Some find it unnerving to look into their eyes."

Torch Karehn and Tamara stood at the front door of the Aerie speaking with a man with slate-gray skin and snow-white hair. He was much larger than the nizarians but wore the same type of one-piece suit.

"Is that a nizarian too?" he asked.

Menphis groaned. "I'm starting to remember the good old days when I would make you do push-ups when you asked too many questions. No, that is not a nizarian. That is a valgt'til. Please tell me you remember them from your reading."

Tadgh thought back to the books he'd read on Maghe Sire. "Of course. They have one of the three Great Castles, right? The trofast have one, the sirians have another, and the last belongs to the valgt'til."

Gnocko looked very amused. "Don't let them hear it's the last one. As far as the valgt'til are concerned, theirs is the only true Castle. Now, pretend to be civilized for a minute. Torch Karehn is waving us over."

Tamara ran to Menphis and the two embraced. "Thank the goddess. We were so worried when you didn't come back. What happened?"

Menphis kissed her cheek. "Long story. When did the nizarians get here?"

"A few hours ago," Tamara said. "Come. Let me introduce you to Elmontrazar. He's a special envoy with the nizarians. Elmontrazar, I'd like you to meet my…" She inhaled and glanced at Menphis. "I don't actually know how to address you."

Tadgh leaned forward. "The term you're looking for is baby daddy. He is your baby daddy."

Menphis snarled at him.

Tamara blinked. "I don't think I'll use that term. Elmontrazar this is Menphis Bannmerci, father of my son. The young man beside him with the unusual sense of humor is Tadgh Dooley. Both are members of the Brotherhood of Tyche."

"Former member," Menphis added. "I'm a former member."

Tadgh did a double take. "Come again. When did that happen?"

"Just now." Menphis smiled and put his arm around Tamara.

Elmontrazar bowed toward them and turned to the others. "And you must be Gnocko Fnesh and Bethel Shakuul. Tamara has been telling me of your adventures for the last hour." Elmontrazar slowly surveyed the town around him. "If you can call surviving an assault by the undead an adventure."

"Zombie apocalypse," Tadgh corrected. "It's called a zombie apocalypse. And I guess we did survive it didn't we?"

Elmontrazar laughed, a warm welcoming sound. "Yes, it appears you have." He glanced down at the sheath Tadgh wore at his waist. "But, if that is what I think it is, your adventures are just beginning, young Mr. Dooley."

Torch Karehn gasped and ran toward Tadgh. Her fingers touched the black crystal hilt of the Sword of Kassandra. Her eyes asked a simple question.

"Yeah," Tadgh said. "It's safe. We got the Sword of Kassandra back. What about the Sage? Has anyone seen him?"

Torch Karehn shook her head. She glanced down at Gnocko helping Tadgh remember something. Last night he'd asked Gnocko about the Sage only to be told they would speak of it in the morning. But they never had.

Elmontrazar walked over to Tadgh, giving Tadgh a closer look at his features. His almond-shaped eyes were the color of steel, his ears large and pointed. If not for the color of his skin, Tadgh would assume he was an extra from the *Lord of the Rings* movies.

Elmontrazar grinned and whispered to Tadgh. "I assure you I am no elf."

Tadgh's mouth dropped. "Hey, no fair! You read my mind."

Elmontrazar threw his head back and laughed. "More like you thrust your thoughts out so loudly, I couldn't help but overhear them. I've lived with the nizarians for too long. Within Castle Nizaria, communication is almost exclusively telepathic." He leaned forward and spoke in a whisper. "No need to worry, son. I'm an old friend of the Sage. I know where you come from. Your secret is safe with me."

"How did you know we needed rescuing?" Gnocko asked. "Torch Karehn said she couldn't reach you because the nizarian communication device was broken."

Elmontrazar touched the side of his head. "The mind is a powerful tool if you know how to use it. It so happens, we have a young man with us with a special talent for seeing the future."

"Hey guys!"

Tadgh jumped at the familiar voice. Shonn stood a short distance away wearing a nizarian battlesuit. His hair was shorter than the last time Tadgh had seen him but there was no doubt. It was him.

Tadgh ran for Shonn, picked him up in his arms, and spun him around. He kissed Shonn deeper and more passionately than he'd ever kissed anyone in his life.

Sometime later, he was aware that Menphis was clearing his throat. Repeatedly.

Menphis glared at Tadgh. "Do you want to get a room? Wait. Don't answer that question. In fact, I think I'm going to stop asking all questions. Of everyone. For the rest of my life."

Instantly blushing, Tadgh pulled away from Shonn.

"Sorry." He patted down Shonn's battlesuit which, since it wasn't made of fabric capable of wrinkling, obviously did not need to be patted down. "Kind of lost it for a second there."

"No kidding." Shonn, blushing as well, briefly embraced his cousin. When he turned back to Tadgh, he said

"I'm happy to see you too. I wasn't sure how things stood with us because of the whole you-thought-you-brain-washed-me thing."

"Which you didn't do, by the way." This distinctly feminine voice came from a nizarian who, Tadgh realized, stood right beside Shonn. As Tadgh watched, she threw back her cowl and looked back him. Her large black eyes, absence of a nose, and thin lips were instantly recognizable.

Tadgh squealed and pointed at her. "An alien! I knew it." He turned to face Menphis. "I knew it. I told you they were aliens!"

Shonn laughed and kissed Tadgh again. "You're an idiot. I've missed you. This is my tutor, Kisma."

"Pleased to meet you Tadgh. I've heard many things about you." Kisma extended a three-fingered hand and Tadgh shook it, hesitantly. Kisma's eyes went wide. She withdrew her hand and stared up at Shonn. "Oh. Well, I can see why you were so happy to see Shonn. I'm sorry, Tadgh. I don't know if your parents were really there or not but obviously Shonn was an illusion."

Tadgh wrapped his arms around his bare chest. Suddenly, it was not the absence of his shirt making him feel naked. How could you function around a group of people who were all telepathic? There were no secrets, no...

"Wait. Back up a few sentences," he said. "How do you know I didn't use my mind control thingie on Shonn?"

Kisma slipped the cowl back over her face. "Telepathic, remember? I've been Shonn's chief instructor since he joined us. If anyone had played with his mind, I would know."

"Oh." Tadgh blinked. He didn't dare look into Shonn's eyes at the moment. If he did, he wasn't sure he could control his emotions. "I'm an idiot."

"Pretty sure I just said that." Shonn reached out and held Tadgh's hand. "We'll talk about us later. Right now we have other things to discuss."

***

Tadgh paced outside the council chambers, hands in his

pockets. Thankfully, someone had found him a change of clothes. Wearing a clean white tunic and red pants, he felt less exposed. It also helped that there were no mind readers nearby.

"This is ridiculous," he said. "Everyone on the island is in the council chamber except me."

"Hello." Bethel raised her hand. "Sitting right here." Still wearing her armor, she sat on a wooden bench beneath a large stained glass window.

Tadgh narrowed his eyes at her. "You know what I mean. Besides, I'm more than half convinced the only reason you're here is to make sure I don't wish for the ability to teleport and leave with the Sword of Kassandra."

Bethel shrugged. "That might have been mentioned."

The council chamber doors opened, and Elmontrazar motioned for them to step inside. The large room was decorated with dark wood furniture and rich carpets. Thick drapes hung over long thin windows along the back wall. In the center of the room was a rectangular table with ten chairs on either side. He knew some of the people around the table but not all of them. Dozens of strangers stood nearby in a section designed for citizens to listen to council discussions.

Tadgh went to the only empty seat which just so happened to be at the head of the table.

He glanced around the table one more time and realized one face he had expected to see was missing.

Elmontrazar answered the question before Tadgh could ask it. "He's gone. One of the Pharocai is taking him back to his home in Trelium as we speak. After everything that happened here, Gnocko needed to see his family."

Tadgh bit his lip. He understood completely. He knew now that Shonn was still alive, but he had no confirmation about his parents. He would give anything to be able to see them again.

Torch Karehn stood at the foot of the table, her eyes glued to Tadgh. "I apologize for making you wait, Tadgh, but I'm sure you comprehend the magnitude of the situation."

Tadgh put his hands on the table. "No, honestly, I'm not sure I do. No one will talk to me about what this sword actually is. All I know is it fell out of the Void and now I'm stuck with it." He pulled at the belt around his waist. "I've tried to remove this thing, you know. It won't come off. How the heck am I supposed to bathe with this thing on?"

Menphis put his head in his hands. "Priorities! Is that seriously all you can think about right now?"

Tadgh glanced at Shonn. "Well, sort of."

Kisma, sitting beside Shonn, began to giggle.

Elmontrazar, who sat close to Torch Karehn, leaned forward and turned to face Tadgh. "As soon as you used the Sword, its power became intertwined with you. I happen to be something of a fieldbender. Perhaps I can devise a way for you to remove the belt and sheath for short periods of time so you can…" He glanced at Shonn. "Bathe, as you say. But you are forever bound to the sword. That's why we're meeting now. To discuss what happens next."

Tadgh felt his anger rise. "You mean you're discussing what to do with me?"

"Quite honestly, yes," Tamara said. Her face looked drawn and tired. Tadgh wondered briefly if she had slept at all the night before. "Tadgh, over a hundred thousand people died on this island, including many that we knew and loved. The forces of darkness came here for one reason. To put the Sword of Kassandra in your hands so you could open the Void and release Dispayre. They nearly succeeded."

Tadgh jumped up and slammed his fists against the table. "Do you think I want it to happen again? Last night was the worst night of my entire life, and I've had quite a few really crummy days. In the last few months, I've watched someone I love beat to death in front of me. A demon turned me into a monster and tricked me into becoming a killer. I've been kidnapped. Several times. Tortured. And last night I had to choose between saving the lives of my loved ones or destroying the world. I made the right choice. So stop treating me like I'm a situation. I'm not a problem. I'm not something you can fix. I'm a person, and you had all better start treating me as such."

Menphis looked at Tadgh with soft, understanding eyes and motioned for him to sit down. Tadgh looked at each of the faces around the table first, daring them to speak against him. No one said anything until he'd returned to his seat.

"Like I said," Torch Karehn said. "I apologize. We all do. But I'm afraid you are more than a person Tadgh. You are also a situation. Combined with that sword you are powerful weapon that in the wrong hands...."

Tadgh interrupted her. "I am not a weapon. I am not a thing. I will not be used by anyone. Is that clear?"

Torch Karehn opened her mouth but Elmontrazar spoke first. "What would you have us do, son? Allow you to head back to the monastery so you can finish your training? The Sword of Kassandra is bound to you and, from what we've seen, you now know how to use it. I believe you've learned everything you can from the Brotherhood of Tyche. And, if you did return, what would happen the next time the Quadumvirate send the armies of Dispayre to attack? Because they will attack again. Are you willing to risk the lives of the people at the monastery for your precious freedom?"

Tadgh thought of the people at the monastery and some of his anger dissipated.

Elmontrazar sighed. "We don't want to imprison you, but you have to admit, it's not safe for you to be out in the world. We believe we have a solution. It may not be the only one. We're open to suggestions. Are you at least willing to hear what we propose?"

Tadgh took a deep breath and nodded.

It was Shonn who spoke. "Come back to Castle Nizaria with us. When Elmontrazar said he was something of a fieldbender, he was being ridiculously modest. He's probably the most respected fieldbender on the planet. If anyone can figure out what to do with the Sword of Kassandra, it's him."

Menphis spoke next. "And as I said last night, Castle Nizaria is the most secure place on the planet. The Quadumvirate would have to mount a ful-out war to get you if you're inside there."

"Let's not be coy." Elmontrazar folded his hands together and placed them on the table. "Because full-out war is likely what happens next. We had a victory today, a large one. But this defeat will anger the Quadumvirate. Whatever Myan and the others plan to do next will be bigger than this. And perhaps more desperate."

"Grandwyn and I are heading there, too." Tamara glanced briefly at her son. He sat on the floor nearby speaking with Re-dha, the young girl he helped rescue from the mall. "At least for the time being. The demons used my son to get to you once. I won't have him used again. Also, as I'm sure you're aware, the nizarians train fod sel-onde. They're working with Shonn. I hope they can help Grandwyn as well."

"I'm not going back to the monastery either," Menphis said. "I'll send word to Instructor Mal as soon as I can. But I won't leave my son again. I just can't."

"And there's me." Shonn lowered his eyes at Tadgh, giving him what could only be called puppy dog eyes. "If you come to Castle Nizaria I might get to see you once in awhile."

Tadgh grunted. "No kidding. We'd see each other every day, wouldn't we?"

Kisma began to giggle again. "That picture in your head. Is that what you think a castle looks like?"

"Yes." Tadgh narrowed his eyes. "Is Castle Nizaria larger than that?"

Kisma smiled. "Much bigger. Much much bigger."

A part of Tadgh was still angry. The people around this table had discussed his fate without asking for his opinion first. However, the part of him that didn't want to hit something realized everything they had said made sense. It wasn't safe to go back to the monastery. And, with the Sage nowhere to be found, he had no idea where else to go.

"Okay," he said. "I'm in. Let's go to Castle Nizaria."

Epilogue

On the fifty-third level of Castle Dispayre, Gaysun Defksquar sat on a cold stone floor. He was alone in his cell, hands and feet bound with darkstone chains. As a geognost, Defksquar had a degree of control over metal but the power dampener around his throat prevented him from breaking free. He was severely wounded: several broken ribs, his left eye swollen from repeated blows to the head, and burn marks on his chest.

'Is this really how my story ends?'

Last night, he had made it clear to the interrogators that nothing they could do to him would make him talk. He would never reveal the secrets of the fieldbender guild of Karaj Robat. The guards knowing glances and low laughter told him they didn't care if he ever spoke. Afterwards, they had beat him for what felt like hours.

The door to his cell opened and in walked the Oracle herself, Myan. She was the most intimidating trofast he'd ever met, even worse than Amir Durgen. With her long, muscular frame, she looked like a Rheiballough in bipedal form. Although most trofast had light mauve skin, her skin was dark and mottled from many years of extensive use of the Damatamen herb. She stood before him wearing barely concealed rage.

"Ah, the mighty hero." Myan knelt before him, a cruel smile on her lips. "I came to tell you today is your last day as a mortal. Savor it."

Defksquar tried to turn away from her eyes. She grabbed his chin, forcing him to look back at her ice-blue eyes.

"It's truly been a pleasure watching your interrogation these last few weeks," she said. "A nice break from the tedium of tracking and slaughtering the infidels. In your prime, so long ago, you were a worthy opponent. An honorable soldier. Even recently, you bested Amir Durgen's forces on the Plains of Tananya. But now look at you." She took out a white cloth from the pouch at her waist and wiped blood and sweat from his face. "So…pathetic. Weak. Of course, this is to be expected. All those who refuse to acknowledge our Lord as the one true savior will die. It is simply a question of time."

"Dispayre is a monster, not a god," Defksquar said.

"Blasphemer!" Myan grabbed him by the hair and knocked his head back against the wall, just enough to rattle him. Defksquar cried out in pain as Myan stood, putting the white cloth back in her pouch.

"Do what you want with this body, Myan. I've convinced myself that I'm dead already. You have no more power over me"

Myan chuckled. "Ah, there's where you're wrong. I have a way to make your suffering eternal. We suffered a defeat last night on the isle of DunDegore. It was foolhardy to trust that puny demon, Bes. He failed us and his superiors. My visions show me Bes is now somewhere in a cell similar to this one." She smiled. "Only with more fire and barbed wire. Of course, I foresaw this, all of it. I knew the plan would fail, but the other members of the Quadumvirate outvoted me. But after last night, we all agree it's time to turn to a more traditional method of building our army."

Defksquar felt a chill flash through his body. He realized the only reason Myan would tell him this is she had no doubt he would never leave the Castle alive.

"How?" he asked.

She stood in the doorway, hesitating a moment before answering. "Why, my dear Defksquar, you are to be given the greatest of honors. You will be turned into an Umbral Knight."

She left the room, allowing Defksquar time to process this turn of events. If he didn't escape, Myan would turn him into an Umbral Knight, a cybernetic undead monster with no individual will. It was a fate worse than death.

A light flashed in the corner of the room.

Defksquar squealed in shock. A minute passed without event. Then the light flashed again.

'What is that?' Going to the door, he pressed his ear against the wood and listened. He heard no sound to indicate the guards were coming.

The light flashed again, brighter and clearer this time. Defksquar walked to it, watching as the light flashed again. This time an image appeared showing the face of the last man on the planet Defksquar wanted to see.

"Kill me now," he grumbled. "What do you want?"

The image of the Sage responded. "What I want is for you to die a long, slow painful death. But, thanks to your friend Tempertin, that's not going to happen. I'm going to rescue you."

Defksquar snorted. "You? You're going to rescue me? Forget about why you'd be willing to do that, how could you get me out of here?" Defksquar took a step back and studied the illusion of the Sage. "Actually, how are you doing this? The Castle has layers upon layers of security. Alarms should be sounding if you're…"

The Sage shook his head. "I'm not doing this. I've acquired an assistant. An unwilling one, but an assistant nonetheless. A dem straki. His fieldbending won't set off the alarms. Now, unfortunately, I can't just teleport in and teleport out. Trust me, I've tried. Repeatedly. The defenses of the Castle are too strong. We'll have to do this the hard way."

"I'm running out of time. When will you get here?"

The Sage's image looked up. "We're already here. I'm standing in Scandalon Woods looking up at the Castle now. We'll be inside shortly."

"What do you need me to do?"

The Sage looked back at Defksquar. "Survive. I should get to you in the next twenty-four hours. Can you do that?"

Defksquar glanced back at the cell door. "I think so. But hurry. They…"

The image of the Sage disappeared leaving Defksquar, once again, alone in his cell. He had no idea how the Sage was going to rescue him but, after their brief exchange, he found one thing he thought he'd lost.

Hope.

Coming in summer 2015:
The Backward Pawn

What's Next – The Worlds of Maghe Sihre and Earth
Have you ever read a book that changed the way you think about fiction? For me it was actually two books, *Desperation* by Stephen King and *The Regulators* by his pseudonym Richard Bachman. The amazing thing about these books is they are versions of the same events told simultaneously in two different worlds. *Desperation* is a literary horror novel; *The Regulators* is more pulp fiction. That gave me an idea.

Two worlds. Similar problems. Shared characters. Different genres.

Council of Peacocks
If you're interested in the origins of the Sage/Wisdom and how he gained his powers, check out *Council of Peacocks*. It is the first in the Activation Series. On that world, he is known as Wisdom. He trains a group of half-demon young adults to fight a group of evil sorcerers, the Council of Peacocks. The Council plans to use the Verdenstab to take over the planet.

That book also has the first encounter between Defksquar and the Sage/Wisdom. If you want to know why the Sage/Wisdom was convinced Echo/Andy was dead, *Council of Peacocks* also has that backstory.

Beyond the Black Sea
As for how the Sage/Wisdom ended up on the planet of Maghe Sihre, put Book Two in the Activation Series, *Beyond the Black Sea*, on your to-read list.

To follow Tadgh's adventures, check out *The Backward Pawn* next year.

ABOUT M. JOSEPH MURPHY

Joseph Murphy was born and raised in Ontario, Canada. He earned his geekdom at an early age. He read *X-Men* comics from the age of 8 and it only went downhill from there.

As a teenager he wrote short stories and wanted to be the next Stephen King. Instead of horror, however, he kept writing fantasy stories. After surviving high school as a goth with a purple mohawk, he studied English and Creative Writing at the University of Windsor.

When not writing, Joseph works as Lead Accounting instructor at a local college. He lives in Windsor, ON (right across the stream from Detroit, Michigan) with his husband, two cats, and a shy-but-friendly ghost.